A NOTE ON THE AUTHOR

PETER WALKER is a New Zealander who has lived in London since 1986. He worked for seven years on the *Independent*, and three on the *Independent on Sunday*, where he was Foreign Editor. He has also written for the *Financial Times* and *Granta*. His first book, *The Fox Boy*, and his second, *The Courier's Tale*, were both published by Bloomsbury in 2001 and 2010 respectively, and were widely praised.

Some Here Among Us

PETER WALKER

B L O O M S B U R Y
LONDON · OXFORD · NEW YORK · NEW DELHI · SYDNEY

Bloomsbury Paperbacks
An imprint of Bloomsbury Publishing Plc

50 Bedford Square   1385 Broadway
London   New York
WC1B 3DP   NY 10018
UK   USA

www.bloomsbury.com

BLOOMSBURY and the Diana logo are trademarks of Bloomsbury Publishing Plc

First published in Great Britain 2015
This paperback edition first published in 2016

British Library Cataloguing-in-Publication Data
A catalogue record for this book is available from the British Library.

ISBN: HB: 978-1-4088-5667-3
TPB: 978-1-4088-5668-0
PB: 978-1-4088-5670-3
ePub: 978-1-4088-5669-7

2 4 6 8 10 9 7 5 3 1

Typeset by Hewer Text UK Ltd, Edinburgh
Printed and bound in Great Britain by CPI Group (UK) Ltd, Croydon CR0 4YY

MIX
Paper from
responsible sources
FSC® C020471

To find out more about our authors and books visit www.bloomsbury.com.
Here you will find extracts, author interviews, details of forthcoming
events and the option to sign up for our newsletters.

For Liz and Louis

There are many here among us who feel that life is but a joke. But you and I—

Dylan, 'All Along The Watchtower'

Contents

Prologue

One thing was plain – Morgan Tawhai had been expelled from Fairfield Boys High. But why? What did he do? What was the crime that sent him flying at an early age and with no right of appeal from that estimable seat of learning?

The four of them looked at one another. No one really knew what to say. There was Morgan's elder brother, Lucas, clearly unhappy that the subject had come up. There was FitzGerald, always the diplomat, looking just as unhappy. There was FitzGerald's new wife, Inga. Inga's eyes were shining. She had never known Morgan but she was keenly interested, being inquisitive by nature. And there was Radzimierz Radzienwicz who had raised the question in the first place.

Morgan himself was not present, nor would he ever be present, to throw any light on the matter. He had been dead now – it was incredible to think of it – for more than thirty years.

'Wasn't it something to do with tennis shoes?' said Radzimierz Radzienwicz, who, mercifully, had been known since childhood as Race.

'*Tennis* shoes?' said Inga.

'Sneakers. Plimsolls. What did we call them then? *Sandshoes*. Didn't he pinch a pair of sandshoes from someone's locker?'

A faint rubbery whiff of old scandal and the school corridor came into the room. They were in Lucas's house by the beach. Race and Inga and FitzGerald had never met Lucas before. They had come down the coast from Auckland on holiday and they called in to see him only after some delay and debate among themselves.

'Well, you know, Morgan – he was brilliant,' said FitzGerald who sometimes wished Race could keep his big trap shut. As he remembered it, Morgan hadn't just taken the shoes from the locker. He had written his name in blue biro on the underside of their tongues. It was that, deemed unforgivable by the school authorities, which propelled him at high speed from Fairfield Boys High, amid no doubt many painful family recriminations.

'He was always top of the class,' FitzGerald went on. 'He just sort of knew more than the rest of us. *What is the name of the liquor flowing in the veins of the immortal gods?* Only one hand went up.'

'And?' said Inga, stretching out a tanned and sandalled foot. Her toenails were lustrous, plum in colour.

'And what?' said FitzGerald.

'The liquid flowing in the veins of the gods,' said Inga.

'God,' said FitzGerald. 'I mean we were thirteen, fourteen. We'd think how the hell would we know? But Morgan knew.'

'Yes. But what is it?' said Inga.

'Ichor,' said FitzGerald.

'*Ichor,*' said Lucas and Inga together – Lucas startled there was such a word, and Inga as if just checking.

'I - c - h - o - r,' said FitzGerald.

Outside, the waves broke and fanned up the black-bouldered sand. It was a great rainless summer storm. The windows of Lucas's house were lightly salted, everything beyond them vague as if seen through smoked glass. In a way, naughty, brilliant Morgan had become almost immortal himself. His friends had never forgotten him. They still talked about him when they met, and wondered what had actually happened to him. Here they were, for instance, come to look at his grave, for what that's ever worth.

'Shall we go?' said Lucas, shouldering up from an armchair. They went out into the booming, sunlit gale. The family grave-yard was surrounded by a picket of trees about a quarter of a mile across the paddock. They set off, FitzGerald and Inga going on ahead. From a distance, Race noticed Inga's good ankles, her air of elegance. She might, he thought, have been heading into Harvey Nichols or Bloomingdale's or some such – so Race framed it – hellhole, but instead there she was crossing the rough grass beyond the shadow of a tall pine that was growing alone in the middle of the field. Under the tree the ground was dusty, bare, ribbed with roots, cobbled with sheep-shit. It was strange, Race thought just then – he caught a faint ammoniacal tang – that he had never noticed the tree when he had been there before, crossing that field in the company of the long-vanished Morgan. He must have just blocked it out, he thought, for after all it was a Norfolk Island pine, and in those days he and his friends disliked the species, the poor Norfolk being so very symmetrical, so neat and regular in brachiation, each one forming a great, green capital 'A', that it was much favoured by the authorities who planted it up and down school drives, outside prisons, on the perimeter of sports fields, along beach fronts – on 'marine parades' especially, all over Australia and New Zealand – A A A A A A A – on account of those very qualities – neatness, order, regularity – which he and his friends, then aged twenty-one or twenty-two, naturally held in low esteem. Now, decades later, he saw how wrong they had been.

It was beautiful, this great green A creaking in the cloudless gale – dark, doughty of trunk, each branch laden with glossed claws of green – a 'star pine', cousin of the monkey-puzzle, the hoop pine, living masts of Gondwanaland still growing on long-separated shores of the Pacific.

Race and Lucas walked on beyond the tree's shadow, and then Race paused for some reason and looked back up at it, and Lucas stopped as well to see what he was looking at.

'We used to climb that when we were kids,' said Lucas, squinting into the sun. 'Morgan and I. We'd climb right to the top and then just jump out.'

'Jesus, Lucas,' said Race. 'It's a hundred feet high. What did your parents say?'

'They never knew,' said Lucas, shaking his head at life. 'We'd jump off and leap down through the branches all the way to the ground.'

They stood there, looking up.

'Maybe they did know,' Lucas said, 'but just couldn't watch. We were twelve, fourteen. We were running wild by then. What could they do? We'd climb up there and jump off, or we'd swim out to the lighthouse and climb that and swing from the gantry by our fingertips . . .'

Just then, among the higher boughs, a magpie appeared with his shining badges of white, and then a second swooped around the tree and joined its mate, and at that moment Race not only remembered the very beginning of the story but, as he and Lucas turned and went away across the grass, he felt that he was quite unexpectedly coming to the end of it, the end of the story of Morgan, or at least his version of the story of Morgan whom he had last seen coming fast along the platform of Wellington railway station one Sunday afternoon, coming to say goodbye to Race who was getting on the overnight train, and to tell him that he had in fact slept with the blonde girl the night before, right there in front of the fire after everyone else had left the party, adding that, at the time, the rain was so loud on the roof it sounded like thousands of people clapping.

'Get out of here,' said Race, looking past Morgan at the railway clock at the end of the platform, but he was in fact pleased that Morgan had come down on a grey Sunday afternoon to see him off on the train, and then he had climbed on board and gone along to his seat to speak to him through the window, but he never saw Morgan again because, by the time he got to his seat, the train was moving off from the platform and away through the marshalling yards where the signals were – in his memory at least – shining blue above the wilderness of tracks.

Part I

1967

1

When the horns sounded the first time, and the second, and even the third, Race did not know what they were or where they came from. The sound came blowing in from a mournful distance, from the dark, well beyond the wharves, out in the harbour, out to sea. Race had just left the nightclub alone. At the entrance was a life-size painting of a woman in a feathery gown. She had startled blue eyes and beside her was a column of names, spangled with stars:

Honey Brown
Fanny Hill
Gaye Abandon
Pinky Nightingale
Treasure Chest
Teddy Bare
PLUS PLUS PLUS:
Jewel Box!!!

'Jewel Box!' said Race to the startled lady in her gown of thick paint. He paused, looking up and down the street, wondering which way to go home, and then set off towards Civic Square. He had been to a dance earlier that night, and he was drunk – drunk enough anyway not to notice or at least not to care that he was in fancy dress. He was walking in fancy dress on his own through dark and probably drunken streets. His costume, though, was relatively restrained. He had spent the night dancing with Candy, who was dressed as a bee, and haughty Rosie Gudgeon, who'd gone as Madame de Pompadour and wore a powdered wig a foot high. FitzGerald had started out the night as a samurai warrior and at some point had acquired – but from where? – a Minotaur's head. A kimono-clad Minotaur was still on the nightclub dance-floor, soulfully clutching Madame de Pompadour. Candy, in her bee costume, had vanished. Race didn't know where she had gone. He left the dingy basement club because he was drunk and because the bee had departed, but he felt quite happy all the same, and he turned left and began to walk home. He was wearing doublet and hose, and a cap with a feather in it, but apart from the white ruff around his neck, and the feather in his cap, he was dressed all in black: in a dark and drunken town his costume was not too different from that of some kid in skinny black jeans. He had just reached Civic Square when the horns began to sound from far away. Race did not recognise them. He had been living in the city a year and a half and had never heard them before. Then, at the fourth or fifth blast, so mournful and solemn, the sea-fog appeared – two billows of fog, eight, nine, ten storeys high – coming up parallel streets from the docks. They reached Civic Square at the same time, they silently turned left and right at the intersections, rolled towards each other, met, and came forward as one. The last thing Race saw before a general blotting-out was a border of red-and-white flowers planted near the council offices. He stood there a moment, pleased for some reason at the sudden evanescence of the prim municipal blooms. Then he walked on. There was no passing traffic, no sign of life or other existence. The only sound was the intermittent rising and falling of the sad fog horn.

Then, a few yards ahead, Race saw someone coming towards him. Even in the fog the figure suggested haste and agitation. It came forward, stopped, bent down, straightened up and darted forward again, and then stood in front of him.

'Morgan,' said Race.

They stood a yard apart in the mist.

Morgan looked at Race without any sign of surprise.

'Oh,' he said, 'Race Radzienwicz.'

'What are you doing?' said Race.

'I'm looking for something,' said Morgan.

He bent down and examined the pavement at the foot of a parking meter beside them.

'What?'

'Something I lost.'

'You want some help?' said Race.

'Possibly.'

Race bent down and looked at the ground as well.

They went to the next meter and repeated the action.

'It might help,' Race said, looking into the gutter – he noticed its clean, dry walls – 'if I knew what I was looking for.'

'Not necessarily,' said Morgan. 'If you saw it, you'd know.'

'How did you lose it?'

'I put it down,' said Morgan. 'Somewhere round here. *Somewhere . . . or . . . other.*'

He was, Race realised, quite drunk as well. Morgan had also been at the fancy-dress ball at the university, although he had not worn fancy dress. Nor had he gone with a partner. Race had seen him at about midnight, dancing alone, with absorption, right up by the stage, almost under the guitar-necks of the band.

'It's not here,' said Morgan, 'and I know it's not down there—'

They had reached the intersection and Morgan stood looking into the mists of Wakefield Street.

'I didn't go down Wakefield Street, so I can't have left them down there, now can I?'

'Them?' said Race. 'I thought it was an it.'

'It's an it and a them,' said Morgan.

'How can it be?'

'How can it not be?' said Morgan. 'Most things are.'

'Cut it out,' said Race.

'All right,' said Morgan. 'It's jewellery. They are several separate jewels, forming a single item of jewellery.'

'Jewels!' said Race. 'What kind of jewels?'

'Rubies,' said Morgan. 'Or possibly amber.'

'Where did you get them?'

Morgan didn't answer.

'And why leave them in the street?' said Race.

'I heard the police coming,' said Morgan, 'and so I hid them.'

'The *police*?' said Race.

'Oh, OK,' said Morgan, in the tone of a man burdened by many unreasonable demands. 'First I went to the fancy-dress dance. It was *quite* a good band, I thought.'

He stood at the corner and sang:

> *There must be some way out of here*
> *Said the gaoler to the thief*

His voice was light and rather hoarse.

'Joker,' said Race. 'It's joker, not gaoler.'

'Gaoler's better,' said Morgan.

Race screwed up one eye to consider this in the fog – the sacrilege of re-writing Dylan.

'Then after the dance, I came downtown and went to that dive you go to,' said Morgan.

'I don't go to it,' said Race. 'I went to it once in my life, tonight.'

'I went to your filthy dive,' said Morgan, 'and I met some people there who asked me to a party. One was called Pinky, and one was her girlfriend, and one was this beautiful girl called Butterfly. And I went to the party and I was dancing with Butterfly and then I kissed her. Then I left and came down here and broke a shop window and took a ruby necklace.'

'Oh,' said Race.

He thought for a while.

'But, I mean – *why*?' he said.

'Well, I was dancing with Butterfly,' said Morgan, 'and she and I went out in the back garden and we kissed. This was a party up on The Terrace and we went out the back, and we kissed and then Butterfly said: "Excuse me. I have to have a pee." And she went over to the wall and lifted her skirt and she pissed against the wall. Butterfly was a boy! And I thought "Oh, boy! What am I doing here?" and I got out of there. I ran away and I came back downtown and took this necklace.'

'Oh,' said Race.

'Then I heard the police coming,' said Morgan, 'so I put it down by a parking meter and walked away. And then I realised it wasn't the police, it was only a fog horn, and now I can't remember which parking meter it was.'

'I see,' said Race.

He looked at Morgan in the dark, concealing his surprise. He was surprised not only at what he had just been told but that Morgan had told him at all, for after all they were not friends, they had never been friends since the day they met: Race remembered the occasion clearly. He had walked into FitzGerald's room six months earlier, at the beginning of term, and there were two men prowling round, watching each other like wrestlers before a clinch. One was Adam Griffin, FitzGerald's new room-mate, whom Race had met once or twice already that week. The other he had never seen before. Griffin started to speak:

> *They said "You have a blue guitar,*
> *You do not play things as they are,"*

'*Things as they are*,' said the other, '*are changed upon the blue guitar.*'

'*But play, you must*,' said Griffin, '*a tune beyond us, yet ourselves.*'

'*A tune upon the blue guitar*,' said the other, '*of things exactly as they are.*'

Race had no idea what they were talking about. He stood leaning on the door-jamb, listening. Griffin was short, fair, stocky, and had a stutter. He fixed you with an imploring blue eye as he stuttered, although now, Race noticed, the stutter had gone. The other man was tall, slim, Maori, wearing a fisherman's black jersey and needle-cord jeans.

'*The morning still deluged by night*,' said Griffin.

'*The clouds tumultuously bright.*'

'*Like light in a mirroring of cliffs—*' said Griffin.

'*Rising up from the sea of ex.*'

The sea of ex! Race pretended not to be impressed. And he felt a little envious as well, he had to admit it: at most he and FitzGerald could sing a few lines of 'Sloop John B' together – *We sailed on the Sloop John B! My grand-daddy and me!* – but these two, they had whole poems by heart, it seemed, they could read each other's minds. He was also beginning to feel some irritation. This was his territory, after all. FitzGerald was his best friend. They had been friends in childhood, and although they then moved to different towns and went to different schools, they had kept up their friendship. Now they were in the same hall: Race regarded Fitzgerald's room almost as his own. But these two strangers hardly glanced at him when he came in.

'*We shall sleep by night and forget by day,*' said Griffin.

'*Except,*' said the other, '*the moments when we choose to play—*'

Then they both chanted, '*The imagined pine, the imagined jay!*' and they laughed and swiped hands like basket-players.

'What was all that about?' said Race, coming off the door-jamb.

'All what about?' said the other man.

'The guy with a blue guitar,' said Race.

'It's, it's, it's—' said Griffin.

'It's "The Man with the Blue Guitar",' said the other.

'This, this—' said Griffin.

'Who's the man with the blue guitar?' said Race.

'This is Morgan,' said Griffin.

'You don't know "The Man with the Blue Guitar"?' said Morgan.

He studied Race intently, without warmth.

'No,' said Race.

'*Really?*' said Morgan. His amazement appeared to be genuine.

And then Race felt not just envious, but ashamed as well, and more irritated than ever. 'Some guy with a blue guitar!' he thought, and from that point on he decided to steer clear of Morgan or treat him warily, but in fact there had been no need to take that precaution: Morgan showed no sign of wanting his friendship, or anyone else's for that matter, apart from Griffin's. He and Griffin were very close, almost inseparable in fact: after a while they even seemed to resemble each other physically, like two statues which look quite different but which have been carved by the same hand – Griffin, short, stocky, with his anxious blue eye, his cowl of fair hair, Morgan slim, dark, calm, remote. Race crossed their path from time to time, but since that first meeting he and Morgan had hardly exchanged a word. Yet here was Morgan now, in the fog, in the depths of the night, calmly relating what anyone else might have regarded as private matters if not deep secrets. Kissing a boy called Butterfly . . . stealing a ruby necklace . . .

'How did you break it?' he said.

'What?' said Morgan.

'The window.'

'With a bottle,' said Morgan.

'What sort of bottle?'

'A milk bottle,' said Morgan.

'A milk bottle!' said Race. 'You can break a plate-glass window with a milk bottle?'

'I did,' said Morgan.

They were walking on now, in the direction Race had been going when they met.

'Full or empty?' said Race.

'Full,' said Morgan with dignity.

'Did it break?' Race said, after a while.

'What?'

'Did the milk bottle break as well?'

'Oh, you'd better just come and see,' said Morgan.

They went through the fog and into a narrow lane that led to Manners Street.

'Stop,' said Morgan in a whisper.

Further down the alley Race could see a shop with a broken plate-glass window. There were voices, and muffled laughter. He saw a figure inside the window handing objects out to someone on the pavement. Morgan tapped Race on the shoulder and silently motioned for him to move away.

They went back to the open street.

'That was Pinky!' said Morgan. 'Pinky and her girlfriend.'

His eyes registered disbelief, outrage, at what had just been witnessed.

'What the hell is Pinky doing there?' he said, still speaking in a whisper. 'That was *my* smash 'n' grab.'

2

They walked on, Morgan occasionally looking back in the dark, as if at the source of a great mystery. They arrived at Willis Street and then went up Boulcott, behind St Mary of the Angels, and began to climb the steep stairs of Allenby Terrace.

'Allenby Terrace . . .' Morgan said, now speaking in a normal conversational tone. 'It's a surprise, really, don't you think, that they named a street after Allenby?'

'I don't know,' said Race.

They had stopped at the first dog-leg of the steps, under a streetlight half-hidden by a creeping vine.

'Our troops hated General Allenby. Don't you know the story?'

'No,' said Race.

'I'll tell you the story,' said Morgan. 'It's really the story of someone called Leslie Lowry. Want to hear the story of Leslie Lowry?'

'Yes,' said Race.

'OK,' said Morgan. 'Leslie Lowry, a young soldier, a trooper, is asleep in his tent one night in Palestine, and in the middle of the night he's woken up. Why is he woken? Think of that painting by Rousseau – the lion and the man asleep in the desert. Although Leslie's not woken by a lion but by his pillow. His pillow is moving under his head! Actually, it's not a pillow, it's his kitbag. This is World War One. Leslie's using his kitbag as a pillow and in the middle of the night his kitbag starts to move. What's happening? Leslie wakes up. What's his kitbag doing? Where's it going? Hey – there's someone in his tent! He jumps up. The other man runs away, and Leslie goes after him. Remember – we're in Palestine. It's 1918. Leslie is in camp, surrounded by hundreds of soldiers. It's the Anzac Division. They've been at Gallipoli, and they've been in France and now they're in Palestine. They've just conquered Palestine under General Allenby and now Leslie's chasing a thief through the dark. The thief doesn't stop. He makes for the lines. And then they're out in the desert. The thief's probably fairly young, and fast, and – you can't deny his courage – he's brave, sneaking into a camp of thousands of soldiers to steal a kitbag. Away he goes. Leslie keeps after him. Leslie's young too, and he's probably fairly fit – he's a country boy. He's played a bit of rugby.'

'Wait a minute,' said Race. 'How do you know all this?'

He didn't really care, but he thought that Morgan shouldn't be allowed to talk too long without interruption.

'My uncle,' said Morgan, nodding, as if acknowledging good conversational grammar. 'He was there. He was in the war. He was in the same camp.'

'OK,' said Race. He nodded as well, accepting the formal role of listener.

'So Leslie's after the thief. They're both running over the sand. Maybe the moon is shining, I don't know. Leslie's not shouting. He's saving his breath. He can hear the thief panting and the thief can hear him. And Leslie's gaining on him. He's faster. He's catching up! But then, just as Leslie reaches him, the thief turns. He has a revolver. He fires. He hits Leslie. The shot attracts the attention of the guard. The guard arrives. Leslie is lying on the ground, dying. He's taken a bullet in the heart. No one else is there. Leslie says nothing, and then he dies. The alarm is sounded. The camp is roused. The soldiers mount a search. There are two settlements nearby. One is called Richon le Zion, where Jewish settlers live. The other is called Surafend, an Arab village. The soldiers follow footprints across the sand for two hundred yards but then the ground turns to rock and the trail is lost. But it seems to have been leading towards Surafend. That makes sense. The Jews of Richon le Zion have no form at all when it comes to pilfering from the army camp. They are delighted with the 'English' as they call the Anzacs. They love them. They adore them! The Anzacs have defeated the Turks and sent them packing after four hundred years. 'The day of deliverance has arrived!' the Jews say. They sing hymns, they put up an obelisk to commemorate the battles, though they take it down later.

'But the Arabs – they're another matter. The soldiers already hate them, or the Muslim Arabs anyway. They're gloomy and suspicious, and they steal, they even dig up the bodies of dead soldiers and strip them naked. That's what the soldiers say. Maybe it's true. And now the footprints of Leslie's killer are leading towards Surafend. So the soldiers put a cordon round the village and send a message to headquarters to report what's happened.'

All this was recounted, with several stops, as Race and Morgan climbed the steps of Allenby Terrace, then turned and came up the stairless part of the lane between old wooden houses whose windows were dark. It was nearly four in the morning. The fog had become thinner as they climbed. A few stars could be seen above the chimneys. Race and Morgan were taking their time. They both felt a kind of false sobriety – the nightclub, the fog, the business with the milk bottle and the broken window and jewels, possibly rubies – all that seemed a long time ago. Here they were on Allenby Terrace at four in the morning, enjoying the experience, almost political, of being the only people awake among many dark houses.

'The troops wait all night,' said Morgan. 'Morning comes. Nothing is moving in Surafend. The village is holding its breath. Then the order comes from army HQ. *Withdraw.* Remove the cordon, stand down, go back to camp. The men obey. And as they leave, they see some men slipping out from Surafend, away into the desert. *There goes the murderer!* That's what the soldiers think. And they're enraged. One of their mates is dead and nothing is to be done. HQ doesn't want any trouble with the Arabs. The British have just conquered Palestine, and already offered the Jews a national home there, and the Arabs are in a state of alarm. They're gloomy and suspicious and frightened. The British want to soothe their fears. The last thing they need is an Arab revolt. They're prepared to overlook minor matters. Any pilfering in the camp is blamed on Australians. But our boys can't agree with that. Leslie Lowry is not a minor matter. He's their mate. He's a 21-year-old. He's been shot dead in the sand-hills and the killer's going scot-free. So they decide to take matters into their own hands. The next night a hundred of them, maybe two hundred, slip out of camp and surround Surafend. No one knows exactly what happened next. The troops said they sent for the headman at sunset and told him to hand over the killer, but either he wouldn't or he couldn't – well, how could he, if the killer's run away, which the soldiers think he has, so the whole thing makes no sense in fact – but, in any case, no killer is produced and then the soldiers go in. They go on a rampage. No firearms are used. They don't want to wake HQ. They're armed with pick handles and horse traces – iron collars covered in leather – you know, the weapons of a lynch mob. The Arabs are outnumbered and disorganised. The soldiers later said they spared the women and children, and the old men, but they would say that, wouldn't they? What really happened? All the reports in the soldiers' own words use the same language – horrible language that won't state the facts but has a grin on its face: "We *taught* them *a lesson* . . . They needed a little *discipline* . . . They were *dealt with* . . ." In other words, it was a massacre. They hunted the men down and beat them to death with axe-handles. Castration is mentioned. Rape. Bodies are thrown down wells. The figures are all over the place. Forty dead. Maybe a hundred. Maybe more. All for good old Leslie. Then the troops forget to be discreet and set fire to the village. Finally, the screams and the flames are noticed at HQ, but by the time the MPs arrive, it's all over. The troops have gone and the villagers have been killed and the village is in ruins.'

'Wait a minute. Where's your uncle in all this?'

Morgan stared at him, his eyes light.

'He stayed in camp. He had nothing to do with it.'

'How do you know?'

'If he had been there he'd hardly have told us all about it, would he?'

'OK,' said Race.

'He was probably on the side of the Arabs by then. And so was Allenby. Allenby was in a fury. The next day he paraded the troops and refused to return the salute of the New Zealand commander. That was unheard of. And then he laid into them. *Cowards* he called them, *cold-blooded killers*. They had to stand there and take it. Everyone was terrified of Allenby. If you wanted someone to play the Minotaur, Allenby could have done it without the mask. He had a huge head and tiny little eyes like mica chips. Bull Allenby he was called. They're all there, standing at attention in the sun. *"Brutes. Cowards. Killers. Scum."* This was incredible to them because they saw themselves as world-class heroes. They were the heroes of Gallipoli. They were the heirs of the Crusaders. Richard the Lion-heart. They had conquered the Holy Land. They marched into Jerusalem through the Jaffa Gate. And now they're the scum of the earth. He never retracted, he never forgave them. And they never forgave him. Yet here we are now, boys, on Allenby Terrace!'

Morgan was suddenly quite light-hearted. They were sitting on a fence consisting of a series of posts connected by smooth wooden planks just wide enough to form a seat. Morgan in his fisherman's jersey and Race in his black Renaissance costume were sitting there, each with his leg crossed on his knee, just before the dawn.

'And that was it,' said Morgan. 'That was the massacre of Surafend. And that was the start of the Middle East crisis. When you hear about Arab attacks and terrible Israeli reprisals – massacres and demolitions and all the rest of it – and you think 'Who taught them that?' – there's the answer. *We did.* It was us. The Jews at Richon le Zion had been plagued by the Arabs of Surafend for years. They were delighted with what happened. "So the Arabs needed a *little lesson*?" they said. "Now we know what to do." '

They walked on up to The Terrace. The fog had almost gone. The streetlights high on Brooklyn hill could be seen quite clearly, and even those far away on Miramar and along the Petone shore.

'It was us,' said Morgan again.

He looked up and down The Terrace.

'That's where the party was,' he said suddenly, pointing south along the street. He stood looking down the hill.

'You know,' he said with an air of detachment, 'maybe I knew Butterfly was a boy all along.'

'Really?' said Race.

'Well, you'd think so, wouldn't you? I mean there is a major difference here. She sort of reminded me of some kid I used to know. Maybe she *was* that kid.'

Here we go again, Race thought.

'Maybe that's why I broke the window,' said Morgan. 'I had to make amends.'

'Amends?'

'I had to make it up to someone,' said Morgan.

'Who?'

'Liddy. I thought: "I have to give Liddy something beautiful." '

'Who's Liddy?' said Race.

'Lids, Liddy, Lydia my girlfriend,' said Morgan. 'I had to make it up to her. Going to a party and kissing Butterfly! What would she think? What would I think if she did that to me?'

'I don't know,' said Race. 'I've never met her.'

'Of course you've never met her,' said Morgan.

'I've never heard of her before,' said Race.

'She lives a hundred miles away – there's your reason,' said Morgan.

'Oh,' said Race.

'Palmerston North,' said Morgan, 'is where she hangs her hat.'

'Her hat?' said Race.

'Yes, her hat,' said Morgan testily. 'She's going to be a vet,' he added, as if spelling out the link.

'I don't know anything about her,' said Race.

Morgan looked at him thoughtfully. 'I know her better than most,' he said. 'And I know one thing: she loves me.'

He paused.

'And I thought, "I've done her a grave harm," ' he said.

The dawn was in the sky. It was time to go. They were near the corner of The Terrace and Salamanca Road. Morgan crossed the street but Race stood where he was.

'I go this way,' said Race, pointing towards Brooklyn hill where his parents lived.

Morgan looked back at Race.

'Or maybe I harmed my *idea* of her,' he called out among the silent houses.

They watched each other on different sides of the street.

'Maybe it's the same thing,' said Morgan.

3

Morgan came in late. Everyone else was getting ready to leave, putting on hats and coats. It was cold outside and was just starting to rain, although the rain was so fine it looked like mist through the window. Out in the corridor there was a great clamour: the whole building seemed to be humming and ringing with voices and footsteps. Across the park, crowds were gathering by the law library steps.

'Morgan, you're late,' said Candy. 'He's late,' she said to Race. 'He's always late. Make him a sign.'

Candy was the driving force of their group that day. She had organised the boards and sticks, hammers and nails, the pots of paint and brushes to make their placards. Race was still on the floor, on his knees, painting the last signs. 'Stop The War' 'Stop The War' 'Stop The War'. He was getting bored with this train of thought. He was kneeling on the floor in FitzGerald's room, one of the two which FitzGerald shared with Adam Griffin. Fitzy had done very well in the room department. He had installed himself – how had he managed it? – in the best set of rooms in the whole hall of residence. He, naturally, had taken the inner of the two, while quiet, shy Griffin had to be content with the outer, but they each had a tall window that opened onto a balcony looking out, beyond high pillars, to the harbour and the city and the eastern ranges across the sea. The only drawback to the rooms was their central location. There on the T-junction of the ground-floor corridor, Griffin and FitzGerald had an endless flow of visitors – anyone coming back from lectures or on their way to the dining room or the common-room after dinner or even going to the showers with a towel round their waist tended to drop in . . . it was Grand Central in FitzGerald's room or Grand Bloody Central, depending on FitzGerald's mood. Right now there were ten or twelve people there – FitzGerald, of course, and Griffin and Griffin's new girlfriend, Candy Dabchek, and both the Gudgeon sisters, Rose and Dinah, and Chadwick, who was from California, and Race Radzienwicz, and handsome Rod Orr who couldn't care less about the war in Vietnam but who hated to miss out on a party and who thought this might turn into one in due course. Even Lane Tolerton was there, and who ever expected to see him on an anti-war march, in his brogues and Prince of Wales tweed? And now here was Morgan, coming in late. He, alone, was hardly ever seen in those rooms, which was odd because Adam was his closest friend, but Morgan didn't like a crowd. Or perhaps he didn't like *this* crowd. But here he was, slipping through the door as if to say 'Well, I'm here – but not really.'

'Make him a sign,' commanded Candy. Race, kneeling on the carpet, picked up his brush. He looked at the signs the others had painted. They were more interesting than his, he had to admit it. '*They make a Desert and Call it Peace*' said Griffin's, in letters of yellow and green. *Fuck Off Maxwell!* FitzGerald had written in psychedelic swirls to excite the police. General Maxwell Taylor and Clark Clifford, special envoys of the US president, had arrived in the country that morning. At that very moment they were down at parliament, trying to persuade the government to send more troops to Vietnam. The city felt electric, there was gloomy exhilaration in the air, as before a storm. Down on his knees on the old brown floral carpet, Race picked up his brush and started to paint, in the shape of an arch –

ALL YOU NEED

The letters were purple and blue, and edged with red. Race enjoyed doing this: he felt as if he was not only outlining but slipping in among the trees of an interesting new wood. A few days before, in London, the Beatles had sat in front of TV cameras in the studio in Abbey Road and sung the single word 'love' nine times over and then, sang it seventy more times in various strophes. Within minutes, the song was known around the world. It was the first live international TV hook-up. In the eighteenth century a young man like Jean-Jacques Rousseau, composing a song in Geneva, would be amazed to hear it being sung on a street corner across the lake only *ten days* later. 'All You Need Is Love' leapt three oceans in half a second. The satellites which broadcast it were each fixed in one spot high above the earth, although in fact they tended to wander about a bit, pushed this way and that by the infinitesimal pressure of sunlight and faint irregularities in the earth's gravitational field. They were built by the same company as the bombers which, that year, were pounding Vietnam *back to the stone-age*. 'All You Need Is Love' rang down through the exosphere. Making the arch of blue and purple letters, which also reminded him of the trunks of a wood on a hill, Race slightly miscalculated the space. He had to run the last two words together:

He then dipped the brush in the red and wrote below the arch:

LOVE

and edged the letters with maroon.

'How's that?' he said, sitting back on his heels.

'It's fine, it's great, we're late,' said Candy. She picked up the sign and thrust it at Morgan. Morgan took it and said nothing. Chadwick, the Californian, who had just come back to the room for a coat, saw the sign in Morgan's hand.

'Oh, yeah – that should do the trick,' he said, jeering slightly, pushing his fist through his coat sleeve. 'That should stop the Pentagon in its tracks. *Love, love, love!*'

'The town of Abdera,' said Morgan, looking at Chadwick as if he was very far away, 'was the vilest place in all of Thrace. What with poison and assassinations, there was no going there by day. It was worse at night. But one day the play *Andromeda* was put on and the whole town was delighted with it, especially the speech "O love, love, prince of gods and men." '

'Jesus, Morgan,' said Chadwick, looking offended.

'In every street, in every house, that was all that was heard: "O love, love – prince of gods and men," ' said Morgan. 'The whole city caught fire like the heart of one man and opened itself to—'

'Jesus Christ!' said Chadwick. He turned to Race appealing for support. But there was no time; they were late – Candy and Race were already going out the door, Morgan followed, and Chadwick came out last; they clattered down the stairs to the basement and through an outer door which led to a shortcut to the park, and crossed the park in the rain which was still as fine as mist, and then joined the march which had just begun to wind down Salamanca Road towards the city.

'So what was that all about?' said Chadwick, coming up along-side Race a few minutes later. '"The town of Abdera was the vilest place in all of Thrace." I mean, don't you think that was just a little weird?'

'I don't know,' said Race.

'I think it was,' said Chadwick. He touched Race's forearm confidentially. 'I think it was definitely weird,' he said, 'and I think he is definitely weird.'

Chadwick usually had a fantastic Californian geniality to him, as if all problems could be dissolved with a little blast of sunlight, but now he had taken against Morgan. He had been outplayed. He wanted Race to join forces with him. But Race had no desire to join forces against Morgan. In the first place, Morgan was already almost a loner, which meant, in Race's view, you didn't gang up on him. Secondly, though, and more important, he showed no sign of caring or even noticing if all the forces in the universe were against him. This gave him the air of someone with a valuable secret. 'He *knows* something,' Race had come to think. 'He knows something we don't. I wonder what it is.' Chadwick read some of this in Race's expression. He gave up and danced backwards a few yards to join the Gudgeon sisters. The procession reached The Terrace; chants began to echo among the office blocks. The rain began to fall more heavily. High above the street the windows were crowded with office workers watching the march. They looked down on the marchers angrily, as if allowed up from their desks for a minute or two only on that condition. The police had just deciphered FitzGerald's sign and dashed into the crowd to seize it. FitzGerald resisted. There was a scuffle. FitzGerald disappeared, somehow with an air of triumph, into a paddy-wagon. The rain-cloud darkened overhead as the crowd reached parliament. It was then just on noon. Inside the building the talks with the Americans had been going on for two hours. The prime minister suggested an adjournment for lunch. He led his guests through the building and, passing the windows, he stopped to give his guests a view of the demonstration outside. He was pleased at the size of the crowd. He had no desire to send more troops to Vietnam. He could plead public dislike of the war. Just at that moment, as he and the envoys stopped to look at the crowd and the rain-cloud came in low over the city, someone turned on the lights and the crowd saw the little golden lamps of chandeliers come twinkling on deep in the parliament building and three grey-headed men looking down from a tall window. There was a sort of mumble, a baying, a booing: someone shouted something about guns and butter. A man leapt over the barricade and swerved past the police guard towards the steps of parliament, which were wide and impressive as befits a public building, but also unusually steep. He began to run up this cliff of stairs, but his progress was slower than he expected. Two plain-clothes men went after him but they were slow as well. All three toiled towards the great front door like figures in a dream. Then one of the policemen made a dive and caught the man by the ankles. At the same time, a fight had broken out further west near the cathedral, where pro-war demonstrators began to scuffle with the Trotskyites. The police made a charge. There was a dipping and swirling of placards like gunwales. ALL YOU NEEDIS rose briefly then fell from view. The prime minister and his visitors turned and went away to their lunch. And quite suddenly the flurries came to an end as if a gust of wind passed over a body of water and left it calm again – the Trots and the pro-war crowd stopped fighting, the workers on the cathedral scaffolding stopped cheering them on, the man on the steps and the police running after him had vanished as if they had never existed, and the gulls settled down again, folding their wings comfortably on the marble heads and the up-flung hands of various statues. Chadwick appeared by Race's side.

'Let's go,' he said. 'The old bores are starting.'

An old man with a clear, ruddy complexion and a noble expression had unfolded a little aluminium step-ladder in front of the crowd and he sprang up the first three steps.

'Comwades!' he shouted, twirling his hand up like Lenin.

Chadwick and Race went away down the grassy slope towards the Cenotaph. And there was Tolerton as well, zipping past in his expensive tweed jacket. He saw Race and Chadwick and came over.

'I think that calls for a drink,' he said. 'I don't mind a little anti-war rioting, no less than the next man. But spare me the dialectic.'

And there was Candy Dabchek as well; she was alone and looking around in all directions. She saw the others and came to join them.

'Where's Adam?' said Candy. 'Where's Morgan? Where's FitzGerald?'

There was a discriminating furrow on her brow, as if those present were all very well, but she was used to the best. Candy's family was rich. Her father had a chain of 'fashion' stores – discount, mainly, in poorer suburbs – and wealth gave her a sense of entitlement. She had thick pale hair and big dark eyes, which sometimes looked alarmed, sometimes accusing. None of her features would have amounted to much on their own but she had decided that she was going to be beautiful and so she was – that was the impression she gave. She was beautiful, and determined, and somewhat sly as well: Griffin had met her one fine day coming out of FitzGerald's bedroom. It was about eleven in the morning and she was in tears at the time. He comforted her, he made her a cup of tea. FitzGerald had the reputation as the heartless Casanova of the group. Candy always denied later that she had slept with FitzGerald, although she had, and in point of fact she continued to do so occasionally after she became Griffin's girlfriend. Morgan, who watched closely over his friend, suspected it, but said nothing as he had no evidence. Griffin sensed Morgan's protective posture but if anything he resented it. He felt their relative positions had reversed. He had a girlfriend now, he had no need of Morgan's protection. Still they formed a trio, Candy and Adam and Morgan, though at times there was a certain silence in the bonds between them, and Adam's stutter did not go away. Candy filled in the silence with her chatter. Just then she caught sight of a coloured arch – ALL YOU NEEDIS – coming down the hill among the crowd.

'*There* they are,' she said. 'Oh, *there* you are, where on earth did you get to? I was hunting everywhere. What about Fitzgerald, do you think they'll charge him?' She chattered on as they left the Cenotaph and walked around to Cable Car Lane to catch the cable-car up to Kelburn again, stopping on the way for fish and chips and then a drink in a pub, leaving behind their placards in a rubbish bin outside the pub like umbrellas in a stand. The cable-cars going up the hill were all crowded with people coming from the demonstration. With lectures cancelled or boycotted, every-thing looked and felt different. You thought of the stage direction

in another part of the wood. When they arrived at Kelburn, someone was playing music across the park and suddenly it was an
early winter evening, the sky turning slightly pink. Tolerton had
bought some wine in town, and as they came out of the station
they turned and went away to the right. That in itself felt – what? –
revolutionary. Up until then, any of their group getting off the
cable-car at Kelburn automatically turned to the left and went
round to the dormitory, or straight across the park to the student
cafe, the libraries, lecture rooms. No one ever took the other
direction to the botanic gardens at the top of the hill. What was
there for them? Flowers, lawns, a wood from which sometimes at
night you could hear owls calling. And yet this time and for no
clear reason and without even any discussion they turned right
and drifted up the hill, past the old observatory and the upper
lawn and into the manuka wood above the rose gardens, Tolerton
holding a wine bottle by the neck, Candy, Adam in a long paisley
scarf, the Gudgeon sisters, Rod Orr, Chadwick and Race, and
Morgan bringing up the rear.

Race had a vague idea that they were under Chadwick's gener-
alship. Chadwick was from Los Angeles. He was black as well,
which added to his authority, though no one could have said
exactly why. He was quite well-off; his father was a wealthy dentist.
Chadwick had been sent out to New Zealand when his parents
decided that the US was a dangerous country for a young black
man, even one whose father was a wealthy orthodontist, to grow
up in. What safer place than distant New Zealand? He had been
at school in Pasadena. Pasadena! At dusk in Pasadena, according
to Chadwick, you could see not one, or two, but three great rivers
of headlights and tail lights, the tail lights all glowing red, stretching away in different directions into the LA penumbrae. It

sounded like the future, it *was* the future – rivers of red tail lights flowing away to the horizon. Chadwick had been at school in Pasadena during the Cuban crisis.

'We really thought we were going to die,' he told Race. 'We were at school and the air-raid sirens went off. It was only a drill, but what did we know? Nuclear war was looming and then the sirens start. We're under our desks! Then someone saw these missile silos opening on the hill-tops. We didn't even know they were there! And everyone started running around screaming, *"It's really happening!"'*

Race liked this story. He saw the kids under the desks, and he thought of the desks in the American school system – thin, plywood veneer, maybe kidney-shaped? And he liked the way that Chadwick did the kids running round screaming: he put both of his hands in front of him and waved them like Mickey Mouse, his eyes and mouth opened wide.

'And all for what?' said Chadwick. 'Cuba, obviously, but what was the real reason? Economic theory. Who should own the means of production? Nuclear Armageddon – maybe the end of the world – over that. Thanks, guys.'

Chadwick looked into Race's eyes with his clear grey gaze.

'We were fourteen then,' he said, 'and now we're twenty, and we're not going to let 'em do it again. Fuck them. That's what's happening now. All the rest of it – the long hair and sex and drugs and all – they're just bonus extras, you know, thrown in for fun.'

They were coming through the manuka wood into the Dell where, in summer, Shakespeare was put on – *Midsummer Night's Dream, Two Gentlemen of Verona* – but now the Dell was cold and dark. Chadwick and Race followed the others down the slope and then along the gravelled path at the side of the rose gardens. The rose gardens were also cold and in shadow, but the fountain was playing and the roses were in bloom. There were some people walking around, bending here and there to sniff at a flower, their hands behind their backs.

'That's what they do,' said Race. 'They put their hands behind their backs to show they're not going to steal the roses. But all it shows is that they've thought of stealing them. It shows they have *mens rea*, a guilty mind.'

He had picked up this phrase from Tolerton and Rod Orr who were law students.

'No. You haven't grasped it at all,' said Chadwick, who was also a law student and who disapproved of Race's use of legal terminology. Race was studying biology. 'In any case, it's nothing to do with your state of mind,' Chadwick said. 'When you're bending over you keep your balance better with your hands behind your back.'

He stopped and bowed deeply over a rose, his hands behind his back like a royal male, to prove the point. Then they walked on. Ahead of them on the path was a long black car with government plates. Race glanced in as he went past. Three Asian men in suits were in the back. All three were gazing impassively at the rose gardens through the closed window. Race guessed they were official visitors who had been sent on a tour of the city's sights. The chauffeur, a little turkey-cock of a man, ex-army by the look of him, wearing a red tie and black blazer, stared straight ahead with an angry expression. Race and Chadwick walked past, and then they paused at the end of the drive where a set of stairs led up to another lawn.

'I didn't mean that about the drugs,' said Chadwick. 'The drugs are important. LSD is real important. Did you know that LSD was synthesised the *same month* that nuclear fission was achieved in another lab five thousand miles away? Call that a coincidence? I don't think so.'

'So what do you think?' said Race.

'I think it was *sent*,' said Chadwick, and he stopped to look into Race's eyes, his pleasing way of adding emphasis to a declaration. They stood at the bottom of the steps to consider the matter. Morgan, who had fallen behind the rest of the party, was drifting along the gravel drive on his own. He came up behind the long black car and then without apparently taking thought or even increasing his pace, he vaulted onto the boot of the car and then onto the roof, and took a few steps forward and then stopped.

Four heads, three Asian and one turkey-cock, jerked upward as one. Disbelief was written on their faces. There were *footsteps* above them! Morgan stood there peacefully for a moment, outlined against the hillside woods. Then he walked forward, stepped down on the hood and back to the ground, and continued along the gravel drive. No one spoke. No one else moved, not even the angry-looking chauffeur. Chadwick and Race were half-screened by the branches of a tree at the foot of the steps and Morgan had not seen them watching. He had leapt on the car solely to suit his own requirements and he still did not appear to notice their presence as he came along the path and nor did Race and Chadwick speak a word to each other, but they both turned quickly and went up the steps so as not to be seen as Morgan came along.

4

'It says here,' said Race, rolling up a magazine and, reasonably enough, he thought, under the circumstances, swiping FitzGerald on the back of the head with it, 'it says that every era has its own blind spots. What do you think? What would you say ours are?'

FitzGerald, at the wheel of the car, said nothing. His eyes were fixed on the way ahead. They were driving on an unsealed country road. A cone of dust rose behind them, filling the rear window. All the roadside foliage was laden with dust, which gave the landscape a wild, slovenly air.

'The question doesn't make any sense,' said Rosie Gudgeon, who was in the front seat between Race and FitzGerald. 'If we knew what our blind spots were, then we wouldn't be blind to them, would we?'

'But that's why they change,' said Race. 'One day people realise the blind spot is there and then they do something about it. That's history.'

The car was an old Chevrolet sedan. The cracked leather bench-seats gave off the dry, dusty smell of ancient summers and old barns. There was still a cobweb in the back window. Race and FitzGerald had bought the car off the side of the road for $100 a week earlier. The vendor was a white man in his mid-fifties who seemed to be on the point of rage. A sprightly green oak shaded the transaction. Race lifted the hood and looked at the engine, then walked round the car and looked at the tyres, but he really knew nothing about mechanics, and the middle-aged vendor knew he knew nothing, which only added to his irritation. They handed over the $100 and drove away into the summer. It was ten days before Christmas. Now in the car seven days later were Race and FitzGerald and the Gudgeon sisters – tall, confident Rosie and short, sweet-natured Dinah – and Rod Orr, and Panos Carroll, one of FitzGerald's school-friends who had come up from the South Island to join them on the road trip. They were driving around the wild coast between Opotiki and Gisborne. The dust rose up behind them, the long white road stretched ahead. 'Bang!' went the stones on the chassis. 'Bang! bang! bang!' The goblins of summer were rapping from below. 'Freedom!' they were saying. 'Sea! Sunburn! Nakedness!'

'*I* think it's a good question,' said Dinah who was reading *Middlemarch* in the back seat. 'Everyone in *Middlemarch* goes round toying with these little silver-handled whips while they're talking.'

'Whips! What for?' said Rosie.

'To whip their horses.'

'Oh, well,' said Rose.

'But I bet they never thought how odd *that* would seem one day.'

'They're not people, Dinah,' said Rose. 'They're characters in a book. They don't think things that aren't written down.'

'Why not?' said Dinah. 'You think things that aren't written down.'

'But I exist, darling,' said Rosie. 'They don't exist.'

'Of course they exist,' said Dinah.

'Not like I exist,' said tall, brown-limbed Rosie, in her sarong and bikini top. She turned to FitzGerald, laughing.

'What do you think, sweetie?'

'Me? I'm lost,' said FitzGerald, watching the road.

Rosie leant over and kissed FitzGerald's ear. Dinah put *Middlemarch* up in front of her face. *'Bang!'* went the goblins under the car. *'Bang, bang!'* The mood in the Chev was not good. All had gone well until the day before when, in the twinkling of an eye it seemed, everything had changed. It began with a voice calling from the road. Panos was alone on the beach when he heard it. Race was way out in the surf. Dinah had set off on a long walk along the shore with *Middlemarch* – every so often you saw a parasol of white gulls rise and hover, then settle again, to mark her progress. Fitzgerald and Rosie had gone off somewhere together. Then Panos heard the voice calling and saw Rod Orr on the coastal road – he could just see his sandy head bobbing along above the low dunes. Panos went up to meet him but on the way a faint noise caught his attention. He stopped and looked at the tent, which was closed. He unzipped the door and saw two naked bodies entwined. FitzGerald and Rosie were making love! The zip sang! Panos was outraged. He had been under the impression all week that Rosie had been flirting with him, which in fact she had. He marched away to greet Rod, his face like thunder. Down at the edge of the surf, Race also caught sight of Rod above the dunes. He was amazed. He had deliberately not invited Rod on this trip. He had found of late that he was uncomfortable in Rod's presence – he hardly knew why. What was Rod doing here now? How on earth had he located them along a hundred miles of empty coast?

Race went up into the dunes as well and reached the tent. Rod and Panos arrived down from the road at the same time. The tent zip sang again. Rosie emerged, tying her bikini top.

'Sorry, everyone,' she said. She laughed her husky, musical laugh. 'We didn't *plan* this, I promise. We just looked at each other and went "Wow!"'

'Yes, that's it: "Wow!"' said FitzGerald lazily from the orange-tinted interior.

'*What* a scene!' said Rod, pretending to be joyful, the sandy-haired Cupid of the match, yet he was feeling hurt at Panos's distracted air and by Race's cool greeting. Within a few hours everyone found they had feelings they could not express. Dinah came back from her walk and was disapproving of her sister, and jealous as well. Panos was angry, and jealous of FitzGerald. FitzGerald and Rosie decided they would now rather be off on their own, yet that was impossible – there was only one car, and hardly any passing traffic, much less public transport, was to be seen. Race meanwhile had realised that someone had been in touch with Rod all the time, guiding him in, so to speak, by phone. Had everyone been in on the secret? Everyone adored Rod, the entertainer, the charmer – sandy-haired, wanton-eyed Rod.

We went to the animal fair,
The birds and the beasts were there

Rod sang from the back seat as they drove away the next morning. Race now felt *he* was the outsider in his own car. And Rod, for his part, was still feeling hurt. The fact was – he loved Race! He was to be punished for that, apparently. That was why he had not been invited on the trip. And yes, it was true – Rosie had secretly kept in touch with him for the last week. She had rung from road-side phone boxes all the way, and told him exactly where they were. He had come hitch-hiking after them. And why not? They were all his friends as well. But now everyone was at odds . . .

The further they drove, the rougher the country became. Fences were scanty or non-existent. Brown cattle wandered the road. A bull stood its ground as they approached, and shook its head. A cow and calf went lumbering ahead of the car for half a minute then crashed away into the dust-hung scrub and stood there, eyes white-rolling. The cone of white dust filled the rear window.

'Stop the car!' said Race suddenly.

The road had turned away from the coast and they were crossing a wide inland plain. FitzGerald pulled over and stopped the car. Race got out and stood on the road.

Far away in the back country rose a single, steep-sided, table-topped mountain; there were one or two chasms in its side, dark, faint and secretive, like the folds in ancestral clothes.

'Look at that!' said Race, but no one in the car was interested. No one, as far as he could tell, was even looking at the view. The wind hummed in power-lines above. A line of willows marked the course of the river across the plain, the willows a-shimmer, as if the water had taken aerial form just in order to dance in air. Race kept his gaze on the mountain in the back country. It reminded him of something – it was like the frontispiece of an old book, he thought, some famous book he had never read. There were tiny dots of birds flying into one of the chasms. Just then he thought of something else.

'Morgan!' he said through the car window. 'Doesn't he live round here somewhere?'

'I think maybe he does,' said FitzGerald.

'We should go and see him,' said Race.

'We should,' said FitzGerald.

'Who's Morgan?' said Rosie.

'Morgy-baby,' said FitzGerald.

'I don't know who you mean,' said Rosie.

'You know Morgan,' said FitzGerald. 'He used to come to my rooms sometimes.'

'We'd just call in,' said Race.

'We would,' said FitzGerald.

'But will I like him?' said Rosie. 'I might not like him.'

'I don't,' said Rod Orr. 'I don't like him, I don't like him, I don't like him – end of story.'

'I do,' said Dinah. 'I hardly know him but I think he's adorable. He's just like Will Ladislaw.'

'*Who?*' said Rod Orr.

'Someone in *Middlemarch*,' said Dinah.

'Oh,' said Rod. Then he laughed a little wildly: he had heard disappointment in his own voice.

'That's it,' said FitzGerald. 'Three against two. Let's go and see Morgan.'

Race got back in the car and FitzGerald began to idle forward.

'What about Panos?' said Rosie. 'What does Panos think?'

'Panos doesn't know Morgan,' said Race. 'How would he know Morgan?'

'I know Morgan Tawhai,' said Panos. 'He was at school with us.' For some reason he found himself speaking in a sepulchral voice.

'He was at school with all of you?' said Race. 'I didn't know that.'

'Then he was expelled,' Panos said.

'Expelled!' said Rosie. She looked disapproving. Rosie's and

Dinah's father was a senior diplomat. At times, when it suited Rosie, who had lived in Paris and Washington and Rome, she liked to play the *grande dame*. Now, in her bikini top and sarong, she looked down from a great height at anyone who had ever been expelled from school.

'But you know, he was the clever one,' said FitzGerald. 'He just knew more than the rest of us.'

'Such as?' said Rosie.

'I don't know—' said FitzGerald.

'What is the name of the liquor flowing in the veins of the immortal gods?' said Panos from the back seat.

'And?' said Rosie, putting her pretty brown foot up on the dashboard.

'Ichor,' said Panos.

'*Ichor?*' said FitzGerald. 'God, I'd forgotten that. Ichor. OK. That's it. Let's go and see Morgan.'

They drove on. A Maori farmer with a pair of round spectacles was ploughing a dusty field beside the road. His glasses flashed in the sun. There was a barn with a round roof behind him. *The big baboon by the light of the moon was combing his auburn hair*, sang Rod from the back seat. It was late December – midsummer in the South Pacific. That same day, on an Apollo mission halfway to the moon, the first photograph of the planet Earth was taken by a man far out in space. This was not known to those in the car. The last radio station had gone out of range two days before. Joe Cocker was singing 'With a Little Help From My Friends' as the signal faded. They drove on north looking at the signposts – Raukokore, Gisborne, Opotiki, Tikitiki, Cape Runaway. At the next settlement they went to the pub and had a drink. Rosie slipped upstairs and took a shower in an upstairs room, without management noticing, and then descended the stairs grandly, her hair in a towel like a turban. Then they went to the post office and got directions to the Tawhai property. Sunset was reddening the sky when they crossed an old wooden bridge out of town, the planks rumbling beneath them. The red in the sky was reflected on the river and beneath the reflection you could see brown boulders on the bed as they headed into the dusk to find Morgan Tawhai.

5

'Trouser creases,' said Rod Orr. 'I mean why have sharp edges on the front of trousers? *Why?*'

'No,' said Race flatly. 'No moral dimension. There has to be a moral dimension.'

They were talking about the blind spots of the age again. FitzGerald was still at the wheel. Dusk had fallen. They were driving along a narrow coastal plain; sand was blowing across the road in the headlights.

'How do you mean "moral"?' said Dinah.

'It has to make people think: "How could they *do* that?"'

'Such as?' said Dinah.

'I don't know,' said Race. 'Child chimney-sweeps. Slavery. Ducking-stools. What do we do now like that?'

'Oh, God,' said Rosie in the front seat. 'War. Dental caries. Eating animals.'

'Trouser creases,' said Rod Orr.

The car made a muffled lurch and stopped. They had gone off the road.

'OK,' said FitzGerald to forestall other comment. 'OK. OK. OK.'

They got out and stood in the dark. The road, as far as could be seen, ran in a straight line across the narrow plain but where they were was a slight dog-leg before a low concrete bridge that crossed a creek. In the blowing sand, FitzGerald had missed the dog-leg and gone straight ahead. Both front wheels of the Chev were in a sandy depression. Water was beginning to ooze around the tyres.

'OK,' said FitzGerald, again. 'OK.'

'Will you please stop saying OK,' said Rosie. She gave a husky, pleasant, somewhat heartless laugh. 'If there's one thing that this isn't—' she said.

'OK,' said FitzGerald. He looked at her with a glint. Rosie got back in the car, this time in the back seat.

'This has nothing to do with me,' she said. 'Let me know when we're ready to leave.'

'It does have *something* to do with you,' said FitzGerald. 'But stay there. You'll be useful there. You can be ballast.'

'Oh, good,' said Rosie. 'Rod! Come and be ballast with me.'

'I'd better not,' said Rod. He looked anxious. Race and Panos were already collecting branches and stones to put under the front tyres.

'No, go on, Roddy,' said FitzGerald. 'It's a good idea. We'll need the weight.'

Rod sat in the back of the car with Rosie. Dinah reappeared out of the dark. She was carrying some white dog-roses she had found growing beside the road.

'Roses,' said Dinah. 'There must have been a house here once.'

There was not a light – not a star, not a candle – to be seen in any direction, along the coast, inland, or out to sea. The night wind was warm. It blew through the scrub making a caressing sound.

'Imagine *living* here,' said Rosie, looking out the window.

Something white lifted and fell in the distance. It was a wave breaking out at sea, quiet as the sheet floated by a bed-maker.

Race, Panos and Fitzgerald went to work packing stones and branches under the front tyres. Dinah sat in the driver's seat. Then she put the car in reverse and revved the engine while the three heaved at the front bumper. In the back seat Rosie was telling Rod about a party she had been to that winter in Repulse Bay. After a while, an hour or so, the Chev came back on the road and they drove on. This time Race stood outside on the running-board on the passenger's side to see the way ahead. Sand was still blowing across the road in the headlights. Riding outside, holding onto the top of the window frame with one hand, Race began to feel wild exhilaration. The sky had cleared and inland hills stood up like pyramids against the stars.

'Whyever did they get rid of running-boards?' Race yelled in the window.

'Blind spot,' said FitzGerald.

'No. No moral dimension,' said Rosie.

The headlights shone on the flanks of a sandy hill. The sand looked like treasure in the moving beam. The road went up the side of the hill and came round onto the face of a cliff. FitzGerald slowed down. The Chev took up the whole of the narrow cliff road. Looking down, Race saw his sandshoes on the running-board and, far below, the suds of ocean. Up ahead a beam of light swept around the sky, once, with alacrity. Then, after a long delay, it came round again. Then the road sloped down and they came to another coastal plain, and the road came to an end.

'We're here,' said FitzGerald. He stopped the car on the verge.

It was very quiet. About a hundred yards in from the road was a house in a stand of trees.

'Jesus,' said FitzGerald. 'It's the back of beyond.'

They got out of the car.

'We can't possibly go in,' said Rosie, looking at the house. 'It must be past midnight.'

'We don't have to go in,' said FitzGerald. 'We can sleep right here.'

It was midsummer night. The wind had dropped. Stars were out in their thousands. *Ruru!* an owl called loudly, quite nearby. FitzGerald and the others took their bedding, sleeping bags and pillows, out of the boot and laid the bags on the grass right there in front of the car. The grass was a strange variety, growing straight out of the sand. Race shucked off his shoes and trod on the ground experimentally. He felt the sand, cold and silken, below the blades. He went on some way into the grassy dunes, and then stopped and looked back at the car, and the distant house, and the rumpled night-land of hills and bush.

The owl called again, quite loud. After a pause, another answered in the middle distance.

And then, finally, another – *ruru!* – far, far away, like a sound formed by the midnight stars themselves.

The Chev was of pre-war manufacture: from a distance it looked like an old upturned bathtub. Race couldn't see the little humps of his friends any more. They had gone straight to sleep – it was as if they had disappeared into earth. He went further on, down into valleys of cold sand, and up again on the ridges. Ahead of him was a grove of trees, and in the distance a vague pallor – the sea, still out of sight. Race set off to the grove and reached it and stepped in, and then he saw that it was not a grove but a single great tree, like a house, with a star shining here and there through the joists. Standing in the house Race then, for a full minute, felt a kind of happiness, as if he had achieved something solid, true – but what was it? Just to be there, at that hour, awake? He walked out of the tree shade and saw that the sea was now in view. There was one more dark clump of trees across the dunes, just before the beach.

'I'll go as far as that,' he thought, 'then I'll go back.'

He went on over the dunes. The trees he was heading for suddenly looked lonely, a last outpost at the end of the world. Yet beyond them the whole sea was now brimming as though it knew that it was midsummer night as well, and was bringing in the dawn early, the waves making a kind of sizzling sound like bolts of cloth being unrolled from the horizon. But then, just before he reached the trees, Race stopped. His heart began to pound. There were people on the beach! Four or five men were in the shallows, coming forward, then idling there, silhouetted against the hollow waves.

At the same time as he saw these figures Race believed, in point of fact, there was no one there at all. It was late – he had gone too far from the car – he was in total solitude.

Quickly, guilty almost on account of his ontological alarm, Race turned and went back fast over the shadowy dunes, back to the Chev, the old upturned bathtub, and he got into his sleeping bag and laid his head down and almost immediately went to sleep behind the back bumper, on the grass, under the stars in their thousands.

'*My mother*,' said a voice, '*is going to kill you.*'

6

Race's first thought was that something was on fire. Then he realised that the sun was burning the back of his head. He opened his eyes and looked straight across the road. Morgan was leaning on a five-barred gate looking back at him. The sky was deep blue. The sun must have been up for hours. Cicadas sounded like gunfire. Morgan put his finger to his lips. The others, this meant, were still asleep.

But just then they all began to wake as well, like birds coming in to land at the same time.

'Oh, oh, oh . . .' said someone.

'*Ahhh.*' Someone else made a comfortable sigh.

'My mother,' said Morgan in a clear voice, 'is going to kill you.'

'Really?' said Rosie, with a tone of keen interest. 'Will she *really*? Why is she going to kill us?'

'She will kill you,' said Morgan, 'for sleeping here at the gate instead of coming up to the house.'

'We couldn't possibly come up to the house,' said FitzGerald. 'It was one in the morning.'

'Two,' said Rosie, yawning and stretching her long brown arms and twirling her hands experimentally.

'That just makes it worse,' said Morgan. 'Every rule of Maori hospitality you've broken.'

Despite his tone, he was amazed. Visitors – for him! It had never happened before. His father told him to invite people to the farm, but he never had. He thought of asking Adam and Candy but decided against it. 'It's too far,' he said. 'No one will come.' He had gone down to the gate at six that morning just to see whose car it was parked on their doorstep – itself a rare sight – without thinking it would be anyone he knew. Nor had he recognised the first sleepers from what he could see – a tousled male head, a bare female shoulder. Then he saw Race asleep behind the car. For a moment, Morgan imagined Adam and Candy might be there as well, but he looked at all the sleepers again, one by one, and he knew they weren't. He watched them for a while, wondering what had brought them there. He looked at Race. Where *was* he, Morgan thought, just then? Race was undoubtedly present there, in the sun, on the kikuyu grass by the car – what an old crate, Morgan thought, how did that get all the way up here? – but where did he, Race, imagine he was at that moment? A thousand miles, half a lifetime, away?

Then Race opened his eyes and looked across the narrow road. Morgan put his finger to his lips. But the other sleepers began to stir as well, one after the other.

'Every single rule in her book,' said Morgan.

A brown colt had come pacing up behind Morgan and put its head over his shoulder as he spoke. Morgan hoisted the great head and swung it away.

'Back *off*,' he said.

It backed off and nodded its head three times, then began to crop the grass. 'You'd better come up and face the music,' said

Morgan. They all got up and got dressed and, leaving their stuff on the ground or on the fence posts or draped over the car doors, which they left open, they crossed the road and through the gate into the big paddock. The colt pretended to take fright and galloped joyously in a great arc around the fence-line. The sun was burning down. Even in the middle of the paddock the cicadas sounded like a war zone. As they came near the house, two or three dogs stood up from the kennels under a row of pines and began to bark, throats lifted, plumes of their tails waving slowly. A woman came out on the veranda and stood watching them approach. Magpies, the Australian magpies, were bugling in the morning glare.

'There's my mother,' said Morgan. 'Every single rule in her book . . . These are friends of mine,' he called.

'Friends of yours!' said Morgan's mother, coming down a step or two. 'Oh, my heavens. You didn't sleep on the roadside?'

'We couldn't possibly have come in,' said Rosie. There was a musical quality to her laugh. 'It was at least two in the morning.'

'Morgan! Your friends should have known to come in!'

Mrs Tawhai looked formidable. There were stern lines on her face and an aureole of iron-grey hair around her head.

'I told them,' said Morgan. 'If only they could behave properly like decent Maoris. Mum was probably still up at two in the morning,' he said to the others. 'She listens to these radio programmes on maths all night. She's crazy about mathematics.'

His mother looked at Morgan steadily as he made this remark.

'Short-wave radio,' said Morgan. 'All she can hear is whistles and pops.'

'He mocks me,' she said. 'His own mother. Oh, my goodness. Sleeping at the gate!'

She came down off the steps and was introduced to them one by one, and then she led them around the side of the house through the orange and lemon trees and into the kitchen through the back door. There she began to make breakfast. Everything was old-fashioned. There was a green wooden dado around the walls of the kitchen, and a single tall sash-window. The window was filled from top to bottom with steep green hillside. The sound of baaing sheep came from the hill and from the yards out the back.

'Morgan, I'll need the shearers' teapot,' Mrs Tawhai said.

Morgan went out to the shearers' quarters and after a few minutes came back with a brown enamelled pot that could hold a dozen or fifteen cups. The tip of the spout was chipped black under the enamel. Tea was made and Mrs Tawhai fried tomatoes and eggs and bacon, and Morgan made toast. Then there was more toast and marmalade and coffee was brewed.

'Coffee,' said Rosie. 'Oh, my God. Real ground coffee!'

Mrs Tawhai looked reproving but all the same she was pleased. Her kitchen crowded with her son's friends talking and laughing!

'Morgan,' she said. 'The toast!'

The toast was burning. Smoke briefly blued the air. There was a brief rumble at the back door, the beating of a soft drum. It was the sound of someone knocking the heel of a rubber boot against a concrete step, and then Morgan's father stepped in. He was stocky, shorter than his wife, dark-skinned, with a piercing eye. He seemed delighted to find six strangers in his house eating his food. In thick grey socks, he advanced noiselessly first to Rosie then to Race, as if selecting the leaders, then to Rod Orr, Dinah, Panos, FitzGerald in turn. He had the manners of a courtier, a duke.

'It's a pleasure, a great pleasure,' he said. 'We tell Morgan to ask his friends up here. "Ask them up," we tell him but he never does.

"It's too far," he says. And it is. We're in the back-blocks here, I know that. But here you are! How long can you stay?'

'We can't stay,' said FitzGerald. 'We have to be back in town on Christmas Eve.'

'You'll stay tonight!' said Mrs Tawhai, looking shocked.

'Not even tonight,' said FitzGerald. 'We have to be in Wellington in two days. We can only stay today.'

'Today! Morgan, they're only here for one day. What are you going to do?'

'I don't know what they're going to do,' said Morgan. 'I have to work.'

'Morgan!' said his mother.

'I'll be cutting scrub,' said Morgan. 'Fifty acres of scrub I'm cutting these holidays.'

'You're not cutting scrub today,' his father said.

'I'll look like Charles Atlas by the end of summer,' said Morgan.

'He's not cutting any scrub today,' his father said to Rosie as if stating a known fact.

'Inches on in all the right places,' said Morgan.

'I go up the hill and cut scrub with him sometimes,' Mr Tawhai said. 'But we're not allowed to talk. Even at smoko, we're not allowed to talk. "The Aborigines in the desert," he says, "sit under a tree to save energy and don't talk." "We're not Aborigines," I say. "We're not in the desert." "Ssshhh," he says. "You're wasting energy." So we sit there on the hill like two blocks of stone and never say a word.'

7

After breakfast, Mrs Tawhai took Race into the hall and showed him various family photos and mementoes. She pointed to a picture of an old man in a top hat, and a sword sent to him by the Queen of England, and a photograph of a boy in uniform, slim as a wand, standing in front of a cannon's mouth.

'This boy swam out in a storm and saved people from a shipwreck,' she said. 'This one' – the man in the top hat – 'at a single word from him, three thousand warriors became Christians.'

The sun sent light straight down the hall, stained pink and yellow and green by a glass door at the end. There was the sound of laughter outside on the veranda. The girls had had showers and then gone out to the garden, their heads wrapped in white towels like turbans. Mrs Tawhai frowned at the man in the top hat.

'Three thousand warriors, singing hymns in the field,' she said. 'The chiefs went up and down the ranks beating anyone who didn't keep perfect time. An English bishop who came to visit fainted away on the spot.'

She led Race away to find the others. They went through Morgan's room which opened onto the veranda. The room was dark. There was a grey army blanket pinned up over the window.

'A blanket!' said Mrs Tawhai. 'Not even a curtain will do. It has to be a blanket. He has to be in the dark first, he says, to do any work, and then he turns a light on.'

She hooked back the blanket from the window, and stood looking around the room.

'He doesn't like it up here, really,' she said. 'The sheep or the shearing or any of it, not really.'

She looked at Race with a burdened expression.

'He ran away, you know,' she said.

'Morgan?' said Race.

'Morgan,' she said. 'He ran away from home. He was missing for weeks.'

'Why did he run away?'

Mrs Tawhai shrugged. 'Some trouble at school. Nothing, really. He was thirteen, fourteen. But he was sent home and he was here with us and then he vanished. He headed for the horizon. Plus, he picked up various children on the way. And they all ran away with him.'

'A sort of Pied Piper,' said Race.

'He was a Pied Piper! He was their leader, I do know that much. He was thirteen, fourteen – the others were only ten, eleven, twelve. But they got all the way to Ninety Mile Beach and no one ever spotted them. Do you know why?'

'Why?'

'They slept in cemeteries,' said Mrs Tawhai. 'Maoris are very superstitious. They wouldn't dream of going into a cemetery at night. But Morgan didn't care. He's never cared about things like that. They were as safe as houses there. No one ever looked in the cemeteries. He was missing for weeks.'

She stood in the veranda door and looked down at Morgan and

his visitors; they were talking and laughing in the shade on the south side of the house.

'Weeks!' said Mrs Tawhai. She went down into the garden.

On the table in Morgan's room was a typewriter with a piece of paper furled in it. Race rolled the paper so he could read the whole page:

The para-poets arrived at dawn,
In waves they came, rocking
Through the morning shades,
The golden rocking-cradle air,
They couldn't hide or fire back, it was
Easy to shoot them as they fell,
Or simply shoot their shrouds –
One bullet in the silk and down
They whistled – crash! – but still more came,
Thumping on roofs, in trees, the onion patch,
Then stopped to smoke a fag
Under the olives, behind the jakes,
And only then they opened up, began to sing,
Declaim, compose, complain,
Declare, opine, put on corduroy,
Velvet, polka-dot, take wine –
'The youth who has never aspired' they sang,
'To ride the clouds unfurled
'Of what use is his life to him,
What use is he to the world?'
The locals ran at them with brooms,
With foot-long spanners, monkey-
Wrenches, but the girls fell in love all the same,

Offered them water – them!
The invaders! – and bared their breasts,
Oh yes, but thats

'That's *what?*' Race thought. He stared at the page. He had never thought of a poem being half-finished before. It was like seeing a fire burning alone in a wood. Then abruptly he wound the page down again, and stepped out on the veranda and down into the garden. Plans were being made to go for lunch at the pub twenty miles back along the coast.

'Morgan, I want you to wear one of your good shirts,' said Mrs Tawhai. 'I don't want you going in there looking like a vagabond.'

'Mother thinks we dress badly,' said Morgan. 'We're just *scruffy*.'

'I didn't say that. I just found myself agreeing with Grammaticus the other day.'

'Who's Grammaticus?' said Dinah.

'Old Prof. Blaiklock in the *Weekly News*,' said Mrs Tawhai. 'What did he say? "I wish the undergraduate gown was still in use. Nothing is served by the cult of the tattered sports coats and bohemian disregard for hair and dress." '

At this, they all laughed – not too loudly – no one wanted to offend Morgan's mother – but merrily enough all the same. No one wore old sports coats any more. Condemning the fashions of youth, Prof. Blaiklock had chosen one a few years out of date.

'He's old, he's retired,' said Morgan. 'You know the old guy who checks out the books at the library? I'm sure that's Grammaticus.'

'What rubbish,' said Mrs Tawhai. 'Professor Blaiklock is a distinguished scholar. He will not be checking out library books to undergraduates.'

'Well, it looks just like him,' said Morgan. 'Where's the *Weekly News*? Race, help me find the *Weekly News*.'

He and Race went through to a sitting-room on the other side of the house.

'Liddy and I are breaking up,' said Morgan.

The panels of the sitting-room were carved with tall Maori figures. Their eyes were shell. Between the legs of each figure was a smaller one – the next generation.

'She wants to finish it. I don't know what to do. There's nothing I *can* do, not from here.'

Morgan picked up some of the papers on the floor and glanced at one or two magazines left open on the sofa by the fireplace. The grate had ash in it from the previous winter.

'The weekends are worst,' he said. 'I can't sleep. I keep thinking of her being more or less raped by some rich red-neck farmer she thinks she's in love with.'

'Go and see her,' said Race.

'I have,' said Morgan. 'It didn't work. I went to Palmerston to see her. She went out every night and left me there in the flat.'

'Well, I never met her,' said Race, not knowing what to say.

'I don't know how I stood it,' said Morgan. 'She made it plain I was of secondary importance.'

'Drop her,' said Race.

'She loves me,' said Morgan. 'I happen to know that. But she loves this social whirl she's in. One I despise.'

They stood there under the shining-eyed figures.

'Here we are,' said Morgan. 'The *Weekly News*.'

They went back to the group in the garden on the shady side of the house.

'Here, you see,' said Morgan.

They all looked at the picture of Grammaticus above his weekly column. He had a noble, Roman-emperor air to him.

'Definitely the crazy old guy at the library,' said Morgan.

'Nonsense,' said Mrs Tawhai.

Mrs Tawhai took the *Weekly News* and began to read aloud. 'Watching this summer's student turmoil in Paris was the philosopher Cioran, one of the gloomy band who have emptied life of meaning. "Human history," he writes "is an immense cul-de-sac. Life is a passionate emptiness, all truth is a hoax." Hence the amusement on the face at the gallery of the Odéon, while the students bawled for a brave new world below.'

She read on a little, to herself, then handed the magazine to Morgan.

'Mum adores Grammaticus,' said Morgan.

'Morgan's great-grandfather had three thousand fighting men at his command,' said Mrs Tawhai. 'At a single word from him, all three thousand became Christian. And now *he* doesn't believe in anything.'

'It's a different era,' said Rosie.

'Come here,' said Mrs Tawhai.

Morgan stood up and went over to his mother.

'I want you to wear your good white shirt,' she said.

'OK,' said Morgan.

She looked at him. His hair was touching his collar.

'*Look* at you,' she said.

Suddenly, before he could move, she put the tip of her finger on her tongue and smoothed his eyebrows, one, then the other, a fierce lion with her cub.

Late that afternoon, after lunch in the pub, they drove back to the farm, Race at the wheel this time, and they dropped Morgan at the five-barred gate and then Race turned the old Chev round in the narrow road and they drove away.

'Didn't Morgan look *sweet* standing there in his white shirt,' said Rosie, and for some reason she laughed, as they rode away in the dusk and went up around the cliff-face road.

8

At the end of the summer Race and Panos took the night train from Wellington to Auckland. They had both decided to go and live there that year. Panos had been studying medicine in the South Island. Now he wanted to become an actor. Race was still studying biology. He only wanted a change of scene. Auckland was a big city by comparison to their home towns. It was sprawling and hazy, laced with motorways. The sea at the city's foot looked dirty in dawn's early light. Ships sailed away east into a morning glitter. Grapefruit and oranges grew along suburban avenues, anyone could pick them. On the train, he and Panos spent a lot of the journey chatting up two sisters in the seats opposite. Race then spent the first days in Auckland buying textbooks and visiting real-estate agencies. At night, he and Panos and the two sisters, one a beautician, one a hairdresser, went to the movies and then back to the girls' flat, which was piled high with feminine clothes, on the floor, on the sofas, on every hook and rail. After a week, Race had found a place to rent, an old cottage between the university and the railway yards. He moved in, but after three days Panos had still not put in an appearance.

On his third night there alone, Race woke just after midnight. He stared at the ceiling. His heart was pounding. He could still feel the heat of the sun on his face in the dream he'd just woken from. It was a simple enough dream: at the start he was climbing a tree, going up round the trunk as if on a rough spiral stair. In some places the branches were difficult to get through, he felt the prickle of pine needles in his face and sticky resin on his hands. Then he noticed that someone else was climbing above him. He stopped and looked up and saw that it was Morgan. Morgan stopped climbing as well, and looked down at him with a most stern and penetrating expression. It was as if he was examining Race's fitness for the most serious test that could ever be imagined.

But nothing was said, and Morgan then turned and began climbing again and Race began to climb as well and followed him up through the highest branches to the top of the tree and even there Morgan did not stop – he just went on out into the air, and Race reached the top of the trunk which was as slender as a whip – he felt his handhold waver – and he too went on up into the air, after Morgan, who without looking back turned and flew out over the sea. They went a long way out, flying a little higher all the time it seemed – Race saw the breakers below, and the sea beyond the breakers, and then the deep blue of the ocean ahead, and they flew on, Morgan never looking back, and then Race saw a series of towers or windmills standing on the horizon. At first these were small and faint but as they grew larger he began to feel afraid. Morgan was flying on, but Race knew if he went beyond the line of towers in the sea there would be no chance of return. He looked back: he could still see the land, though it would soon be out of sight. He looked ahead. Morgan was still flying on, and he never looked back, and then Race turned and headed for the land, saw the green back-wash of the breakers below him, and then came in to land, the sun and wind beating on his face, and then he woke.

He lay staring at the ceiling. At first he felt only wonder, and then some alarm. It was the most vivid dream he had ever had, and it had left a kind of fearful livingness in the room. A sound of clanking came up from the rail-yards and a blueish light from the yards went tracking across the ceiling. Race began to feel sad and sorry for himself as well. The cottage was old; the air was musty; the bed-springs sagged. Even the old wardrobe at the end of the bed had a gloomy forbidding appearance. And he was quite alone. There had been no sign from Panos that he would ever show up. Race had a feeling that the dream had come *because* he was alone. It had come for that reason and then it had gone, but it had woken him first, to ensure that he remembered it. He lay there for a long time and his heart stopped pounding and he went back to sleep.

In the morning the sun was shining. He got up, dressed, ate some breakfast, then packed his bags and stepped out onto the veranda. He remembered the key and stood there for a minute wondering what to do with it. It was an old-fashioned iron key, long and thin, dank, with the faintest bloom of rust. For three days Race had carried this with him, out to his lectures in the morning and back to the cottage in the early evening. The air that met him when he came into the house in the evening was musty, heated, sad – no one had spoken in it or had thought a thought in it since he had left in the morning. He had come to dislike the weight of the key in his pocket during the day. It was a proof of the solitude waiting for him at home. Race had never spent any time alone before. He was lonely, and irritated with Panos, and embarrassed at his situation. And now an element of fear had arrived. That was one drawback to living alone, he thought: it was unsafe. Dreams, far too vivid, could come and get you, and then wake you in order to record them. He had the key in his hand and he looked at it again. Then he brought his stuff out on the veranda, locked the door, dropped the key through the letter slot and, hoisting one bag on his shoulder, walked up the street in the sunshine, and never went back there again.

Part II

2001

1

'A visitor for you.'

'For *me*?'

'A visitor for you,' said Candy, 'in the form of – *ta dah!*'

'Granddad!' said another voice. 'How are you?'

A tall young man strode into the room. A very old man was sitting alone at the end of a gleaming wooden dining table. A knife, a fork, a spoon, a soup plate on a linen mat, salt and pepper shakers and a glass of red wine were in front of him. At his neck he wore a napkin rather spotted with soup. He looked at the young man with strained blue eyes.

'How am I?' he said. 'I'm *old*.'

'But lookin' good, Grandpa. Lookin' pretty snappy.'

'I am in my ninety-third year,' said Bernard. 'And I may say I feel every minute of it.'

'You're going to do the ton for me, I know it,' said the young man. 'One hundred years old! I'm relying on you now.'

'What a horrible prospect,' said the old man, looking pleased.

'Come on. I bet you're having a good time.'

'A good time?' said Bernard. 'Let me show you how I spend my time.'

Bernard laid down his spoon, stood up and, exaggerating his totter, went across the room to the sofa where he sat down, then flung out his arms to represent every emptiness.

Candy sighed.

'He had Merle in to get him up,' she said to her son. 'Then the chiropodist came. Then I spent an hour with him and he told me all about the 1947 snow storm. Didn't you, darling?' she cried, bending down to her father-in-law. 'The 1947 snow storm!'

'What about it?' he said curtly, looking up at her. Bernard had been one of the leading ophthalmologists in the United States. His sharp blue eyes had gazed into the orbs of tens of thousands, including Eisenhower, John Foster Dulles and Marlene Dietrich.

'Where's Dad?' said Toby to his mother.

'Race?' said Candy. 'Oh, he'll turn up like a bad penny. Sorry. I shouldn't say that. Your father will be here for Thanksgiving.'

'Toby has come home for Thanksgiving,' she called to Bernard.

'As to that,' said Bernard, 'in all my years here, no one has made it absolutely clear to me who is thanking whom for what.'

Toby laughed. He looked lovingly at the old man, who was not in fact his real grandfather but the father of Candy's second husband, Chip. When Race and Candy had divorced, Toby was six. Race, so it seemed to him, suddenly vanished off the face of the earth. But he and the old man had formed a bond. Bernard bought him a bicycle and took him cycling, at ruthless adult speeds, on the Rock Creek trails. He taught him sailing, and even, in his eighties, took up wind-surfing with him on Chesapeake Bay. Chip, by contrast, had no aptitude with children. He looked through them, though without malice. He was a journalist; he had a column on the *Washington Post*, and he could not identify any child as one of his significant readers. 'I write for eight significant people inside the Beltway,' he once said. 'The million and half others are a pleasing superfluity.' Race, in the meantime, had not really disappeared, but he no longer lived under the same roof, and for a few years after splitting up with Candy he did travel more often than before. Toby, in boyhood, lived under a windfall of postcards, mostly ultramarine in hue, underwater scenes from obscure tropic shores, Sulawesi, Socotra, various Gulfs. Race was a marine biologist. Toby developed a dislike of the underwater blue. What was the hold it had, the mermaid draw, over his father? He connected it somehow with his mother's love for Chip; in childhood he developed a distaste for the formidable ardours of the adult world.

'If it's the Indians we're thinking of,' said Bernard, 'perhaps an orgy of remorse rather than gluttony might be in order.'

Toby beamed at him.

'Toby's just come from England,' Candy called. 'He's at school in England now.'

'*England!*' said the old man, startled. 'I was born in England.'

'Yes I know, Granddad,' said Toby. It was an elementary piece of family lore. It was probably one of the reasons that he, Toby, had gone to live there himself. He had left London ten hours earlier. London had been dark, damp, gloomy, lit by a dim silver lamp nearly hidden by clouds. Here, everything was hard, cold, bright, dry. The lawns in northwest Washington looked as though they'd had military haircuts. No rain had fallen in the DC area for forty days. Several strangers, Slavic, black – a cab driver, a porter at Union station – had informed Toby of this fact since he'd arrived. He had almost forgotten the easy address between fellow Americans. The idea of a porter at a London station – *were* there any? – engaging in un-ironic chat even about the weather seemed remote. The English, he thought, lived at another depth of the atmosphere, like fish in another zone of the ocean. Before leaving for Heathrow that morning, he had run along two long, damp, brown-carpeted avenues to return Jojo's overdue books.

Jojo had called from Honolulu to remind him about them, before she flew east and he flew west to meet in Washington.

Inside the library, a young male librarian – obese, gay, besprin-kled with dandruff – was reading a story to twenty pre-schoolers camped on the carpet.

'Now, who knows what a skeleton is?'

'Oooh. Arrgh.'

'It's *bones*,' said one, in gloom.

'That's right,' said the librarian. 'All of you – hold up your arms. Feel that? That's bone. We're all made of bone. If we got rid of all . . . *this* . . . we'd be skeletons too. This is a story about a man called Mr Skeleton. Say "Hello, Mr Skeleton." '

'Hello, Mr Skeleton,' said many sepulchral voices.

Toby, rightly or wrongly, could not imagine this scene in American accents.

From the sofa, Bernard looked around his sitting-room with a patrician air.

'It's not a bad sort of place, I suppose,' he said. 'They generally serve a drink about now.'

'Would you like a drink?' said Toby.

'Yes,' said Bernard. 'I would.'

'What would you like?'

'What would *you* like?' said Bernard cagily.

'I'd like a vodka,' said Toby.

'It's three in the afternoon,' said Candy. Her hair was in two wings, thinner than it used to be, and silvered and elegant.

'I'm on holiday,' said Toby. 'I've just flown the Atlantic.'

'*I* will have a vodka as well,' said Bernard.

'Oh, let me do it,' said Candy and she went away to fix the drinks.

'I don't know who she is,' said Bernard, as his daughter-in-law left the room, 'but she seems a good sort of woman. Are you married?'

'No,' said Toby.

'Like your father,' said Bernard. 'Running off after every bit of skirt.'

Toby listened calmly to this remark which was in fact baseless. Bernard mused on the sofa, his eyes bleak.

'My own father took *agin* me, I never knew why.'

Candy came back in with vodka, glasses and ice on a tray.

'Toby's girlfriend's arriving tonight,' she called. 'Jojo. She's Australian. She'll be here for Thanksgiving as well.'

Bernard sipped the vodka with an elaborate pucker, and shuddered.

'This is rather good,' he said.

'She and Toby live in London,' called Candy.

'My brother Reuben, of course,' said Bernard, 'married a girl from London. A pretty girl, without a single, solitary thought in her head.'

'Toby's studying there,' said Candy. 'He's studying popular culture.'

'Haw!' said Bernard, in the tone he reserved for the latest example of human folly that came to his notice, but he looked kindly at the young man.

'I suppose you live in *digs*,' he said.

'I suppose so,' said Toby who never used the term.

'I lived in digs,' said Bernard, 'once upon a time.'

He paused for a long time, looking at the carpet.

'He sent me *shitty* letters,' he said.

'Who?' said Toby. He was amazed. In all his days, he had never heard Bernard use foul language.

'Father,' said Bernard. 'The old man.'

Candy sighed again. 'He's obsessing,' she said. She spoke at a conversational level, confident that Bernard could not hear. 'At the moment it's his father,' she said. 'He goes on and on about him. Last summer it was Eisenhower. Nothing but Eisenhower. And there's the snow storm in 1947. We still have a lot of that. He's polishing it all up for eternity.'

' "*Good riddance*",' said Bernard. 'Imagine writing that to your own son! I was seventeen. I'd gone to university in Manchester. "*I'll be as glad to see the back of you as you will be of me.*" That's what he wrote to me. Of course he didn't write it himself. He was quite blind by then. He dictated his letter to Reuben. And Reuben wrote on the bottom: "*Take no notice of the old bugger.*" Ha!'

Toby looked out the window. Bernard had bought the house on Barleycorn Street in 1958. A white pick-up truck went fast down Barleycorn and at the corner sounded its horn – a sort of fanfare of trumpets. A tall black woman was walking up the street. She suddenly stopped, as if seized by dread, and searched through her leather shoulder bag. Then she went on up the hill at a leisurely pace. Another fanfare sounded much more closely. Toby looked nonplussed, then he grabbed at his phone in his inside jacket pocket.

'Hello, Plum,' he said. 'Where are you? What? Can you? Really? Will I pick you up? Of course I'll pick you up. OK. OK. OK. Yes. I'll come and get you. I know. I know. I know. OK.'

He hung up, pressing a key, frowning down at the little phone.

'That was Jojo,' he said. 'She just left Honolulu. She's on the plane. She can see the sea.'

But Bernard's eyes were closed. His drink, forgotten, was on the square arm of the sofa. Candy chose not to be impressed that Toby had just spoken to Jojo who was looking down 30,000 feet at the ocean.

'I *never* use that phone thing on the plane,' she said. 'I'm just terrified of what it might cost.'

She collected Bernard's drink from the sofa arm and put it on a coaster on the table, and picked up his soup bowl, spoon, knife, fork and the linen table mat. Toby followed her out to the kitchen and stood there. He turned on his heels one way, then another. He opened the fridge and looked in. Every centimetre, every last millimetre was jammed with pickles, sauces, chutneys. Chip liked condiments. Toby sighed. Nothing, he thought vaguely, had changed in the whole of his life. On the fridge door was a litter of magnet-held data – photos, crayon drawings, scraps of paper with addresses on them.

'What time does she get in?' said Candy.

'Uhhhh . . . late,' said Toby absently.

'Do you want the car?' said Candy.

'Nope,' said Toby. 'I'll take Caspar's truck.'

'Caspar!' said his mother.

Toby didn't answer. He was reading an essay in a childish hand on the fridge door:

Robert Ripley

of Ripley's believe it or not started his collection of amazing facts as a caratoonist for the New York Globe. Then he went to find every unusual thing of life: such as an sub machine gun with a

curved barrel for shotting round corners and over obstercals. He
searched 747000 miles for more material and found a snake
trying to eat itself and a tooth pick mermaid.

'Who wrote this?' said Toby.

'Romulus,' said Candy.

Romulus was Merle's younger son. Merle had been coming to the house every day for six years to get Bernard up and dressed in the morning. Merle was from Jamaica. Her mouth was deeply downturned; in winter she wore a man's pork-pie hat. She was a clever and thoughtful woman; over the course of the years she and Candy had become friends. Romulus was eleven. Candy, who taught remedial reading, took an interest in his education. She did not approve of Merle's elder son, Caspar, who treated his mother, she believed, with young black male indifference. As teenagers, however, Caspar and Toby had formed an alliance which appeared to be in place despite the Atlantic. They must have been in touch already, she thought. Who knew how 21-year-olds communicated across space and time?

'A tooth-pick mermaid?' said Toby.

'*I* don't know,' said Candy.

'Then we're going out to Middleburg,' said Toby.

'Middleburg!' said Candy. 'What time does she get in?'

'Midnight,' said Toby.

'Why on earth are you taking Jojo to Middleburg at midnight?' said Candy.

'We're going to see the meteors,' said Toby. 'It's the Leonids tonight. It'll be dark out there. We're going to see a meteor shower.'

Candy shrugged but she was impressed all the same. She felt a little lonely as well. Who would ever ask her to see a meteor shower in dark Virginia? She looked at her son from behind – tall, brown-haired, narrow-headed: she liked looking at the back of his head and the cusp of hair in the nape of his neck. But still he was just a child! Just as he used to as a boy, for instance, he now put the coffee grounds in the sink and turned on the waste-disposal switch and peered in, watching. There was a rich grinding of metal jaws, then they whirred freely again.

'In-*sink*-erator,' said Toby, just as she remembered.

'*Chantilly lace and a pretty face,*' sang Jojo, '*she walks with a wiggle and she talks with a giggle . . .*'

They came to an intersection and turned west on Route 66 towards Middleburg.

'Route 66!' said Jojo. 'Get Your Kicks on—'.

'Darling,' said Toby.

'Yes?'

'Are you going to sing your way right across the US road map?'

'Yes,' said Jojo. 'Yes. I think I will.'

'OK,' said Toby. 'Just so's we know.'

'We,' said Jojo.

'Caspar and me,' said Toby.

'This is not the real Route 66,' said Caspar. 'That goes from Chicago to, God – someplace.'

'They changed it,' said Toby. 'Can you believe that? The most famous route in America and some jerk, some board, changes the number.'

'They did?' said Caspar. 'Why did they do that?'

'You wonder,' said Toby. 'You have to ask yourself.'

He glanced at Jojo out of the corner of his eye. She's angry, he thought. Jojo had thick, short blonde hair and mid-brown eyes. She looked as if she was internally heated, with no need for a naked flame in order to catch fire. Her colouring was the same as his mother's – Toby was aware of that, and saw no need to examine the fact further. He guessed there was some psychological weight in it and he didn't care. Jojo's eyes, side on, sweetly protuberant in the passing night lights – streetlights, headlamps – were transparent. He put his arm around her, his hand was resting on her shoulder. She was in the middle of the cab between Caspar who was at the wheel and Toby on the door. Toby moved his thumb left and right, a gentle arc, on her skin just below her collar bone. Jojo shrugged at this caress, as if at an insect touch.

'She's mad with me,' he thought. 'I wonder why.'

The American sky, the horizon, was all lit up as if expecting visitors from space. The pick-up turned down a narrower road, hem-stitched with dark trees. After a while the lights of a police cruiser appeared in the distance, coming towards them, and went past.

'He'll be back,' said Caspar, nodding his head several times as if agreeing with someone else.

Caspar was thin and dark, and clever like his mother. He worked part-time as a security guard at the mall at Tyson's Corner and studied business administration at night school. He looked sure of himself and rather amused at the human race: he didn't seem to mind or even notice that he was right in only about the same proportion of cases as the rest of mankind.

'So who's there?' said Jojo.

'Where?' said Toby.

'At your place. At your mother's.'

'Oh, well,' said Toby, feeling relieved. It was a normal question, he thought, perhaps he and Jojo had resumed normal communication.

'Well,' he said, 'there's Mom, and Chip, my step-father—'

'Step-pop,' said Caspar.

'Step-pop,' said Toby.

Chip had once referred to himself in this style and the boys, then teenagers who found everything adults did richly comic, had heard him.

'And Granddad. He's my man.'

'What does he do?'

'Oh, Lord,' said Toby. 'He's retired. He sits on the couch.'

The police cruiser came up behind them. Its lights flashed red and blue in the mirror and the siren sounded a single wail.

Caspar pulled over. The road ahead was very dark. The state trooper came up to the driver's window. He peered in at Caspar. He looked worried, like a man presented with grievous household bills. He took Caspar's licence, then asked him to step out of the vehicle. He and Caspar went to the back of the pick-up and stood in the headlights of the police car. Then Caspar was left standing there while the trooper walked round the pick-up to look at it. Caspar stood motionless and looked at the back of Toby's and Jojo's heads. The trooper bent down at the passenger window. Toby pressed the button and the window came down.

'Where you folks off to?' said the trooper.

'Middleburg,' said Toby.

'To see a comet,' said Jojo.

The trooper looked at her sharply, picking up the accent.

'Meteors,' said Toby. 'It's a meteor shower, officer.'

The policeman suddenly looked relieved, thankful.

'Oh, I heard about that,' he said. 'You folks have a good evening now.'

He went away and spoke to Caspar who came back and got in the cab of the truck. The trooper came back and looked in the passenger window again.

'Where you from?' he said to Jojo.

'Australia.'

'Australia!' he said, smiling. He didn't sound the 'l'. 'Orstraya,' he said again. 'You folks have a good night now.'

They drove on. The police car stayed where it was for a while then did a sudden U-turn and went away in the other direction. In Caspar's truck, they all thought separately about the encounter for a minute. Jojo started to laugh.

'Did you see?' she cried. 'That was *so* funny.'

'What was so funny about it?' said Toby.

'He had sugar on his chin,' said Jojo. 'I couldn't work out what it was. Right there.'

She touched Toby on the upper round of his chin.

'Good,' he thought, 'we're all right again.' He thought briefly of growing a beard just under his lower lip.

'Icing sugar,' said Jojo. 'He must have been eating a sugar doughnut. All alone in his police car. In Virginia.'

'Yeah, that's funny,' said Caspar.

'So what *did* he do, before he hit the couch?' said Jojo, reverting to the subject of Bernard.

'He was an eye surgeon,' said Toby. 'He cut corneas.'

'Is that a pun?' said Jojo.

'No,' said Toby. 'He's in the ophthalmologists' hall of fame.'

'Ha,' said Caspar.

'I'm serious,' said Toby. 'There is one. Bernard went to the

Soviet Union to learn some new technique. Radial corneal surgery. He used to go there a lot. When he came back he would go talk to the CIA. He kept his eyes and ears open in Russia. "You were a spy," I said to him. "I was not a spy," he said. "They used you," I said. "On the contrary," he said, "I used them. *I* was against the Soviet Union before those boys were even born." '

'Here we go,' said Caspar. They stopped at a wide gate with a sign that said: Mickie Gordon Memorial Park. Caspar drove in and they went bumping over the open grass.

'Plenty people had the same idea,' said Caspar.

Other headlights were roving slowly in the dark, and more parked cars and SUVs showed up here and there in Caspar's own headlights.

'Here, I guess,' said Caspar, stopping. 'It's all the same view, hey?'

He pointed skywards with his forefinger. They sat there for a moment, then unbuckled seat belts and all got out of the vehicle.

'We have sleeping bags, we have airbeds, we have blankets, we have coffee, we have a little whisky to go in the coffee,' said Toby. 'And cushions.'

'I'm going to take a look around,' said Caspar and departed, vanishing instantly on the unlit sward. One smudge of horizon light showed, in the east, from Washington.

'So,' said Jojo. 'Just what, I mean just what exactly, is all this?'

'What do you mean?' said Toby.

'I mean just what exactly are we here for?' said Jojo.

'What do you mean "what are we here for?" We're here for—'

'What I mean,' said Jojo, 'is why are we here, with him?'

'Who?'

'Caspar.'

'Don't you like Caspar?'

'I like Caspar. I'm crazy about Caspar. But I want to see you. I want to be with you. I haven't seen you for three and a half weeks, twenty-four and a half days, and I look forward to flying in and meeting you and seeing you and here we are out in the middle of nowhere with Caspar and whisky and coffee. I'm jet-lagged, remember. I've flown eleven thousand miles. I want to see you and I want to go to sleep.'

'I thought you'd *like* it,' said Toby. 'I thought you'd like doing this. You've never been to America really, only LA, and I thought you'd like it driving out here into the country, I thought you'd like to see the Leonids. I mean we could turn round and go straight back to town and creep around the house not waking everyone, though we'd be bound to wake up Mom and Gillian, not to mention Bernard, though he's stone deaf, and Chip, he's a whole lot of fun, I can tell you, but if that's what you want, then we'll do that.'

'Well, how do I know if that's what I want?' cried Jojo. 'I've never met your mother so how do I know if I want to wake her, though I've always wanted to come to Washington and meet your family but that's hardly *this*, is it, *here*, is it?'

She waved her arm, unseen, at the night.

'Well it is,' said Toby, 'in a way it is, I mean there's Washington right there' – he pointed, also unseen, at the light pollution – 'and here am I, and Caspar more or less grew up at my house—'

'Oh, Toby, all I wanted was to be alone with you, is that so bad, is that so difficult?'

'Well, I wanted to be alone with you, too, that's why I thought of coming straight out here instead of Barleycorn Street with the whole family breathing down our necks, that's why I asked Caspar for the truck and then he said "Sure," but then he said "I want to see those meteors too." So what was I supposed to say? "No, no – I'm taking your truck and you can't come"? Could I say that? Could I?'

'I don't see why not. Why not? Why did you need his truck anyway?' said Jojo. 'You've got a car. Haven't you got a car? Why do we need his truck?'

'Well, I thought we could lie on the flatbed and, you know, look *up*. I thought it would be nice. I thought that would be fun,' said Toby, but his heart was sinking. Why didn't he take Candy's car? he wondered. Why *did* he take the Caspar option? Was Jojo right? Was he secretly avoiding being alone with her? Jojo had accused him before of not loving her – not sufficiently, not intensely, entirely. Was she right? Or was it rather that the more she accused him, the less sure he felt of himself, and then the less he did in fact love her, for causing this uncertainty, this anxiety?

'*Aha*,' said Caspar, manifesting himself out of the dark. He leaned in and turned on the cab light. He looked amused. He gave the impression, in fact, of having overheard the conversation between the unhappy lovers. A lesser spirit might have been affronted by what had been said, but Caspar was not. It was not in nature, his expression seemed to say, it was beyond the realms of possibility, that he should be surplus to requirements.

'Let's get us comfortable here,' Caspar said, shining a torch into the back of the pick-up. '*Any dam' nigger can make himself comfortable*. That's the wisdom my Wesleyan forefathers handed down to me.'

He leapt onto the back of the truck and wrapped a blanket round himself.

'Where's these shooting stars anyway?' he said.

He held out his hand.

Jojo, despite herself so to speak, put one foot on the tow-bar and let Caspar haul her up. Caspar had a gap between his two front top teeth which for some reason added to his air of self-assurance. He was not only amused, his teeth indicated: he knew what to do next. He now lit a marijuana joint and inhaled deeply.

'This – this – this—' he said, pointing at the joint while also trying to hold his breath during utterance, 'is necessary to appreciate the *scale* of the solar system and its – uh – uh – attendant families of – of – of—'

Jojo laughed. Toby felt relieved. There *was* a problem, he thought. He had a problem, they had a problem, but for the immediate moment the problem would not present itself. He unzipped the goose-down bag and put it round Jojo's shoulders, and then he pumped up an airbed with the plastic hand-pump.

'Where you folks headin'?' said Caspar, standing against the night-sky in his blanket. 'Orstraya? Well, I'll be doggoned. You have a nice evening in Orstraya, you hear?'

Jojo laughed again. Toby lit the halogen lantern and put it on the roof of the cab. Someone screamed across the dark field. Some teenagers went past in a car with its doors hanging open.

'Oh, yeah – let me tell you my dream the other night,' said Caspar. 'I was in this house in Washington and I saw my watch start to run backwards. Then my beer glass, when I emptied it, filled up of its own accord. "It's a Scharnhorst variation," I heard a voice say. "A local, limited backward run of time. Quite rare. Rather interesting."

'It had a kind of British accent, this voice. Then there was another one across the street. Another variation, I mean. I can't remember what it was, but it was a much bigger one. Then I was on an old-style streetcar and we went crashing down the hallway of a house and then we were all sitting down to dinner. That was all right, except it was a Baltimore streetcar and we were in Washington. "Oh well," said the voice. "It's the break-up of space-time. It's the end of the world. But it's nice to see it being done so well. So . . . British." '

There was a pause.

'Whaddya think?' said Caspar.

'Fairly nuts,' said Toby.

'Yeah, yeah, but you don't get it,' said Caspar. 'This dream was about *you*. She's got a British accent.'

'I have not,' said Jojo.

'And you – you got a little twang. I can hear it. You're turning English on me.'

'I do not have anything remotely resembling a British accent,' said Jojo.

'Remotely resembling,' said Caspar in a British accent.

'Cheek,' said Jojo.

Caspar did not answer. At work as a security guard he had been trialling the use of a motorised scooter. He now saw himself scooting along endless passages of the mall, skimming through the crowds, a head taller than all of them.

'These shootin' stars,' he said dreamily, 'these shootin' stars, they were left behind in 1776. These are *American* meteors coming your way tonight, folks.'

'I don't follow,' said Jojo.

'Well,' said Caspar. 'This comet swings by the sun every thirty years, but the debris doesn't hit us for another couple of hundred. And here comes the 1776 crop of thistles now.'

'*Oh!*' went a voice out in the dark as Caspar was speaking.

'Tempel-Tuttle, that's the guy who found it,' said Caspar. 'Crazy name, crazy guy.'

From different parts of the field people started calling out.

'*Oooh!*' they went.

'*Aaaah!*'

'Oh, wow,' said Jojo. '*Wow . . .*'

Out of the constellation of the Lion, the debris of Tempel-Tuttle streamed above them in the night.

3

'Radial keratotomy,' said Bernard, 'is the name of the procedure. As well as that, of course, we used the cryolathe, which freezes the cornea tissue and then lathe-cuts it just as you would cut the lens of a pair of glasses.'

He looked sharply at his listener to make sure she was attending, and also – she had the feeling – to check the state of her corneal tissue. She was a diplomat's wife. Her name was Heloise. She was a handsome spare-boned woman with black hair drawn back in a – what was the word, Toby wondered – barouche, barrette, barrique? Her husband, the *chargé d'affaires* at the Belgian embassy, sat further down the table. These were the kind of people Chip often found and brought home. He felt that they added lustre to his dinner table, in this case, a Thanksgiving table. Heloise was on Bernard's right. She felt slightly trapped but she brought all her powers to bear on concealment of the fact. Toby watched Bernard with, as usual, admiration. The poor old nonagenarian who wasn't quite certain where he was – a displacement Toby didn't necessarily buy – had vanished. Bernard sat at the head of the table in his excellent grey suit, his cuffs were gleaming, his small, neat head was combed, and gleamed as well, as with a kind of exo-cranial intelligence.

'Now Voltaire—' he was saying.

On his other side sat Candy. Also present were: Chip, Toby's sister Gillian, Jojo, Race, Race's date from the marine biology department, Chadwick and his wife Laura, Merle and Romulus.

'Merle is coming for Thanksgiving,' Candy announced a week before. 'I have more reason to give thanks for Merle than anyone else on the planet.'

A place was set for Caspar but he hadn't showed up. It was four in the afternoon. As usual, Toby thought, Candy had got up to some tricks with the seating plans. She loved arranging seating plans. This time she had put Toby next to Race's date. But why? Only to annoy him, he guessed. He didn't want to meet Race's date. He didn't like Race's dates. He had never in fact reconciled himself to the divorce of his parents. On the other hand, he didn't much like seeing Race at Barleycorn Street. He loved his father but on these family occasions there was this forced cheer in the air as if they – Race and Candy – were secretly looking back at something complex and sad and far away. Was it their break-up? Or was it the fact they had married at all? That was a fear of Toby's.

'I myself played a part – a small part, but I am pleased to think a useful one,' said Bernard, 'in designing the microkeratome, which, as you may know, has an oscillating blade to open a flap in the cornea. At one stage I went to sit at the feet of the illustrious José Barraquer, in Bogotá. Now José was a very odd chap – he adored fish—'

'Adored what?' said Heloise.

'*Fish!*' said Bernard irritably. 'But Slava – he was a genius. Slava—'

'Who is Slava?' said Heloise.

'Slava?' said Bernard. He looked at Heloise sternly. Was the woman mad, or was she just playing games? Everyone in the world knew of Slava Fyodorov who had invented radial keratotomy.

'It's all a question,' he said, 'of flattening the curvature of the cornea. The funny thing is that Slava discovered the procedure purely by accident—'

Candy and Merle were bringing in the soup. They placed a bowl in front of each guest.

'*Do* all start,' said Candy.

Jojo took up her dessert spoon and dipped it in her soup. A flicker passed across Heloise's face; she raised one eyebrow by less than a millimetre. Then Jojo realised what she had done. Then Gillian took up her dessert spoon and dipped it in her soup as well. Death to tyrants! That was what she meant. Toby loved his sister for that. And the two of *them* could have been sisters, he thought, looking at Gilly and Jojo laughing silently, side by side. He himself was still not getting along with Jojo. There was a freeze in relations. After two nights sleeping in his old bedroom they still had not made love. Strange, he thought. At fourteen, fifteen years old, in that very room hadn't he, nearly asleep, imagined sumptuous orgies, and now there he was, with a woman a foot away, and he did not know how to cross the space between the two beds. The decals on the wall were the same, and the woven rug with the picture of a brown bear by a waterfall, a friend from childhood, was still on the floor between them.

'Delicious, the soup,' said Laura Chadwick. 'Artichoke, I think.'

'One of Slava's patients was a young ruffian who got into a street-fight,' said Bernard. 'His glasses were broken and glass pierced his eye. After Slava removed the splinter he found that the patient's sight had quite improved. A deep radial incision, you see.'

'I see!' said Heloise.

'The last twenty years of my professional life,' said Bernard, 'you might say I spent *fine-tuning* the results of a street-brawl in Moscow.'

'Wonderful,' said Heloise. 'How old are you, my dear?'

Bernard did not hear the kindly note of condescension.

'I am ninety-two years old,' he said, 'which is to say, I am in my ninety-third year.'

'Wonderful!' said Heloise. 'It can hardly be credited.'

Bernard basked in the flattery.

'You may not credit it,' he said, 'and I may take no credit.'

'Your parents also lived to a wonderful age?'

'My mother and my father both. My father, of course, had the finest physique in the British army. His measurements just about matched the Great Sandow's, except that Father's thighs were an inch longer and he was accordingly shorter from knee to ankle. He often wondered if this hip-to-knee length gave him his facility as a horse-rider. He was one of the best riders in the army, you know. He was often mentioned in despatches.'

Heloise was drinking her soup, nodding all the while to show she was up with the play, with the Great Sandow, whoever he was, and Bernard's father's thigh-length.

'The Boer War, that is,' said Bernard, 'which was before your time. He was a great horseman. Even after he went blind he had a tremendous way with horses.'

'Your father went blind!'

'Nothing that couldn't be fixed in a trice today. But in those days. Before lasers . . .'

'Do you think,' said Heloise, 'that you took up your field of medicine because your father was blind?'

'That I have often asked myself,' said Bernard. 'And the answer is: *Perhaps!*'

'Fear,' Chip was saying at the other end of the table. 'Fear, and a deep, deep respect for American power. That's the psychology we have to aim for in the Arab street.'

'Brute force, in other words,' said Chadwick.

'He tamed a rig at Sloman's stables that no one else would go near,' said Bernard.

'A rig?' said Heloise.

'A stallion that has been only partly castrated. They are dangerous animals. They feel somewhat bitter towards mankind. But Father mastered that horse, even though he was almost completely blind. He was a man of very high temperament, and a handsome man as well.'

'How wonderful,' said Heloise.

'But, you know, he took *agin* me,' said Bernard.

'*Agin?*' said Heloise.

'He took against me,' said Bernard.

His face reddened.

'I never knew why,' he said.

'Never mind, dear,' said Candy on Bernard's left. 'He gets upset about this,' she said to Heloise across Bernard's back.

'*Good riddance!*' said Bernard.

Everyone turned towards him.

'Imagine that,' said Bernard, 'to your own son!'

'Don't worry about it, dear,' said Candy. 'It was a long time ago.'

'It *was* a long time ago,' said Bernard. 'That's the trouble, you see. I can't – you can't – find your way back. Not by any means.'

A look of anguish crossed his face. Candy patted Bernard's left hand with her right several times, and reached at the same time with her left for the long, silver serving fork to spear not one but two roast potatoes, which she knew Bernard liked, and put them on his plate. Bernard took no notice of these ministrations. He was staring at the table cloth trying to remember something. He put both hands on the table, ten fingertips on the edge of the white cloth, looking now, somehow, like an earnest boy.

When I do count the clock that tells the time,

he said,

And see the brave day sunk in hideous night;
When I behold the violet past prime,
And – and – and sable curls, all silvered o'er with white
Then of thy beauty do I question make
That thou amongst the wastes of time must go—

'Never mind, darling,' said Candy. For Bernard had stopped reciting. His eyes were filled with tears.

After a moment's pause everyone began talking to one another again, at first rather gently, and then in ordinary tones.

'After we finish up in Afghanistan – then it's time for Iraq,' said Chip. 'Hit Iraq! Then Iran. Then Syria. "*You're next!*" That should be our message.'

'Forget Iraq,' said Chadwick. 'Forget Syria. Pakistan is a bigger problem. If Pakistan blows . . . And of course none of them is the *real* problem. China is our *real* problem.'

Race was not speaking but he listened peaceably. This was not his field. Chadwick had been in the State Department for thirty years. Chip despised the State Department. He stated the fact openly in his column in the *Post*. 'The Department of Nice' he called it. Race was a marine biologist. He taught at the National University. His speciality was proto-zygomatic disguise – camouflage, cryptic colouring, in invertebrates, in octopi especially.

'Our real problem,' said Chip, 'is folks who attack America and kill thousands of her citizens in her streets and you people in the Department of Nice who won't face up to the fact.'

'Invading Iraq isn't facing up to the fact,' said Chadwick. 'It's a thousand miles in the wrong direction.'

'In Europe—' said the Belgian husband.

'Europe!' said Chip in outrage. 'Let me tell you a little story. It's 1988: we have a little problem in the West Bank. The Arabs are rioting. And finally Yitzhak Rabin says: "Go in and beat them. Break their bones so they can't throw stones any more." So they went in and broke their bones. Lily-livered liberals condemned him. *Europe* condemned him. But the voters liked it and he won the next election, and then what did he do? Made peace with the Palestinians. Machiavelli would love this guy! Ok, it was a little rough for a while but in the end – everyone won. If you want to do good you have to be brutal now and then.'

'Oh, Chip, that's just plain wrong,' said Candy. 'Things are worse than ever in Palestine. Plus there are hundreds of people crippled for life by Rabin's beatings.'

'We have to be hard-hearted,' said Chip. 'You want nice. I prefer wise. Read Machiavelli, read Hobbes, read Strauss. America needs a pagan ethic. There's nothing immoral about pagan virtue.'

'Toby,' said Chadwick, turning away as if Chip had ceased to exist. 'How's England?'

Chip recognised the slight and flushed.

'England!' said Toby.

'You like it?'

'I sometimes think I need a diving bell.'

'Toby's studying in England,' said Candy to Heloise.

'What are you studying?' said Heloise.

'Popular culture,' said Toby.

'Define popular,' said Chadwick.

'Popular culture is what doesn't need studying,' said Toby.

'And so?'

'The theory is, it all looks very simple, but it might be doing things that high-brow culture can't even imagine.'

'Example?' said Chadwick.

'Example!' said Toby. He was nervous. Now everyone at the table was listening. Even Chip, who was looking red and angry about something else, was craning at him. He couldn't think. Then Race sent across a sort of bead of light – this was Toby's impression – that hit his chest.

'Well,' he said, 'take 9/11. It was terrible and horrific and everything, and no one was ready for it, and yet it was oddly familiar. Remember those big dust clouds coming down the street and everyone's running away? No one in the State Department saw that coming. No one in big serious novels or big white art galleries had a clue. But we *had* seen it before. It was in Superman . . . Batman . . . Marvel comics. And maybe that's what happens. In America, the words of the prophets really are written on subway walls.'

'And the tenement halls,' said Gilly.

Jojo should have said that, Toby thought, but Jojo was looking remote, as if she could hardly hear what was being said.

'And the tenement halls,' said Toby.

'A few comic books?' said Chadwick, incredulous.

'Popular culture,' said Toby.

'Coincidence,' said Chadwick. 'Superimposed meaning. Wishful thinking.'

'Maybe,' said Toby. 'That's what I'm studying it to see.'

Caspar had slipped into the room and had sat down at the empty place without a word.

'Take *Ghostbusters*,' said Toby. He felt emboldened by Caspar's poker-face. 'Now here's a ridiculous movie. No one could possibly take it seriously. Manhattan invaded by all the old demons of the Middle East. Then, because of official denials, the demons escape – *Boom!* – and New York is under attack. A crazy story – but a much better prophecy than anything *Foreign Affairs* magazine or the *Washington Post* ever came up with. There's even a shot of the explosion framed by the Twin Towers. Then the Stay Puft Marshmallow Man – America at its most innocent – turns evil and begins to tear down our own structures. Perfect metaphor.'

'Manhattan invaded by all the demons of the Middle East,' said Chip. 'That's nice, Toby. I could use that.'

'Thanks, Chip,' said Toby.

He and Chip were both aware they rarely engaged positively.

'I might just use that,' said Chip again, generously. He suddenly wanted to defend his step-son, and to form an alliance against Chadwick. 'You say "because of official denials". What do you mean? What denials?'

'Remember in the movie,' said Toby. 'Some guy from the federal government declares there are no demons. They don't exist. Then the holding facility is shut down and – *Boom!* – they escape. It's just like American foreign policy. "We can do what we like in the Middle East. Nothing can touch us." Boom! September 11!'

'Whoa, whoa, whoa – now just you hold your horses,' said Chip.

'I was in London on 9/11,' said Toby. 'I saw it all from there. There was this guy from Washington, a White House staffer, running round London, panting into one TV studio after the other yelling: "This has nothing to do with Israel." The obvious conclusion was this: *He* thought 9/11 was caused by America's bias towards Israel.'

'September 11 had nothing whatsoever to do with Israel,' said Chip. 'I hate to hear you even suggest it, under my own roof.'

'It's my roof, too,' said Candy. 'And Bernard's roof.'

'It's not an unreasonable argument,' said Chadwick. 'Bin Laden himself said Israel's treatment of the Palestinians was a reason he attacked us, and I guess he'd know.'

'Hitler blamed World War Two on the Jews,' said Chip. 'I suppose you'd say' – Chip put on a simper – ' "And I guess he'd know." '

'I will not have that man's name mentioned in this house,' said Candy. 'It's always the sign of a weak argument when he gets dragged in.'

Bernard had got to his feet shakily. He walked along past all the diners to the sitting-room through the open double doors. Everyone watched him, though as if they were unsure why. He sat down in an armchair and looked back into the dining room, and then beamed at the assembled party.

'Where were you on 9/11?' Gilly asked Jojo.

'I was in LA,' said Jojo. 'We were staying at this hotel and my girlfriend rang from down the hall. It was six in the morning. "Turn on the TV," she said. But I couldn't work the remote and I went down to her room and on the way the doors were open and everyone was talking to each other in their pyjamas. In the Chateau Marmont! You just knew something terrible had happened.'

Heloise's eye was perfectly round. She looked more than ever like the blackbird that hears a worm under a lawn. She was, in fact, puzzled. She had not been quite able to place Merle – she assumed at first she was from one of the Caribbean embassies – perhaps even ambassador – but then Merle had risen from her place and, along with Candy, come and gone from the kitchen with an air of familiarity. Heloise had to consider extraordinary possibilities. Could it be Merle was the *help*? Was this a Thanksgiving Day custom? And who was this youth who arrived late without a word and sat down wearing a dark navy jumper which had – Heloise thought *surely not* – the black suede epaulettes of a security guard or a gas-pump attendant? Who knew the customs of this strange city?

'*Hey!*' said Romulus. 'There's Egypt!'

Candy's cat, jet black but for one white forepaw, had come into the sitting-room and was advancing across the carpet towards Bernard, her tail up, the tip curling very slightly as she paced along.

'Egypt!' said Bernard. '*Darling!*'

4

Chadwick arrived first. The car-park was empty. Chadwick, who didn't drive, was dropped off by a cab. The sky was an innocent baby-blue but the air was icy. The commuter traffic on Jefferson Davis Drive was already in full spate. *Wap, wap, wap* went the air buffets. Chadwick, dancing on the spot, checked his watch and then checked it again, but then, just after seven, he saw Race's old maroon Citroën – just the kind of car, Chadwick thought, that some mad marine biologist would drive – turning in the gate. Race parked the car, and father and son came across the car-park towards him.

'You crazy young *fucker*,' said Chadwick as Toby came up.

'Hey! What did *I* do?' said Toby, laughing, protesting feebly, as Chadwick pretended to attack him and get him in a headlock.

'All that stuff – to Chip Drake, of all people.'

'What stuff?' cried Toby.

'All that stuff yesterday, about Israel and 9/11. *No one* says things like that in this town. Not in this entire country.'

'I didn't know,' said Toby.

' "I didn't know," ' said Chadwick.

'I didn't.'

'Come on, England's turned his brains,' said Chadwick, pushing Toby away and dancing on the spot. Chadwick was wearing a navy ski hat and dark sweats – the costume of a cat burglar – but no one, Toby thought, not even the dumbest city cop, could mistake him for anything but a patrician, a member of the elite, here in the world's marbled capital. They went through the gates into the Arlington Cemetery and began to jog up the hill, around Sherman Drive and under the trees on L'Enfant. Toby ran on ahead. The old guys, as he thought of them, were hardly running at all. They kept stopping to talk, their heads bent under the low-sweeping branches of the oaks on L'Enfant, some of which were still in leaf. He wondered what they were talking about. It must be weird, he thought – dull, detailed, useful – to have known the same person for thirty or forty years or whatever it was. He ran on. He didn't mind being alone. 'I'll come!' Jojo had said the night before when the morning run was first mooted, but when the dawn came and Race texted Toby to wake him and Toby heard the phone's twang and looked over at Jojo asleep in the other narrow bed, he decided not to wake her. It could be adduced as an act of kindness. In fact, he didn't want her to come with him. They had finally made love in that bed, his childhood bed, but there was still something cold between them, a distance. Even the friendly bear on the rug, he felt, childishly, knew that, when Toby's bare feet touched the floor . . . He jogged on a few more hundred yards then turned back to meet the other two coming up under the avenue, and then they all walked up towards the great mansion on the crest of the hill.

In the distance, in the bowl of the valley, there was already a knot of people amid the waist-high tombs.

'Who's over there?' said Toby.

'That must be JFK,' said Race. 'Is that JFK?'

'That's JFK,' said Chadwick.

'I've never been here before,' said Toby, looking at the pillared mansion that rose above them.

'Yes you have,' said Race. 'I used to bring you up here all the time.'

'I don't remember that.'

'Well, you wouldn't. You were two.'

'What were we doing here?'

'We'd just arrived in America. I used to come up here a lot.'

'Why?' said Toby.

'I wanted to climb a hill.'

'Homesick?' said Toby.

'I just wanted a hill to climb,' said Race. 'I suppose I needed a view. Chadwick brought us up here, and showed us this.'

They looked out over the city which in that cold hour seemed both solid – the marble dome, the great obelisk – and as evanescent as foam on the long tilt to the continental horizon.

'So what did you think?' said Toby.

'What did I think?' said Race.

He looked at the city.

'I loved it,' he said. 'I looked at that and I thought there was something old and deep here, which also belonged to me. I can't justify the feeling. And something good, which is always under threat. Internal, mostly. And dark red apples in America . . . I remember that too, when I first got here.'

'Apples, huh?' said Chadwick.

'Very dark red,' said Race.

'What were you doing then?' said Toby to Chadwick.

'Me? I was at the State Department by then,' said Chadwick.

'Was I? No. Yes. I was an intern with Clark Clifford, then I went to State.'

'Who's Clark Clifford?' said Toby.

'Who's Clark Clifford!' said Chadwick. He took a step towards him.

'Not the headlock!' said Toby, dancing backwards.

'Clark Clifford was a great American monument,' said Chadwick. 'In fact, the last time I was here we had just buried Clark Clifford down there.'

They looked down the hill at the innumerable tombstones.

'He's there somewhere,' said Chadwick. 'He was in disgrace by then, but he was still a national monument. So he got an Arlington burial.'

'In disgrace?' said Toby.

'Banking, some banking scandal. Don't ask. Jesus! Bankers! In his eighties he was taken downtown and finger-printed. All the same, he was the man who got America out of Vietnam. That was the finest deed of his life, he told me.'

'You actually knew him?' said Toby.

'I worked for him a couple of years – 1972, '74. I was a nobody, an intern. He was the great insider, about 1,000 light years above me in Washington circles. But he used to talk to me sometimes late in the office. I told him I had seen him at a demonstration. I had been *in* the demonstration. "What was the demonstration against?" he said. "You," I said. That made him laugh.'

'What demonstration?' said Toby.

'Against Vietnam,' said Chadwick.

'Nineteen sixty-eight!' said Race.

'Sixty-seven,' said Chadwick.

'I'm sure it was '68,' said Race.

'He's a marine biologist,' said Chadwick to Toby. 'What does he know? It was 1967. But anyway, it doesn't matter. The important thing is: Clifford remembered it too. I told him where I'd seen him and he said: "I remember that!" He'd been to all these countries to raise more troops for the war and there were no demonstrations on the whole trip, but then he got to Wellington and there we were. Ten thousand kids standing in the rain. He remembered standing at a window and looking down at us.'

'I remember that!' said Race. 'I remember seeing him at the window.'

'*You* were there?' said Toby to Race.

'We were both there,' said Race.

'You guys,' said Toby.

'He even made a joke about it,' said Chadwick. 'He said there were more people out that window than New Zealand had ever sent to the war. But it was an important moment for him, he told me. He looked down at the crowd and he saw the signs, and for the first time he thought "Maybe we're wrong."'

'What signs?' said Toby.

'Oh, the usual thing,' said Chadwick. '*Make Love not War* and so on. He was this big Cold War warrior, you see, but at that moment he thought "Maybe these kids are *reading the tide of events* better than us."'

'All You Need Is Love,' said Race.

'All You Need Is Love!' said Chadwick. 'Maybe that's what changed his mind. Morgan's sign.'

'I painted that,' said Race.

'*You* did? I thought Morgan painted it.'

'I painted it,' said Race.

'And I laughed at it,' said Chadwick.

'Why?'

'I don't know. I just wanted to jeer for some reason. I wanted to bring Morgan down a peg or two. He was so damned aloof. And he turned on me and read me a lecture. *Abdera was the vilest town in all of Thrace*.'

'I'd forgotten that,' said Race.

'I never forgot it,' said Chadwick.

'You two,' said Toby, jogging on the spot.

'I didn't know what he was talking about,' said Chadwick. 'It would take about two seconds to find out today but we didn't have the internet then. But I always remembered that – *The town of Abdera was the vilest town in all Thrace*. Of course I was busy with other things and I never really thought about it, but one day I ran into that sentence again.'

'What *was* that all about?' said Race.

'It's an old Greek play called *Andromeda*,' said Chadwick. 'It's a boy-meets-girl thing. Andromeda is this beautiful girl left chained to a rock by her father to be eaten by the sea-monster. Then Perseus comes by on winged sandals, "cutting a path through the midst of the air", and he sees her and falls in love and he makes this famous speech: "O love, love, prince of gods and men!" The rest of the play is lost. We only know it existed because it was put on in a town called Abdera and the whole place fell for that speech. It was a famous incident. Everyone went around singing: "O Love, O Cupid, prince of gods and men". The story was reported about 100 AD by a Roman called Lucian. I've read it all up now, you see. I'm a world expert on the fragment of *Andromeda*. The story reaches England in the seventeenth century. Hobbes repeats it, then it turns up in Sterne. Lucian and Hobbes both hated the story. They thought the Abderites were ridiculous: "The whole population went round like pale ghosts yelling, 'O Love, who lords it over gods and men!" ' But Sterne – he loved it. He'd have loved to have been there, you can tell: "*In every street, in every house, O Love! Prince of gods and men! The fire caught, and the whole city, like the heart of one man, open'd itself to Love.*" That was Morgan's theory, you see. The same thing was happening to us. 1967. Love, love, love! And this time it was all around the world. And some people loved it, and other people hated it, and they still do.'

'Morgan said all that?' said Race.

'He must have thought that. He knew the Sterne by heart,' said Chadwick. 'He fired it straight back at me.'

'What did Clifford do?' said Toby.

'Well, that day changed his mind, he said. He saw these kids and he thought, "Maybe they're *reading the tide* better than us." That was his phrase. But he said nothing when he came back and he was then made Secretary of Defense. And then he came out against the war. Top guy in Pentagon is against war! The president was furious but what could he do? He'd just appointed him. Everything was going crazy that year anyway. Martin Luther King shot. Riots everywhere. American cities burning. This city right here was on fire. You could smell the smoke in the White House. So LBJ gave in. He started peace talks with the Vietnamese. And it took a few years but, you know, we got out of an unwinnable war.'

They stood under the pillars looking at the city.

'I think there's something bad going on down there right now,' said Chadwick.

'What?' said Race.

'I think they're going to invade Iraq,' said Chadwick.

'Jesus,' said Race.

'Uncle Chip'll be pleased,' said Toby.

'Uncle Chip!' said Chadwick.

He stood musing.

'Then he climbed on the limo roof!' he said.

'He jumped on that limo!' said Race. 'I didn't know you saw that.'

'Who?' said Toby.

'Of course I saw it,' said Chadwick.

'What limo?' said Toby.

But they ignored him. They were looking at Morgan on the roof of a long black car beside a rose garden decades earlier.

There was a faint fanfare of trumpets. Toby dived into different pockets of his sweatpants and took out his phone. He spoke for a while, looking first at the horizon, and then he turned to look at Race and at Chadwick while he listened to Candy. The call ended, and they kept watching him.

'Bernard's had a fall,' Toby said.

5

'Reuben!' cried Bernard, stretching out both arms.

Toby paused at the door. Bernard, sitting up in bed, wore a bandage on his head at a rakish angle. One of his legs was in a cast: his ancient naked foot peeped from the encasement of plaster at the edge of a light blanket.

'Reuben!' said Bernard again. 'Who did *you* marry?'

'I didn't marry anyone,' said Toby cautiously. He came further into the hospital room. Merle was sitting on a straight-backed, plastic-seated chair beside the bed. Romulus was outside in the corridor on a red vinyl bench, doing his homework.

'Oh, dear,' said Bernard. 'You should marry, you know. "It is not good that man should be alone." God said that. Or was it Adam? I forget which. My own wife was here a little while ago. Have you seen her about at all?'

'No,' said Toby.

'Your own wife died,' said Merle. 'Twenty year ago.'

'Oh no, that can't be right,' said Bernard. 'I'm sure someone would have mentioned it. Haven't you seen her at all today? I'm sure *I* have.'

'No, Granddad,' said Toby. 'Merle's right. Your wife died.'

'Either you're wrong, or I'm wrong,' said Bernard. 'Perhaps I haven't been *compos mentis* for quite some time. Oh dear, where is the front door key? I have always made a point of keeping it right *here*.'

He patted the glassed top of the bedside locker.

'He's high,' said Merle. 'He had another shot. Enough morphine to kill a horse.'

Bernard giggled. 'I just don't want to be a nuisance,' he said. 'I want to die so I won't be any trouble to my children. You can drop me off any time, you know.'

'We're not dropping you off anywhere, Grandpa. How do you feel?'

'*Dreadful!*' said Bernard.

'Would you like something to drink?' said Toby.

'I would,' said Bernard.

'Cup of coffee?'

'I wouldn't be wanting *that*,' said Bernard. 'What'll we have? Name your poison!'

'I'd like a cup of coffee.'

'I wouldn't bother with that if I were you.'

Afternoon sunlight, slightly begrimed, shone through the window. Pigeons were cooing out of sight on a ledge nearby, and the sound of traffic on K Street soughed through the double glazing.

'How's your leg?' said Toby.

'My leg?'

'Your femur.'

'My femur?'

'You broke your femur. And your tibia.'

'No, my boy. You must be confusing me with someone else. I have never broken a bone of my body in my life.'

'What's this, then?' said Toby, touching the cast with a light finger.

'That?' said Bernard. 'Oh, I let the girls here do all that to keep them happy. They have very little to occupy their time.'

A nurse came in, addressed herself wordlessly to various checks and balances, covered Bernard's empurpled toes with the blanket and departed.

'I suppose you find these nurses highly attractive, sexually?' said Bernard.

'I guess,' said Toby. 'How about you?'

'Well, I *am* rather selfish in these matters,' said Bernard. 'How about you?' he said to Merle.

'I'm going out,' said Merle, standing up and putting on her hat. 'I have some shopping. I leave Romulus with you for ten minutes?'

'Leave him with me,' said Toby.

He followed Merle into the corridor and stood over Romulus.

'It's you and me, kid,' he said. 'What are you doing?'

'Science,' said Romulus, not looking up from his writing. Toby read over his shoulder:

Our own Sun rings like a bell, according to Nasa scintists. It pulses and make a ringing as it does so. We cannot hear the sounds, but we can see oscillations in our Sun's brightness every few minutes

'Wow,' said Toby.

He went back into Bernard's room and sat on the straight-backed chair with the plump, taut seat which Merle had vacated. *Steatopygia*, he thought.

'I suppose you're wondering about my walking stick,' said Bernard, his eyes closed. 'Of course, I'd like it back because it is an *item*.'

'That's fair,' said Toby.

There was a long pause.

'They said at the Manchester laboratory: "We can't afford Bernard Drake, he's too highly paid," said Bernard. 'I was on thirty shillings a week. But Colin McClintock put in a word for me. He said "He'll be value for the money".'

'I bet you were,' said Toby.

There was a silence. Bernard seemed to have fallen asleep. Toby looked out the window at the westering sun.

'It's the only thing I do well now,' said Bernard, half opening his eyes. 'Sleep, I mean. I am very old . . . And lazy.'

'How are you feeling now?'

'It's very hard at this end of life.'

'I meant today, here.'

'Here?'

'In hospital.'

'Hospital!' said Bernard.

'We're at the University Hospital,' said Toby.

'*Are* we?' said Bernard. 'What are we here for?'

'I'm visiting you. What do you think of the place?'

'They're a bit bloody zealous. I intend to leave shortly.'

'You can't leave yet. You need nursing. There are no nurses at Barleycorn Street.'

'Thank God for that.'

There was a long pause. This time Bernard began to snore. Toby went out of the room.

'Come on, Romulo,' he said.

'Where're we going?'

'Fresh air,' said Toby.

They took the elevator down and went outside and stood in the concourse by the street. Toby lit a cigarette.

'Whyn't you quit?' said Romulus severely.

This made Toby laugh. He took the school book from Romulus's hand.

'Let's have a look,' he said.

' "The earth moves round the sun at twenty-five (25) miles a second round the sun," ' he read.

'Twenty-five miles a *second*!' said Toby.

'That's nothing,' said Romulus. 'The sun's going round the galaxy faster than that. And the galaxy's going somewhere else as fast as hell as well.'

'Oh,' said Toby. He looked along the street. The lights changed, the traffic came forward decorously.

'You'd never know it,' he said.

Two hospital porters came out and stood on the concourse, big men, burly, about thirty, wearing white T-shirts and hospital jackets. Then a third came after them. He was much younger, also black, with a limp.

'You're a good man, Pete,' said the younger man, 'you're giving me advice as a family man, I like that, it's important.'

He was looking anxiously from face to face.

'My kid's eighteen months old,' he said. 'He knows me. His mother calls and says: "He wants a word." "Put him on," I say. "Dadda!" he says. She wants a romantic affair with me again but I don't want it. After we split up she was full of animaversity to me, all kinda stories which ain't true, that I'm a junkie, that I'm a closet, that I beat her up. I never beat her up – she beat *me* up.'

The other two said nothing. Romulus was listening with frowning brow, like a *Times* critic on a first night.

'Pete, you look good, you look well, you always do,' said the man with the limp. 'So do you, Pete, you *both* do. I love you guys even though you used to beat me up, even when I had a crippled knee.'

The two Petes said nothing. The traffic changed again at the lights.

'Come on,' said Toby.

He and Romulus went along the street as far as the intersection. Then they turned back, went in the main entrance and took the elevator up to Bernard's room. Merle was already there, sitting beside the bed.

'Hey!' said Romulus. 'Which entrance you come in?'

'The same one I went out of,' said Merle.

'You must have walked straight past us,' said Romulus in admiration at the universe.

The TV set, hung above the bed and angled down, had been switched on. 'Bloodshed in Gaza!' said a richly timbred voice.

'The news,' said Merle. 'He's asleep but he likes the news when he's asleep.'

'Four boys aged between five and twelve were on their way to class at about seven a.m.,' said the television voice.

'I'm worried about my wife,' said Bernard, opening his eyes. 'It would be foolish to pretend at this point of our lives that we have a lot of time left together.'

Chadwick walked into the room. He was wearing a suit of some magnificence and carrying a newspaper. The dark suit, without any further agency, seemed to change the interpersonal dynamics on the wing. A nurse came in and then a doctor appeared for the first time that afternoon. He glanced briefly at Bernard and then turned to Chadwick to say that Bernard was doing well. Chadwick shot his cuffs and listened to the prognosis. The doctor and nurse went out again. Chadwick sat on one of the tautly plump chairs and winked at Toby.

'Body parts were strewn scores of yards away,' said the television voice.

'I saw smoke rising,' said another voice. 'I went running and I saw pieces of people on the ground – legs, hands. Children's legs and children's hands.'

'Funny business, that,' said Chadwick, watching the television from the side. He tapped the paper, then unfolded it and looked at the front page, and then back at the TV.

'Same old thing,' said Toby. 'Arabs and Jews.'

'I know,' said Chadwick. 'But if a country does something like that – us, the Russians, Israel – the first thing you do is deny it. It's only human nature. States are just like people – more primitive and cruel, but just as cunning. And yet here are the Israelis saying: "Oh, yeah. We did that! That was us all right!"'

The doctor came back in and indicated with an inclination of his head that Chadwick should come out to the hall to talk to him.

'I don't get it,' said Chadwick.

He tossed his copy of the *Times* on Bernard's bed and went out. Merle got to her feet heavily and took the paper off the bed and put it on the third chair. She then went around the bed and picked up the glass water-jug from the locker. She tilted it, looking in, then left the room. Toby picked up the paper to read the story:

It was about half an hour after sunrise. The boys were on their way to school, following the lanes between tumbledown houses and greenhouses and out to a field of bright green peppers. Then they climbed a steep sand dune: there was a roar and the ground shook.

'I have come to a momentous decision,' said Bernard, his eyes closed.

There was a long pause. Toby watched him.

'I have determined,' said Bernard, 'taking full responsibility for my actions, to tell the Surgeon-General that I will not comply with his directive. I consider that I am not in a position to do otherwise. I will therefore *not* go to Cincinnati.'

'Well, OK,' said Toby.

'There is a matter of grave importance which requires my presence here,' said Bernard.

There was another silence. The pigeons cooed.

'I was on the tram with Father,' said Bernard, his voice now light and far away. 'I was reading the paper to him. The headline said: "Woodrow Wilson – Too Proud To Fight". I read that to Father. And a man on the tram said: "Some men fight and some won't." And I said to Father: "You're a poor blind man. *You* won't fight." '

There was another silence.

Bernard opened his eyes. He stared all around in alarm, then he set eyes on Toby.

'*Someone* said that,' he said. 'Some boy – half jokingly – suggested that Father should be in the war. But it wasn't me.'

'OK,' said Toby. 'It's OK.'

A look of fear, and of woe, filled Bernard's eyes.

'It wasn't me,' he said. 'Reuben.'

'That's OK,' said Toby.

He took Bernard's hand – weighty, thin-skinned, dramatically blotched – amazed at the heavy costs of time.

Merle came back in the room with the glass jug of water, now full, and put it on the glassed top of the bedside locker. Toby let go of Bernard's hand. Merle put on her hat, then called: 'Romulus'. Romulus came into the room with his book open. Chadwick followed him in and picked up his newspaper.

'Say goodbye to him,' said Merle to Romulus, pointing at Bernard.

'Goodbye,' said Romulus.

Bernard seemed to be asleep. Romulus jiggled Bernard's uninjured foot under the blanket. Merle smacked the back of Romulus's head without force. Bernard opened his eyes a little and looked at the ceiling. Then he crooked his head on the pillow and looked at Romulus.

'Goodbye,' said Romulus.

'Goodbye, old man,' said Bernard.

He sat up a little more and gazed round at them in mild puzzlement.

'You've all had – plenty of, of, of – what you need?' he said.

'Plenty,' said Toby.

'Very good,' said Bernard. His gaze wandered the room.

'Oh,' he said. '*Look!*'

He pointed at the shining wall beyond the end of the bed. They all looked at the shining plaster.

'Egypt!' said Bernard.

Romulus's eyes started.

'No, Grandpa,' Toby said. 'Egypt's not here. Egypt's at home at Barleycorn Street.'

Bernard gazed at Toby. There was a long pause.

'Of course Egypt is not here,' said Bernard. 'Egypt is a cat. And this *is*, I believe, the University Hospital.'

Part III

1969

1

They were going up the hill fast, in the dark, Adam and Candy and Morgan and Race Radzienwicz. It was raining so hard you couldn't talk, you could only laugh. It was raining with a kind of passion. They were running, and laughing – what did the rain mean by this passion, what on earth did rain want? It was as if it was in a rage or trying to make copies of itself. They ran across Willis Street through the sluicing headlights and under the neon signs of the Hotel St George, and then up Boulcott Street, water sliding in scallops down the steep black pavement. Race had almost forgotten that he was going to miss Chadwick's wedding the next morning. Chadwick was the first of the gang to get married. The night before, Race had caught the train from Auckland. A plane, with the whole wedding party on board, was leaving Wellington at ten-thirty the following day. But at six that morning, sitting in the second-class carriage, Race was woken by a sudden stillness and silence: the train had stopped. The sun was not up yet but he could see the faint green of a field in the early light. Then an announcement was made: there was a slip on the line further south.

Away across the fields stood a factory with the word *F e l t e x* painted on the roof. On the other side of the carriage was a muddy lane with a long queue of cows standing at a gate. After a while the sun came up and for a moment burnished the brick walls of the factory as if to say: 'There . . . *eternity.*' The cows began to move forward with an air of matronly leisure.

'I'm going to miss the plane!' thought Race. 'I'm going to miss Chadwick's wedding.'

At seven-thirty the train moved off, but very slowly, through dew-spangled meadows. It stopped again, lengthily, in a field outside Levin, and again at Foxton station, and in a siding at Otaki. It seemed to Race that the powers-that-be knew all about the wedding and had decided he should miss it. But then at nine-thirty the train set off at speed, racing southward – Paraparaumu, Paekakariki – '*Paekakariki! Where the girls are cheeky,*' said an old man with a white cloth cap across the aisle – Plimmerton, Porirua flashed past – dales and tunnels vanished behind them, mud-flats and flag-staffs and rock-girt seas. At quarter past ten, they emerged from the last tunnel and swooped round the harbour. Across the water planes were lifting off and setting down in the rookery of the airport. At exactly ten-thirty Race walked out of Wellington station with his bag in his hand. There were no more flights to Queenstown that day. Everyone, Race thought, was going to Chadwick's wedding. They were all on the ten-thirty flight – Chadwick and his bride-to-be, FitzGerald, the best man, the Gudgeon sisters, Rod Orr, Lane Tolerton, all the rest of them. This was Race's first trip back since he had moved to Auckland and now he felt all alone in the place.

He stood there under the sandstone pillars feeling hapless, like a man in a cartoon, but what exactly was the joke? Haplessness is the joke, he thought. He took his bag back and checked it at the left-luggage then came out of the station again and walked into the city. He went to several record stores and bookshops and then to a coffee bar and ordered coffee and a roll and read the *Dominion*. Then he walked up to Cuba Street and went to a second coffee bar and re-read the morning paper. 'Something will happen,' he told himself.

At two o'clock his mother, passing in a bus, saw her son standing at the corner of Willis Street and Manners Street. He was looking in a shop window, immersed in study of the contents – pipes, cigars, speciality tobacco. She went up Brooklyn hill on the bus and walked from the bus stop to the house and let herself in and went into the kitchen and sat down on one of the old bent-wood chairs she had inherited from her father, and burst into tears.

'He's in town and hasn't even rung us!' she thought.

She went to the phone to call her husband, but then stopped. He had a busy surgery and didn't like to be disturbed by home-life dramas. In any case, he himself, at the age of twenty-two, a Polish prisoner of war, had escaped from a camp in the Ukraine and walked all the way to freedom across a mountain range into Persia. The tribulations which his wife offered for his consideration sometimes made him roar with laughter.

'Oh well,' she thought. 'After all, he's only twenty-one.' She was thinking of Race but she also saw her husband crossing a mountain pass in 1941 – she saw the ice and the Persian sunlight around him – and she began to feel more cheerful. She went to the piano and sat down to play. She plunged her hands on the keyboard and sang:

> *Down at the end of* lone-*ly street*
> *At* heart-*break hotel.*

Just then Race, down in town, remembered Adam and Candy and Morgan. Had *they* gone to Chadwick's wedding? Had they flown off to Queenstown with everyone else? It occurred to him that they might not have: he hadn't heard their names in any lists mentioned in the preliminary arrangements. It occurred to him as well that Chadwick and those three were not very close – that Chadwick and Morgan, especially, had never hit it off. Perhaps it was hard for them, he thought, to make friends, the only two non-whites in a white crowd. Maybe they thought it would look ridiculous, an alliance based on skin colour. 'I'm only guessing,' he thought, but he decided to walk up the hill to see. Light rain was falling in town, but then it stopped and then started again. An hour later, he stood at the foot of a retaining wall of rain-stained concrete which rose forty feet above the pavement. Inset in the wall was a zig-zag path. Race had only a rough idea of the address. He had heard it but never written it down. He stood and looked at the wall. The rain stains were dramatic, like the graphs of profit and loss. He took the zig-zag path. It led up to a little hamlet of letter boxes in a grove of trees. Higher up, above the trees, he could see the gables of four or five houses. Asphalt paths led off in different directions. Which one to take? The mailboxes were numbered but the paths were not. Is there a guiding instinct which helps the young find one another in their momentous task, to make love and perpetuate the species? He chose the middle path and went up through the trees. The path led up around the side of a house to a small concrete yard. The back door was open. He stepped into a kitchen. No one was there, but the room was warm and smelled of recent frying. He walked through the kitchen into a larger room. There was Candy on her hands and knees on the carpet.

She looked up at him with her great eyes. For a moment he thought she was in some kind of travail or danger and that she must be pleased to see him.

'Don't move!' she said. She spoke sharply though in a mumble. There were pins between her lips.

'Don't mumble,' said Race. He felt hurt at her greeting, the first he had had from any human being all that day.

Candy took the pins from her mouth.

'Sorry, dear heart,' she said. 'I'm making this dress, and I really don't have a clue what I'm doing. Walking on my pattern won't help.'

Race looked down at his feet. He was standing among flimsy sheets of grey paper marked with blue lines.

'You make your own clothes!' he said.

'I'm trying to.'

'I thought you'd get your clothes from Mary-Lou.'

Mary-Lou was the name of the chain of stores Candy's father owned.

'Mary-Lou!' said Candy. 'I would wear something from Mary-Lou! No one in their right mind would wear clothes from Mary-Lou.'

'Oh,' said Race humbly. 'I didn't know that.'

'*So* hideous,' said Candy, thinking of the pale mannequins in the windows of the Mary-Lou outlets, who had sent her to the best schools.

Race stood there unsure of what to do next. A pretty girl he had never seen before came out of the next room. She and Race looked at each other. Candy was suddenly struck by a thought.

'Quick!' she said. 'Morgan just left. He's going to the movies. You must have seen him on the path.'

'I didn't,' said Race.

'You must have,' said Candy. 'He just left. Go!'

The other girl laughed, apparently at Candy's tone of command and Race's air of indecision.

'Go!' said Candy again. 'You'll catch him if you run.'

Race turned and left the house; he went back down through the trees and down the zig-zag and across the street and along the avenue in the direction of the cable-car terminus. Not far ahead he caught sight of Morgan's black hat. The rain had stopped and just then the sun came out under the cloud-eaves in the west, and lit up one side of the boles of the old avenue trees, pohutukawas and planes, as stout as wine-vats or wheat-sacks. Race tapped Morgan on the shoulder. Morgan spun around and stared at him.

'Where did you spring from?' he said.

'I've been at your place.'

'You couldn't have.'

'We must have missed each other on the path.'

'That's not physically possible,' said Morgan.

'I know,' said Race.

'I'm in a hurry,' said Morgan.

'Where are you going?'

'Movies.'

'What are we going to see?'

'Whatever's on at the Lido.'

They took the shortcut to Glasgow Street, went through the campus, past the graveyard knoll with its Celtic cross, down the steep, pine-rooted asphalt track to Salamanca Road and then leapt the Allenby Terrace stairs two at a time and arrived in the heart of town.

'Look at that,' said Morgan, coming into the foyer of the Lido. 'I had a bet with Candy you could get to the movies in twenty-five minutes and you can.'

'We won,' said Race. He looked at the poster. It was for a Bergman film. '*Wild Strawberries*,' Race said. 'We'd better go to the pub.'

'You're right,' said Morgan. 'I've proved that it can be done. There's no need to actually go doing it.'

They went to the pub next door. At six, Morgan phoned the others. At seven Candy and Adam arrived. Race had never been out with the trio before and found he was enjoying himself. Adam's stutter was bad at first but then dwindled away. Candy linked her arms with both Adam and Morgan as if she could hold all three together for ever. Morgan began to tell a long story about Flaubert in Egypt – he had been reading Flaubert's *Letters from Egypt* – and how Flaubert, visiting a Turkish bath in Cairo or somewhere and lying there in the dim hot dripping echoing room, felt this incredible melancholy, and how he, Morgan, always felt the same melancholy just at the point of getting into a hot bath – '*lowering* in', he said. Adam then said that he too felt that same melancholy, and Race was about to say that he – although he was not sure what the end of the sentence would be but he was sure he had something to say but Candy interrupted and said that it was complete balls – that was the expression she used – and that getting into a hot bath was one of the least melancholy things that you could do especially on a winter's day at about, say, seven-thirty in the evening and you'd come in and it was freezing cold outside and preferably raining and you weren't going out that night but staying in and then you had a long hot bath, and if anyone wanted to join you—. Then she stopped and laughed, and

Morgan stopped for a moment too and looked at her. He thought of FitzGerald slipping up the zig-zag path on a winter's evening. He had not seen him there but he thought of it anyway. He went on to say that Flaubert, when he climbed one of the pyramids—

'Oh, still in Egypt, are we?' said Candy.

'Still in Egypt,' said Morgan evenly.

—he found that the top was white with eagle-droppings, with the shit of eagles—

'That's important,' said Race.

'I know,' said Morgan.

'Why is it important?' said Race.

'I don't know,' said Morgan.

'No one else has ever mentioned it,' said Race.

'That's why it's important,' said Morgan, and at that moment they were both pleased with each other and Morgan felt as if he had momentarily slipped the gravitational pull of Adam and Candy, that for the first time for a year or two he was no longer just the third member of a trio, always circling the other two at a distance, often not even visible like one of those bodies in space which scientists can detect, although not by telescope. At ten o'clock when the pub closed they went to the door and saw the rain slashing down on the street, violent, passionate, as if serving aces.

'How're we going to get out of this?' said Candy.

'Taxi,' said Morgan.

'No money,' said Candy, who was careful with money.

'You can come with me,' said Race.

'Where are you going?'

'I'm going to stay at Rod Orr's,' said Race.

'Will Rod Orr mind?'

Race thought of Rod Orr arriving on the road-trip in the summer.

'He'd better not mind,' said Race.

They ran out into the deluge. It was raining so hard you had to laugh. At the top of Boulcott, they turned and went down the hill again towards parliament, then into Silver Lane and climbed the steps to the house where Rod Orr lived. The clouds scudding over the town were filled with the urban glow; everything below was lit up as if by X-ray – the flights of steps, the running figures, the house above.

'How do we get in?' said Candy when they reached the top of the steps.

'We break in,' said Race.

'Are you sure Rod won't mind?' said Candy.

'He'll never know,' said Race.

There was a wild gust of wind and the big cabbage-tree beside the veranda tossed its head. Someone stepped out of the shadow. Candy gave a scream.

'Christ,' said Race to the figure. 'You gave me a fright.'

'Lord love us,' said Candy. 'Who are you?'

'This is Salmond Burns,' said Race. 'I thought you were in England.'

'Scotland,' said Burns.

He stood in the rain-cloud glow, looking sheepish.

'Are you really called Salmond Burns?' said Candy.

Salmond Burns nodded, with his eyes shut.

'What are you doing here?' said Race.

At school Salmond Burns had been the speedy winger, the sprint champ, the golden boy. What was he doing standing in the shadow of Rod Orr's veranda in a rain storm?

'I came to town to see this girl,' said Salmond. 'But she shut the door on me. She laughed in my face,' he added, deciding to reveal what until a moment before he had planned always to hide – the extent of his humiliation.

'Then I drove round but I couldn't find anyone and I thought of Rod Orr. So I came here. Then it started pouring down so I just waited here. I didn't know what else to do. Race! I never thought *you*'d be here. Thank God for that!'

Race was unused to the role of saviour. 'Wait,' he said. He went to the window and pushed at the splintery wooden frame with his fingers. The window went up shakily on a single sash cord. Race swung his leg over the sill and went into the room and disappeared. A light came on through the mottled glass of the front door, and Race reappeared.

'*Yes?*' he said, opening the door a little.

They crowded in past him.

'Are you sure Rod Orr won't mind?' said Candy.

'Rod Orr will be honoured,' said Race.

'I adore Rod,' said Candy, superstitiously. She had an idea that Rod Orr, five hundred miles away at Chadwick's wedding, might be able to see them walking around his house at that moment.

'Look at Rod's wine,' Adam called out from the dining room. He began to read out labels. 'Chateau Talbot. Côte de Beaune. Meursault. Nuits-Saint-Georges.'

'Rod is into wine,' said Candy. 'He's got a part-time job as a waiter at Le Normandie so now he's really into wine.'

'Let's have a drink,' said Adam, picking up a bottle.

'No!' said Candy. 'Not his good wine. Open some plonk.'

They opened a red that looked more humble and went into the sitting-room. Race closed the window where the rain was coming in on the gale. The sitting-room had a red carpet and a faded red velvet sofa and red and yellow curtains with a jaunty pattern of musical instruments – oboes, clarinets – in yellow thread. There were some pot plants on the coffee table and a vine growing up a trellis on the wall.

'Oh, how lovely,' said Candy, sinking onto the sofa. 'Shall we light a fire? It's horrible out there. Did you notice how horrible it was tonight? Did you notice the atmosphere? All those men.'

'What men?' said Morgan.

'Those old men everywhere. In blazers. Old men in blazers on the street.'

'They're remembering the war,' said Morgan. 'What do you expect?'

'I hate Anzac weekend,' said Candy. 'All those old men in their blazers. Glorifying war. The *boys* at Gallipoli.'

'Well, they were boys,' said Morgan. 'They were *boys*. What do you think they were?'

Candy looked baffled. She had had the feeling that Morgan was angry with her, but why? What had she done? Now he was picking a fight with her over war, of all things. War, you'd think, would be safe ground. She wished she remembered more about Gallipoli.

'Gallipoli was absurd,' she said. 'It made no sense. The British—'

'It made perfect sense,' said Morgan. 'Knock Turkey out of the war. Relieve the eastern front. No Russian collapse. No sealed train. No Lenin. No Bolshevik revolution. No Hitler. No World War Two. Seems like a good plan to me.'

Candy gave up. Her brow was furrowed. Did Morgan really hate her? Sometimes she thought he hated her for taking Adam from him. Sometimes she thought he liked her more than he liked

Adam. And what did she think of Morgan as a possible lover? That was dark to her. She turned towards Salmond.

'So,' she said, 'who's the girl?'

'You don't know her,' said Salmond.

'In which case there's no reason not to tell us, is there?' said Candy.

'I don't want to talk about it,' said Salmond.

'What's her name?'

'Sandra.'

'OK,' said Candy, nodding. 'Sandra who?'

'You don't know her,' said Salmond.

'You've said that,' said Candy. 'Oh my God, not *Sandra*!'

'Yes,' said Salmond.

'Sandra Isbister?'

'Yes,' said Salmond.

'Oh my God,' said Candy.

'Do you know her?' said Salmond.

'Of course I know her,' said Candy. 'Who was helping me make a dress this afternoon?'

'Who?' said Salmond.

'Cassandra Isbister.'

She gazed at Salmond with an expression that was kind and contemptuous. It was brave, and foolish, was what her expression meant, to fall for Sandra Isbister.

'Everyone falls in love with Sandra Isbister,' she said.

'Not me,' said Adam.

'Not me,' said Morgan. 'I've only met her once.'

'Not me,' said Race. 'I never heard of her before.'

'You *did*,' cried Candy, turning on Adam. 'You said you thought she was incredibly attractive.'

'Only because you asked me if I thought she was incredibly attractive, and I said I c-c-c-could see why people said so.'

His stutter was back. He had felt the tension between Candy and Morgan and he was angry with Morgan for that.

'She *is* incredibly attractive,' said Candy. 'She looks an ordinary little thing at first, then you realise she's incredibly attractive. It's not her hair, it's not her eyes. They're just grey eyes. It's her walk. It's her body. She has – *jouissance*.'

No one said anything.

'I'm being objective,' said Candy. 'You might give me the credit for that.'

She turned back to Salmond.

'Wait a minute,' she said. 'You're the one who's been to Scotland?'

'Yes,' said Salmond.

'She told me about you! She told me about this guy who was coming back from Scotland and wanted to take her out.'

'Did she?' said Salmond.

'Oh – my – God,' said Candy again. 'You saw her tonight?'

'Yes.'

'And she shut the door in your face?'

'Yes.'

'So then you came here?'

'Yes.'

'To see Rod Orr?'

'Yes.'

'A shoulder to cry on?'

'Sort of,' said Salmond.

'Oh, dear,' said Candy. 'That's just incredibly funny. I'm sorry. I shouldn't laugh, but it *is* funny.'

'What's funny about it?' said Morgan.

'It was Rod who put her off you,' said Candy. 'He said – I'm sorry, I'm just repeating what he said – he said you were this, well, rich country boy who dresses like Prince Charles or someone and doesn't have a clue about what's going on.'

'Is that what he said?' said Salmond. His face went red.

Candy looked slightly guilty about her cruelty but she nodded. Salmond got up and went into the dining room and came back with a bottle of Chateau Pomerol and a bottle of Chateau Talbot, both of which he opened.

He tipped wine into their glasses.

'The thing is,' said Morgan, 'that it worked.'

'What worked?' said Race.

'Gallipoli.'

'No it didn't,' said Race.

'It nearly worked,' said Morgan. 'We got to the top.'

Candy stood up and left the room.

Morgan stood up too, and then climbed on the coffee table and looked at the wall as if it was very far away.

'What are you doing?' said Race.

Morgan didn't answer. His fist was clenched near his heart as he looked at the wall.

'What's he up to?' said Race to Adam.

'I d-d-don't know,' said Adam.

'I'm the monument on Brooklyn hill,' said Morgan.

'I don't know any monument on Brooklyn hill,' said Race.

'Well, exactly,' said Morgan. 'No one goes near it any more. That's why I'm going to the trouble of standing on this table to show you. OK, so I'm the war memorial on Brooklyn hill. I'm the statue of a soldier. What am I looking at?'

'I don't know,' said Race.

'Some people say that I'm looking at the ships sail away to World War One. But that doesn't make sense. If I'm a soldier, why would I be standing on Brooklyn hill watching the troopships sail away to war?'

'I don't know,' said Race.

'It doesn't make any sense,' said Morgan.

'So what are you doing?' said Race.

'I'm looking at Constantinople,' said Morgan. 'I'm on the top of the hills at Gallipoli, and I'm looking east, at the lights of Constantinople. Because that's what happened. We got there. We took the heights. The Wellington boys, the Maori boys. And they *were* boys,' he said, looking down the hall where Candy had gone.

Adam got up and went out of the room.

'We got to the top,' said Morgan. He followed Adam with his eyes. 'The plan had worked. It was just like the *Iliad*. Troy was only fifty miles away from Gallipoli. A lot of people at Gallipoli thought they were in the *Iliad*.'

Salmond went back to the dining room and came back with more bottles, a Chablis and a Nuits-Saint-Georges, both of which he opened.

'Steady, lover-boy,' said Morgan. 'It's only a girl.'

He held out his glass. Salmond filled it.

'The Greeks took Troy. We didn't take Constantinople,' said Race.

'*Exactly*,' said Morgan.

'What I don't see,' said Salmond, 'is why she should take any notice of Rod Orr.'

He was kneeling, hunched, in front of the fireplace.

'Women like disinterested advice,' said Morgan.

From his armchair Race looked down the hall. It was only a small house with a dining room off to the right of the hall and a bedroom off to the left and a kitchen at the back. He could see no one down there in the dark. A fire was now burning in the grate. Salmond was feeding it screws of newspaper.

'In the *Iliad*,' said Morgan, 'there's this big debate – whether to stay and take Troy or to sail home. Thersites said "Let's go home" and so Achilles beat him with a golden rod.'

'Who's Thersites?' said Race.

'The ugliest man who ever came to Troy,' said Morgan. "*Squint-eyed, lame, hunched, pointy head crowned with fluff. He cared not what he said as long as he raised a laugh. 'Let's all sail home,' he said, 'the king can go fuck himself.' 'Silence,' said Ulysses. 'No mortal worse has come to Troy,' and he beat him with his golden staff.*" It was the same at Gallipoli. We took the heights. We could see the lights of Constantinople. We could have done it. But what happened? This journalist arrived. No worse mortal ever came to Troy. He only stayed for three days, listened to all the worst opinions he could find, and then went to London and made a fuss. He cared not what he said as long as he caused a stink. The British panicked and abandoned the campaign and so then we packed up and sailed away.'

Salmond stood up and went over to the window. He stood on a chair and took down one of the red curtains with golden oboes and clarinets on it. Then he wrapped it around himself and lay on the floor.

'There's the difference,' said Morgan. 'Thersites got beaten with a golden rod, Murdoch got a knighthood. Then he founded an empire. They bought up the local paper here the other day. And that's still the Murdoch racket: find the worst opinions you can, then package them up and sell them to the people you got them from.'

Race looked down through the house from his armchair. He could see no one down there in the dark.

'That's the racket,' said Morgan.

'Where have they gone?' said Race.

'To bed,' said Morgan. He stepped off the table.

'To bed!' said Race. There was only one bed, he realised, in the house. 'There's only one bed,' he said.

'They have priority,' said Morgan. 'They get the double bed. Sex has priority. Troy was all about sex. Who gets Helen? Who gets Candy?'

'Who gets Sandra Isbister?' said Race.

He looked at Burns wrapped in the red curtain like a chrysalis and apparently fast asleep.

'Who gets Sandra Isbister?' said Morgan, bowing his head as if acknowledging the oversight.

Race looked down the hall and saw Candy come out of the kitchen. The kitchen and hall were still dark but he saw her walking carefully, carrying two glasses of water. She was naked. Race felt a cool pang in his throat and chest. Candy went through the bedroom door which was ajar; she opened it with one foot, there was a brief glow from a bedside light, then the door was closed.

'That's what the *Iliad* was all about,' said Morgan. 'Who gets the girl? Who gets the double bed? That's always the big story. What about you?' he said. 'What's your version?'

2

Race then told Morgan about his love affair the year before. 'She was engaged to someone else,' he said. 'She was in love with him and going to get married.'

'Well, that's a bad start,' said Morgan.

'But he'd gone away,' said Race. 'He was on this ship that had gone to England. He was away six months. She was bored and a bit lonely and her flatmate invited me round to visit, I suppose to cheer her up. I didn't care one way or the other. I went round because I had nothing else to do that night. Then this disaster happened.'

'What disaster?'

'I fell for her. I fell completely in love.'

'That's bad,' said Morgan.

'Maybe it was just that night, in that room – if someone else had been there maybe I'd have fallen in love with them instead.'

'No,' said Morgan firmly. 'To hell with that!'

'OK,' said Race. 'Maybe not. Anyway, it wasn't someone else. It was her. And then I was obsessed. I was crazy about her. I went there every single night. Straight after lectures I would run right across town, I'd run all the way – down Courteney Place, up Kent Terrace. I couldn't take the bus.'

'Why not?' said Morgan.

'I couldn't stand waiting at the bus stop,' said Race.

'No,' said Morgan.

Race wanted to describe the feeling he had when he ran across town every night and reached Kent Terrace where the statue of the queen with her crown on stood among the trolley-bus wires in the dusk. Up the hill was the house where his girlfriend lived. Her name was Bonnie. The road went up the hill and curved round a corner towards her house and the trolley-wires went up too, curving round the corner, and when he saw the statue of the queen among the trolley-bus wires, he felt a shift in his heart as though, in the dusk, that curve in the road, and the trolley-wires on the way to Bonnie's house were changing the shape of his heart for ever. But he couldn't say this to Morgan.

'So what happened?' said Morgan.

'She liked me,' said Race. 'She let me come back to see her every night. We'd play games. We played cards. But mostly we just talked. She told me all about her family and where she grew up and so on. She loved talking. She talked about her fiancé too – to fend me off, you see. I hated that, but still it was better than not being there with her. I let her talk. Sometimes she even kissed me a few times. I mean she let me kiss her. But I always had to leave. I'd catch the last bus home.'

'So then what?'

'Finally one night she let me stay. I was allowed to sleep in the bed!'

'Really?' said Morgan.

'But not between the sheets,' said Race.

'Jesu Criste!' said Morgan. 'What happened then?'

'Nothing,' said Race. 'She went to sleep and I went to sleep. I don't think I really slept. I kind of just dreamed I was asleep all night. I was incredibly happy, you see. I was nearly there. I always thought I'd get her in the end and the fiancé would just never show up or something. Then that night there was a bang on the window. We were on the ground floor. The bed was in the bay-window. We were just about sleeping in the street. I sat up and pulled back the curtain. There's this guy there, angry-looking guy about forty, red face, black combed hair, staring in at me. He's a detective, he says. There's been a murder across the street.'

'A murder!' said Morgan.

'A girl across the street had had a party and everyone left except someone hid in her wardrobe and came out and killed her. I don't know how they knew he'd been in the wardrobe. Well – we hadn't seen anything. We hadn't heard anything. We couldn't help. But I thought: "Here I am, in bed with the girl I love, there's been a murder across the street, and a plain-clothes man is looking in the window. This is it. Adulthood!" '

'Ha!' said Morgan.

'It was just before dawn. I saw the milkman at the end of the street. I even heard a cock crow. Imagine that – someone keeping hens in those old apartments on Mount Vic.'

'Then what happened?' said Morgan.

'That was the end of it. The fiancé came back two days later.'

Morgan burst out laughing.

'What's the joke?' said Race.

'It's not funny,' said Morgan.

'Now she's married him, and I'll never see her again.'

'At least she let you sleep in her bed,' said Morgan. 'What did you say her name was?'

'Bonnie,' said Race.

'Sexy old Bonnie,' said Morgan. 'Liddy – Lydia – never let me sleep in her bed.'

He stood up and began prowling round the room. 'Probably that's why I'm so incredibly fucked up,' he said with aplomb. 'But I happen to know she loved me. I was going to step right in and ask her to marry me. But she loved something else more. The social whirl she was in, with these rich red-neck farmers. Like what's-his-name here.'

He did a neat scissor-leap over the sleeping Salmond Burns.

'He's not a red-neck,' said Race.

'Maybe he is, maybe he isn't,' said Morgan, still prowling round. They were now very drunk, Race realised drunkenly, on Rod Orr's wine. The fire was blazing up. The music was on. Miles Davis was on. Who had put Miles on? The vines seemed to be curling down the wall in slow motion.

'I have this cousin in love with me,' said Morgan, 'but she's sixteen and my cousin and she's none too bright, so that's not much use, is it?'

He took a letter out of his pocket and then began to read aloud:

My dearest cousin Morgan,

Having the opportunity of relaxing I thought of such a charming idea to write. Here's the local gossip not that it's plentiful. Johnny had a big gathering at Cape Runaway. My real parents were there and I was so glad to see them. Johnny was buried on a hill looking down to the old school and the church to be. The church will be named St Johns after him. I didn't pass the army because I'm absolutely dumb and dreadfully sad. I went up to Gisborne for my interview stayed there for a week and of course got involved with a couple of nice looking boys. One mind you was a Pakeha with glasses but a fab Velox, the unknown I would presume, but the first one I went with was a

Maori his name was Charlie Hirini he had a bomb I kind of liked him because he was one of the boys that was interviewed with me. At night I roamed the streets. There was the bogies all in tight skinned clothing waiting in uncivilized places and taking girls on their motorbikes. Just the sight of them made me shrink a little. Came back through the gorge, decided to stay the night at Opotiki then right to Charlie Tuhiwai's wedding. There was Charlie Spoons, Rangi Koroheke, Richard and Gladys, Whata Wairua, Jimmy Rhodes and Jimmy Devereaux. We stayed there two nights so like a flirt I decided to go with Whata, that's Johnny Wairua's brother he's quiet nice but incline to be shy. He called me doll all the way, of course I got the cheap thrills. Martha who is not a friend of mine any more went with Porgy. No doubt I got kisses, kisses that one and only night. Queenie Rolleston is getting married Labour weekend. Dardanelle is going nursing. Mary Cowan's bull jumped the fence and chased Hubert round his truck three times. My photo album is piling up for you to have a look. Rita and Teia are naughty day after day and we still got Ricky and Motu. Well so long, dear cuz, time slips away for another day.

Long Live Love
Please write cousin
Count all mistakes as kisses
Rianora Kingi

'See what a silly girl she is,' said Morgan. 'She wants to make me jealous.'

He folded the cheap lined paper and put it in the envelope and put the envelope back in his pocket.

'Always to hand,' said Race.

'It reminds me of home, that's all,' said Morgan.

'Oh yeah,' said Race.

'*Little boy blue, come blow your horn,*' said Morgan. '*The something, the something the cow's in the corn.*'

Race then remembered climbing up round the trunk of a tree, and Morgan climbing above him, but he said nothing. After all, he thought, it's a damned cheek dreaming of other people. They have no say in the matter. It's not something you mention.

'Life in the country. You have no idea,' said Morgan.

'I have been there, remember,' said Race.

Morgan looked at him. 'Oh, you have too,' he said.

He went to the window and stood on the chair and took down the other red curtain, then got down off the chair and put the curtain around his shoulders and went and lay on the sofa again with his feet up.

'I was watching TV the other day,' he said, 'and these guys were doing a space-walk. They were tethered to the ship and walking around in space and behind them was the earth. But the earth was actually a cliff of blue water seven thousand miles high . . .'

He took the curtain off his shoulders and covered his body with it and then lay back again.

'A blue cliff of water, thousands of miles high,' he said. 'And I was sitting down beside it, watching on TV.'

From his chair Race looked around the room. Burns was on the floor under one red curtain. Morgan was on the sofa under the other. The hall light and the kitchen light were off.

'Where am I going to sleep?' he said.

'You'll have to share,' said Morgan.

Race got up and took off his shoes and lay down on the sofa in the other direction. Morgan's shoes were in front of his face.

'Tomorrow,' said Morgan, 'I'm going to this party in Brooklyn. I've met a girl who's asked me to a party. Candy and Adam are coming. You can come as well. Just don't cramp my style.'

'OK,' said Race.

There was a long silence.

'Your shoes,' said Race.

'What about them?'

'I don't know. They're kind of in my face.'

'OK,' said Morgan. His shoes disappeared, then his bare feet appeared.

'That statue on Brooklyn hill,' he said after a while.

'Yeah?' said Race.

'I always kind of liked him. It reminds me of my uncle. Even though he's not a darky.'

'A *darky*?' said Race. '*Who* isn't?' But then it seemed to him that he fell straight to sleep and never knew if Morgan gave any explanation.

In the morning he woke and saw two bare feet in front of his eyes. For a moment he didn't know whose they were, or even to what species of creature they belonged – those sallow, fanned metatarsals. Then Candy and Adam came into the room and Morgan woke up. Salmond Burns had gone. His curtain was lying on the floor like an empty chrysalis. The others tidied the flat a bit, re-hung the curtains, took the bottles out, shut the windows, closed the door and went away. Race walked down to the station and took his bag from the left-luggage, changed his shirt in the men's room and put his luggage back again. Then he phoned his parents.

'Oh, how *wonderful*,' said his mother. 'You're here, in *town*?'

Race explained what had happened. When she heard that he had missed a plane and been in town only a day, and by accident, his mother felt quite light-hearted.

'Darling!' she called out to her husband, while still holding the receiver. 'Guess what! Race is in town.'

'I know,' said Race's father. 'You told me that yesterday.'

'Shsh!' she said, shaking her head and signalling with her free hand. He looked at her in wonder. Race vaguely overheard this far-off exchange but took no notice. He was used to such negotiations between his parents, between fact and feelings, which had been going on above his head since infancy.

'Are you coming up to see us?' said his mother.

'I'll come tonight,' said Race. 'I'm back on the train tomorrow.'

At six, Race met Candy and Adam and Morgan again and they took a cab up to Brooklyn to Morgan's party. There was hardly anyone there: the hostess, a girl with long, pale blonde hair; two of her girl-friends; a cousin from Melbourne; a neighbour who mowed her lawn. There was a fire blazing on the grate and a white sheepskin rug in front of the fire. The hostess handed round drinks and snacks formally, in a way that didn't happen at student parties.

'I'm not staying,' said Race to the others. 'I have to see my folks. I'll catch a cab.'

'You're leaving us,' said Candy, wide-eyed.

'I'm leaving you,' said Race.

There was a patter on the roof, then a crash of rain. It had been dry and calm all day but now a second storm had arrived. Race called a cab and ran out through the driving rain and went home.

That night he slept in his old bedroom. He had been away from home only a few months but all his belongings had been removed. There was no sign he had ever slept in the room, much less lived in it for nearly twenty years. Everything was in boxes in the basement, said his father.

'You are not one of these sentimental fellows,' he said, stating this as a fact. This made Race laugh.

'I *tried*,' said his mother. She rolled her eyes towards her husband. 'I tried to save something from the wreckage but you know what he's like.'

That night Race played chess with his father, who beat him, as usual, with despatch. He went to bed at midnight in his bare, stripped room. It rained heavily again in the night and he heard the sound of the rain on the roof. Then it stopped and later he dreamed that he got up and went outside and saw the full moon rising at the end of the yard where he used to play as a child. Then he saw that it was not the moon but the Earth, with its pelt of blue seas and continents and all its stories, rising on the full above the pines at the end of the yard where he had played as a child.

At five in the afternoon the following day his parents dropped him at the station. He retrieved his bag and went out to catch his train.

Just as he was about to climb aboard he saw Morgan coming fast along the platform.

'What are you doing here?' said Race.

'I came to see you off,' said Morgan.

Race put his suitcase down. Morgan picked up the suitcase and hefted its weight.

'All this for one weekend,' he said.

'I was going to a wedding, remember,' said Race. 'There's a valuable wedding present in there.'

'What?' said Morgan.

'Pewter,' said Race.

'Pewter?' said Morgan.

'I bought it from Panos.'

'That Greek. He probably stole it from somewhere.'

'Possibly,' said Race.

There was a din of announcement. The train was about to leave.

'That girl last night,' said Morgan. 'I stayed. Everyone else left and I stayed. We made love right there in front of the fire.'

'Go, Morgan!' said Race.

'You should have heard the rain on the roof,' said Morgan. 'It was like applause.'

'Applause?' said Race.

'Like thousands of people *clapping*,' said Morgan.

'Get outta here,' said Race. But he was pleased and surprised that Morgan had come down to see him off and tell him this story. He looked over Morgan's shoulder at the clock at the end of the platform with its yellow face and Arabic numerals. Then the whistle blew and Race climbed up and looked back at Morgan who was looking back at him, his eyes still shining.

'Come down,' said Race, tilting his head towards the front carriage where he was going to sit, and he went along to his seat, but when he got there the train had already begun to move and there was only an empty platform out the window and then they were sliding through the marshalling yards under the signal gantries and then suddenly speeding alongside the motorway and all the traffic was speeding beside them, either going as fast or faster than they were in the same direction or coming towards them faster still, and although it was not even dark yet all the cars speeding towards them had their headlights on, the sure sign of a storm ahead.

3

The three men stood under a streetlight by the steps. Three separate sets of concrete steps came down side by side from unseen houses high above The Terrace. From one of the houses you could hear the engine-thrum of a party. The three men – Morgan, Meiklejohn and Human Sanity – were arguing, though mildly, about what to do next. Morgan was rather drunk. Human Sanity was drunk as well, though not as drunk as Morgan. Meiklejohn had been drinking with them but didn't appear to be drunk at all. He was tall and thin and had an expression of distaste on his face. He was a painter, an artist. So was Human Sanity, whose real name was Hooman Sanatay; he was from Iran. He was short and stocky, with round brown eyes, two black-furred arches of eyebrows above them.

'Let's go to Auckland,' said Morgan. 'First we find some pot, then we go to Auckland.'

'Forget Auckland,' said Meiklejohn.

'We should go back to the party. Why did we leave the party?' said Human Sanity. He pointed up one of the flights of steps.

'Don't be ridiculous,' said Meiklejohn.

'What is ridiculous?' said Human Sanity.

'You were. The party was.'

'I was very happy. I met a girl there who loved me.'

'The fat girl.'

'Fat!' said Human Sanity. 'Meiklejohn doesn't like girls,' he said to Morgan. 'He likes boys.'

'It is quite normal to feel attraction for your own gender – if they are of sufficient pulchritude,' said Meiklejohn.

'Pulchritude,' said Morgan.

'I *assumed*,' said Meiklejohn, 'I was having a conversation with an adult.'

'If we left now, we'd be in Auckland by morning,' said Morgan.

'Why, Morgan, you want to go to Auckland?' said Human Sanity.

'I have this feeling,' said Morgan.

'How could we get there?'

Morgan crossed the road and bent down at the window of a parked car. The driver rolled the window down. There was a conversation and Morgan came back across the road.

'He won't take us to Auckland but he will take us to Kelburn,' he said.

'Who is he?' said Meiklejohn.

'I don't know. I never saw him before.'

'Why will he take us to Kelburn?'

'I said we were incapable of locomotion.'

'You may be incapable of locomotion,' said Meiklejohn.

'Why do we want to go to Kelburn?' said Human Sanity.

'Pot,' said Morgan.

'You have smoked pot?'

'I have smoked pot once, twice, three times,' said Morgan.

'It is good to make love on pot?' said Human Sanity.

'Tremendous,' said Morgan, 'by common repute.'

They crossed the road and got in the car. Morgan sat in the front, the other two in the back. The driver said his name was Clive. He had just finished work on the night-shift, he said, and was on his way to the party that they had come out of. He started the car and drove up Salamanca Road.

'Good party?' he asked.

'Foul,' said Meiklejohn.

'Gee,' said Clive. He glanced at Meiklejohn in the rear-view mirror. He said that one night he had gone to a party in Newtown after the night-shift, and when he got there there was a tiger in the street.

'I remember that,' said Meiklejohn. 'Escaped from the zoo, right?'

'I went into the party and I said, "There's a tiger in the street," and no one believed me. Then they all came to the door and saw it coming in the gate.'

'They shot it, right?' said Meiklejohn.

'The cops shot it,' said the driver.

'No call for that,' said Morgan thickly. 'No need to *shoot* it.'

They drove along Upland Road and into Highbury.

'Stop here,' said Morgan.

'Have a good night, fellas,' said the driver and they stood on the pavement and watched him drive away.

'He was a nice guy,' said Morgan. 'He drove us here for no known reason.'

'Where are we?' said Meiklejohn, looking around with distaste. Suburban roofs stood up like pyramids mildly against the sky; a little television radiance was still leaking at some window frames.

'Friends of mine,' said Morgan.

He pointed at one of the houses below the street. They went down a flight of steps and Morgan beat on the door.

'Shsh,' said Meiklejohn. 'It's eleven-thirty.'

Morgan laughed.

'Bang softly,' he said.

FitzGerald opened the door. He had a motorbike helmet in his hand. For a moment it looked as if he was going to bar the way. Then he took Morgan by the hand and pulled him indoors. He put his helmet down on a table and danced Morgan a step or two round the hall.

'Morgy-baby,' he said.

'You're going out,' said Morgan.

'I'm going out,' said FitzGerald.

'Where the hell do you think you're going at this hour?' said Morgan.

He picked up the helmet and put it on. Then he pulled the dark visor down and looked at himself in the mirror.

'Nowhere much,' said FitzGerald.

Morgan thought: 'Candy!'

He pushed up the visor and looked at FitzGerald. He knew that on Thursday nights Candy stayed at her parents' house in Karori. FitzGerald was going to Karori to sleep with Candy! Morgan was sure of it. But, after all, was that good or bad, or right or wrong? Sometimes, he thought, he just didn't know anything. He took the helmet off.

'Sell me some pot,' he said to FitzGerald.

FitzGerald walked out of the room.

'Stay here,' said Morgan to Meiklejohn and Human Sanity. He followed FitzGerald into the sitting-room.

'Oh, Morgan, I can't sell you pot,' said FitzGerald. 'I don't sell pot. If had some pot I would happily give you some but I don't. In any case, you're drunk. Marijuana would make you doo-lally, crazy, you'd fall down the stairs.'

There was no furniture in the big sitting-room, apart from a new brown-leather couch on an oatmeal carpet. There were no curtains on the plate-glass window. The window looked down a valley towards a high concrete viaduct, empty and all lit up in the night.

'You've slept with Candy, haven't you?' said Morgan.

'Yes,' said FitzGerald. He instantly wished he had lied.

'I thought so,' said Morgan. He walked around the room and then looked at FitzGerald from under his brows.

'That's where you're going now,' he said.

'No it's not,' said FitzGerald.

'Where are you going?'

'To see Sandra Isbister.'

'Sandra Isbister!' said Morgan in wonder. 'I saw Sandra Isbister today! I asked her to come to Auckland with me, and first she said she would and then she said she wouldn't.'

'When are you going to Auckland?' said FitzGerald.

'Now. Tonight! Hey, Fitz! Let's go to Auckland!'

'How?' said FitzGerald.

'On your bike,' said Morgan.

'I can't tonight,' said FitzGerald. 'I have other things to do.'

'Such as?'

'Seeing Sandra Isbister.'

'I'm coming with you,' said Morgan.

'Why?'

'To see Sandra Isbister,' said Morgan.

'You can't come with me,' said FitzGerald. 'You'll fall off the bike.'

'I need to come,' said Morgan. 'To check.'

'Check what?'

'Check it's Sandra Isbister you're going to see.'

'You'll have to trust me,' said FitzGerald.

'Trust you!' said Morgan. 'Sell me some pot.'

'I'll give you some pot,' said FitzGerald. He took out a plastic bag of marijuana and rolled two joints and lit one and passed it to Morgan, who took it, and drew on it lengthily, and put the other in his pocket. Human Sanity came into the room and Morgan passed him the lit joint.

'This is Human Sanity,' said Morgan. 'He won't come to Auckland either.'

'Why do you want to go to Auckland?' said FitzGerald.

'I'm going to see Race.'

'Why do you want to see Race?'

'I don't want to see him. I just have this feeling I'm going to see him. I can't see him if I'm not in Auckland, can I?'

'Not if he is,' said FitzGerald.

'*Whoooo!*' said Morgan, ducking down.

A great dark bird, an eagle, swooped low over the roof of the house – he heard the *huff* of its pinions – and it went on down through the darkness towards the lonely lit-up bridge.

'Where did *that* come from?' he thought.

Where-ere-ere-ere— he heard. His voice echoed so much in his mind that he thought: 'Well, I'll just never get to the end of the question.'

Nev-ev-ev-ev— he heard, fading away like the sound of pinions.

'Maybe I'll just never get to the end of my thoughts,' he thought, and at that all his limbs buckled. He fell on the floor.

'He's fallen down!' said Human Sanity.

FitzGerald and Human Sanity stood looking down at Morgan so primly that he began to laugh. It was hard to laugh lying down.

'No one realises that,' he thought. 'Lying down's no laughing matter.'

'Get up,' said FitzGerald.

Morgan tried to get up. His limbs wouldn't obey him. This also made him laugh.

'You can't laugh when you're lying down,' he thought. 'Yet lying down is inherently funny. And not getting up is funny too. It doesn't add up at all.'

'Hands and knees,' FitzGerald advised, looking at Morgan as at a mechanical problem.

'What's all this?' said Lane Tolerton, coming in the room. He was rubbing his hands and looking pleased at the sight of midnight company. He was wearing a red-and-yellow check dressing-gown. He and FitzGerald had just taken the house together, and Rod Orr had also moved in. Rod's house in Silver Lane was being demolished for office-block development.

'What's Morgan doing on the floor?' said Tolerton.

'I don't know what he's up to down there,' said FitzGerald. He knew Tolerton didn't approve of marijuana.

Morgan was on his hands and knees. He had begun journeying on hands and knees to the couch. It was a long, long way. He thought of pyramids in the far distance. Their tops were white with eagle-droppings.

'Of *course*,' he thought. 'That's what they were *for*! For eagles to perch on.'

'What's the matter with him?' said Tolerton.

'He's drunk,' said FitzGerald.

'He'd better stay the night,' said Tolerton.

'You'd better stay the night,' said FitzGerald, calling out to Morgan as if he was deaf.

'I better stay,' said Morgan. *Stay-ay-ay-ay*— he heard.

'You better stay tonight,' said Human Sanity, who was suddenly anxious to go back to the party at once. Why had he ever left? The plump girl, Trisha, whose party it was, had more or less invited him to stay the night with her. He imagined being in bed with Trisha. But then he remembered that he wanted some of Morgan's pot and that it would be easier to take it from him outside.

'He can sleep on the sofa,' said Tolerton.

'You can sleep on the sofa,' FitzGerald called. Morgan was kneeling now, his elbows on the sofa.

'He's not staying here,' said Rod Orr, who had just come in the room.

'Really?' said FitzGerald.

'Not in this house!' said Rod.

FitzGerald gazed at him in surprise. Rod himself was surprised at his own vehemence, but he liked it. He felt pleased. His eyes blazed. He had been waiting for this encounter, he realised. All his best wine they had drunk. And Race had not even left a note. He still felt hurt at that. And the curtains! When he came back from Chadwick's wedding he found that his curtains had been taken down and hung back to front. Why? What did it mean? It was a code! It must have meant something. Anger surged through him.

'What the *fuck*,' said Rod, 'did you do to my curtains?'

'It's OK, it's OK,' said FitzGerald, who had no idea what Rod was talking about.

'Curtains!' said Morgan. He remembered sleeping under Rod's red curtain. He remembered the golden instruments on the curtain. Race was there as well. 'That's why I have to go to Auckland,' he thought. 'Tell Race what the pyramids were for. Tombs so tall that eagles would come and perch on them.' He saw an eagle in the azure. He wanted to say something about that but the words began to echo again as soon as he formed them.

'He's not staying here,' said Rod Orr, now very calm, as if stating a well-known fact.

'*I* will take him home,' said Human Sanity.

'I'm not staying here,' said Morgan solemnly. Hilarity filled him and almost made it impossible to speak unless he was very careful. 'I mean, look – no curtains!'

'Get him out,' said Rod.

Human Sanity reached under Morgan's arms and hauled him up, and led him into the hall. Meiklejohn unfurled himself from the hallway chair. He looked furious at being left there unattended. He and Human Sanity and Morgan went out the door.

'Wait,' said FitzGerald. 'I'm coming.'

He picked up his helmet and came out onto the front step and closed the door and put his helmet on under the outside light. Then he followed the others up the steps.

'I'm fine, I'm fine,' said Morgan, fending off Human Sanity.

The thought of Rod Orr in a rage made him laugh. Morgan laughed, then fell down the gap between the steps and the house.

'Jesus!' said FitzGerald, looking down into the gap. 'You OK?'

Morgan stood up and laughed, and fell over again. FitzGerald went back down the steps and helped him to his feet.

'I'm leaving you here,' said Meiklejohn. He had suddenly realised how intoxicated Morgan was. 'I'm wasting my time here,' he thought.

He went up the steps to the road and looked back down at them.

'Good*night*!' he said and went away at a fast pace.

'He's gone,' said Human Sanity. 'He is a very irritable man.'

'Give me a hand here,' said FitzGerald.

Human Sanity came down the steps and between them they helped Morgan up the steps and onto the street. They stood on the footpath.

'OK,' said FitzGerald. 'Here I love you and leave you.'

He lowered his visor, got on his bike, kicked down and roared away with such speed that he was at the far end of the road with his words still hanging in the air.

His tail light shone red and then the brake light shone red and both tilted to the ground as he took the corner.

'Sandra Isbister *and* Candy Dabchek,' thought Morgan.

The sound of the bike faded. Morgan felt sad. He wanted to go off on a bike himself. He wanted to go to Auckland. He had something important to tell Race. He stood there swaying. Something very important, but what was it? It was – it was—

'Put your fingers down your throat,' said Human Sanity.

Morgan put his fingers down his throat but nothing happened.

'Give me the pot,' said Human Sanity.

Morgan took out the other joint and handed it over. Human Sanity put it in his jacket pocket.

'Come on,' he said.

They walked along the street a few yards. Morgan thought of Rod Orr's eyes blazing. He laughed. Then he thought of Lucas, his brother, flying down through the pine branches. Morgan leapt at the branch of a tree overhanging the pavement and swung from it for a while. Then he let go. He walked along a bit further, then fell on the ground.

'Get up,' said Human Sanity. He stopped and looked down at Morgan. Morgan's eyes were closed. Human Sanity felt rage. Everyone else had run away. Meiklejohn. The guy on the motorbike.

He'd been left holding the baby! Why should he stay? Especially now that he had the pot. All he had to do was get back to the party and find plump Trisha.

'Get up, black bastard,' he said to Morgan.

Morgan didn't move.

'You black bastard,' said Human Sanity.

Morgan didn't move. Human Sanity saw his mouth twitch.

'Black fucking bastard,' he said.

Morgan didn't move. Human Sanity looked down at Morgan, then stared all around in the dark. There was a phone box at the corner. He went along and rang a taxi. A taxi arrived in about two minutes. It came cruising very slowly along the street. Human Sanity could tell just from its slow deliberation, from the expression of its headlights so to speak, that it wouldn't take Morgan. The cab stopped by him. He got in beside the driver and told him to go along the road. Morgan was lying on the footpath. The driver stopped and looked out at him.

'I'm not taking that,' he said.

'He's asleep,' said Human Sanity.

He jumped out of the cab and heaved Morgan to his feet, then opened the back door with one hand.

'I'm not taking him,' said the cabbie. 'He'll be sick in my cab.'

'No, no. He's been sick,' said Human Sanity.

'I have to think of my upholstery,' said the driver.

'Polstry?' said Human Sanity.

'You try cleaning up after them,' said the driver.

'You don't understand,' said Human Sanity. 'He is bachelor of arts.'

'Ha!' said the driver.

'It's only a short way,' said Human Sanity.

'That's nice,' said the driver. 'Shut my door.'

Human Sanity closed the back door with his foot and the cab drove away. He let Morgan go. Morgan fell on the footpath. A light rain began falling. All the streetlights across the valleys, on Brooklyn hill and Mornington and Melrose, turned hazily gold in the rain. Human Sanity looked around.

'Fuck, fuck, fuck, fuck, fuck,' he said. He went out and stood in the road and waved his arms at an approaching car. It swerved around him not braking and drove on. He went back to the phone box and called emergency.

'Do you require an ambulance?' a woman asked.

'No,' he said.

'Police?'

'Yes,' he said. Then he thought of the joint in his pocket. 'No,' he said.

'Which service do you require?'

'None,' said Human Sanity.

'I have notified the police,' said the woman. Human Sanity came out of the booth and put the joint inside his sock. A car had stopped along the street. He ran along the pavement. There was a man standing looking down at Morgan.

'I can't get him home,' said Human Sanity.

'That's OK,' said the man. 'Up you get, sonny boy.'

They heaved Morgan to his feet and put him in the car.

'There was a tiger at the party,' said Morgan. 'It - it - it - it—'

'It what?' said the man.

'It came in by the gate,' said Morgan.

'Course it did,' said the man.

Morgan fell asleep. They drove three hundred yards around the corner to the bottom of the zig-zag.

'Here,' said Human Sanity, who had dropped Morgan before.
The car stopped.

'We're here!' said Morgan.

'Someone's woken up,' said the man.

Morgan looked out the window.

'That's the zig,' he said. 'Further up's the zag. Just so's you know.'

'He's all right now, see?' said the man. 'It happens to the best of us.'

Morgan and Human Sanity got out the car. The car drove off. They went up the path. Human Sanity took the joint out of his sock and put it in his inside jacket pocket. Halfway up the first section of the zig-zag, Morgan began to stagger. At the turn, he sagged. Human Sanity tried to hold him up, but he went down and lay there.

'Oh, you black fucking bastard,' said Human Sanity. He bent down and looked at Morgan. He slapped his face and looked hard at him again. Then he stood up and stared around. He could see four or five houses high above him, through the trees, but which was Morgan's? There were no lights on in any of them. He was going to start up the path but the thought of knocking on the doors of those high dark houses quelled him. He thought of Trisha. He came back and looked down at Morgan. It had stopped raining. There were even one or two stars out among the clouds. Human Sanity took off his jacket and laid it over Morgan, and he stood looking at him for a moment. Then he turned and ran away as fast as he could down the path and across the street and along the avenue, turning his head again and again and even running backwards for a few paces at a time in case a taxi came along behind him, going the same way as he was into town.

After a while Morgan woke up. The stars were out, the wind blew a little. A few rain drops fell out of the trees and then stopped. He lay there a moment, thinking. Where was he? He had been dreaming that he was in the sun. But then he opened his eyes and found he was in the dark, alone, on a cold hard path. But why? Why was he here in the dark, all alone? He felt sad. He felt bitter at fate. He remembered walking along the road with Human Sanity, but then what happened? He was going to Auckland, that was part of it, but why was he going there? There was something he had to do there. So why had he ended up here on this cold path? He lay there a moment and felt sad and sorry for himself. 'I have never been happy, not once in my life,' he told himself. Then he thought of living in the sand-hills of Ninety Mile Beach with his troop of runaway kids. He was the leader. They lived in the dunes for days. What on earth did we eat? he thought. He remembered one night they looked along the beach in the gloom and saw a pick-up truck parked, nose towards the sea, about half a mile away. He and one of the other kids ran across the sand and crept up to the truck. The fishermen were standing in the surf, their backs to the beach. In the tray of the truck was a single big fish. Morgan picked it up. It was still alive! The scaly hull turned slowly astern in his hands. Then away they ran, taking the fish. They ran along the sand half a mile and up into the dunes.

Then Morgan recalled a detail he had forgotten for years. They had run backwards. It was quite calculated – if the fishermen tried to track them down, all they would find were footprints coming *towards* the truck.

'You little devils!' Morgan thought. 'You cunning little rogues.' He felt almost shocked. Then another detail came to mind. They were naked! They had both stripped before setting off to raid the truck in the dusk. Why on earth did we do that, he wondered. To be invisible, as free as the wind! Morgan sat up. He remembered running naked in the mild night air. A strange garment – Human Sanity's jacket – fell off him. He didn't know what it was and let it fall. Then they had reached the sand-hills and tracked inland and hid on the heights and watched the pick-up. Nothing happened for a while. Then they saw the men come up from the sea. There was a pause, but only for a minute or two – then the headlights flashed on and that old jalopy took off, it came rushing south towards them and went tearing past, fifty, sixty miles an hour, slewing in the sand as if the devils of hell were after it.

Morgan wanted to laugh. 'Those superstitious Maoris,' he thought . . . A vast beach. Dusk. Not a soul to be seen. And the catch of the day – one big fish – gone.

Ghosts!

The truck vanished away in the south.

'And it was only us,' thought Morgan. 'Those crazy superstitious Maoris.'

He wanted to laugh but he felt sad still and he wanted to go home. And to go to Auckland in the morning. He stood up. He must be at the top of the zig-zag, he thought. He took a few steps along the way. The path was tangled with bushes. He was puzzled at that. And there was a faint light down to the left which he had never noticed before. An orange glow, peacefully showing through long stems of the grass. He had come along that path a hundred times and had never seen that a light was there.

'I'll just take a look,' he thought, 'and then – bed.' There was a low fence in the way. He felt sad still, and careless, and daring. He thought of Lucas, his brother, jumping from the top of the tree.

Morgan climbed the little fence and stepped out.

At that moment he saw the top of the streetlight below – a dirty grey helmet – and he felt nothing underfoot and a bolt of dread and disbelief went through him.

'I was only at the zig!' he thought.

4

It was late when Race woke the next morning. He could tell from the silence. The reef-rumble of commuter traffic from New North Road had subsided. It must be after nine. And spring had arrived – he could tell that as well, almost before he opened his eyes. The spring had come in the night, high, warm, unseen. He lay listening for sounds in the house. Nothing. They must have already gone in, Panos and Busoni. He got out of bed and went over to the window and lifted the blind. Yes, there it was: you could see spring had come just from the look of the sky. A flock of little clouds floated above the factory roofs like lambs straying across a field. Broken glass glinted on the grass verge across the street. The panels of the phone-booth had been smashed. The receiver dangled from a metal-spiralled cord. The smell of new-baked bread came from the Tip-Top factory on New North Road. Suddenly Race felt a deep, shocking kind of gloom. *Christ*, he thought, where did that come from? And it stayed with him – a savage black gloom – no, not black, he thought. He saw the blue sky and the green grass and the glass glint in the verge and those were its colours. Maybe it was the spring itself, he thought, the idea of spring in the back streets that depressed him. He stood at the window and felt it turn away and sink into the depths. He went to the wardrobe and put on a shirt and pants and went down the hall to the kitchen. 'House to myself,' he said aloud, but when he came down to the kitchen there was Busoni standing at the bench. Busoni was naked. He liked running round the place naked.

'You still here?' Busoni said. 'I thought you had lectures at nine.'

'I slept in,' said Race.

'Toast?'

'Toast,' said Race.

'Coffee?'

'Coffee.'

'Jews want coffee, Jews want toast,' said Busoni.

'How exactly do you mean?' said Race.

'This waitress I know,' said Busoni. 'She goes round chewing her gum and says: "D'youse want coffee? D'youse want toast?" '

'They want coffee,' said Race.

'And are you in fact Jewish?'

'I have Jewish antecedents. But they jumped ship, our lot. One became a bishop.'

'A *bishop* in the family tree,' said Busoni, rolling his eyes upwards.

'Can I still have coffee?'

'I am preparing your coffee,' said Busoni.

The toaster popped. Busoni went to the old glass-doored wooden cupboard and peered in.

'Hello, little pot of Communist jam!' he said. 'Are you all there is to go on my toast this morning?'

'Communist?' said Race.

Busoni held up the jar like Yorick's skull.

'This here is Commie red-cherry jam from Poland, Poland,' he said.

He put the jam down on the table. The smell of newly baked bread came in a waft through the screen door.

'Hey, hey!' said Busoni. 'It's spring!'

He slapped his upper belly with both hands like a bongo drummer. Then he poured the coffee and swung a cup across the table to Race. He buttered his toast and put cherry jam on it then went out the screen door into the back garden. The screen door banged. The grass was very long. No one had done any gardening out there for years. Race went out the screen door and it banged again. He stood on the back porch with his coffee. Busoni walked away holding two pieces of toast, one in each hand, coffee mug hooked on an index finger. His dog was leaping by his thigh. Busoni held both his arms out wide.

'Down, sir, *down*!' Busoni said. His voice was charged with happiness. A blonde girl walked fast through the dining room behind Race and went into the bathroom. Busoni had a series of girls through his room. Sometimes you heard their screams: they had encountered Busoni's rats, Radio and Television, which were not even white rats from a shop but wild brown baby rats Busoni had found in a nest in the back garden and taken in and trained, and which lived in his room, in the pocket of an old tweed overcoat, and which arrived questing on his pillows in the depths of night. Busoni was an acting student with Panos. Race watched him in the sunlight like someone in a photo – his waitresses, his dog, his rats, his clean shoulder-blades. Then Race felt the shock again – this time a dreary bleakness. It's the spring, he thought. It must be that. Spring arriving in a grimy city . . .

'What are you up to now?' said Busoni out in the long grass.

'I'll go in soon,' said Race. 'What about you?'

'I'll go in later,' said Busoni. 'Just have to get rid of—'

He pointed behind Race and winked.

'Where's Panos?' said Race.

'Early start. It's *The Merchant of Venice*,' said Busoni. 'The quality of mercy is not strained, it droppeth as the et cetera upon the et cetera.'

He crouched down naked and looked in the grass. All his vertebrae were apparent.

'What is it?' said Race.

'Nothing,' said Busoni. 'Snail shell.'

He stood up and closed his eyes towards the sun.

'I thought it was a dollar,' he said, eyes closed.

'The phone box is smashed again,' he said after a moment.

'I saw it,' said Race.

'Saw it get smashed?' said Busoni.

'No. I saw it was smashed, just now.'

'I saw it get smashed,' said Busoni. 'Three in the morning. We were awake. I got up to have a look.'

'Who was it?'

'Maori maiden with raven tresses.'

'Did you say anything?'

'Like what?'

'Like, I don't know, don't smash the phone box.'

'You kidding?' said Busoni. 'She wasn't taking no shit from that phone box or anyone else.'

'I'll ring them,' said Race.

'Good deed for the day,' said Busoni.

Race went inside and the screen door banged. He left his cup on the table and went down to his room and came back and went into the bathroom. The bathroom was still warm and misty with a fleeting feminine scent. He showered, then went back to his room and dressed. He went down the hall and rang the P&T to report the smashed phone box. There was no sign of Busoni and the girl. He made some more toast and boiled an egg then cleared up his and Busoni's plates. Then he went back to his room and took his wallet and keys and picked up his satchel. He opened the satchel and looked in. His lecture notes were there. Race stood at the table in the corner of the room just beside the window where the spring shone in and he looked down at the lecture pads. Busoni and the girl came out on the veranda and kissed outside his window. They didn't see him. Race took his lecture notes out of the satchel and laid them on the table. Busoni came back in the house and the girl went down the steps off the veranda and down steep King Street. Race saw her blonde hair in the sun. He waited a minute or two then took his empty satchel, left the house quietly, and went the other way, up the street to New North Road.

The bus coming from the western suburbs was empty. At Dominion Road, a Samoan woman, slim, handsome, about thirty, got on and came down the aisle.

She stopped and looked down at Race's foot. His foot was in the aisle.

He withdrew his foot.

'Fool,' she said.

She went past and sat at the back. The bus went on to Khyber Pass and Symonds Street. The buds were green on the oaks in the Jewish cemetery and in the high crowns of the oaks below the road in Grafton Gully. The bus turned left into K. Rd. Race pulled the cord and got off. He stood at the corner in the diesel fumes. Yellow buses were labouring up Symonds Street. It was already getting hot. Then the gloom, the dread, hit him again. *Christ*, he thought. He looked at the traffic in the fumes. Then he remembered the night the Chev broke down – no, not broke down, he thought, FitzGerald stuck it in a ditch. It came to him then very clearly, the sweet darkness of the coast when the Chev crashed. *'Roddy, come and ballast with me.'* Dinah coming out of the mild wind holding white dog-roses. Suddenly he had an intense wish, like a passion, to be back there again – not a light, not a star or candle for forty miles, east or west, inland or out to sea . . . *'The coast,'* he thought, *'the dark,* no, *unlit,* no, *the* profoundly *unlit coast.'* He went down Symonds Street under the avenue. The buds were coming out on all the trees. Dock cranes stood blackly at the bottom of the hill. Far away the island cone of Rangitoto was magnified in the haze. Then Race knew what he was going to do. He went along the avenue and through the campus to the library building. In the lobby he saw Ruru. He was shepherding some girls into the lift.

'Going *up*!' he said. 'First to ninth.'

No one knew quite how Ruru had appointed himself elevator man in the library building. None of the lifts in the other university blocks had an operator. *Ruru.* Tiny, ancient, sad boxing-champ eyes trebly pouched, fly-weight champion 1935. A song he wrote in the war had made him famous, but now people had forgotten

Blue smoke goes drifting by,
Into the deep blue sky

'Going up, son?' he said to Race. His pork-pie hat was tilted over his eyes.

'No thanks, Ruru.'

Ruru held the lift. He called Race over with a side-tilt of the hat, one hand on a button to keep the doors from closing.

'These girls,' he said to Race. 'They're beauties. Belles. That's why I take the care I do.'

'You take care of them, Ruru,' said Race.

'Belles of the ball,' said Ruru. 'That's the French for it.'

'You look after them,' said Race.

'Someone has to, son,' said Ruru. He touched Race's hand with a cool, dry finger. 'It's not safe today,' he said. 'Not in lifts.'

He gave Race a deep solemn look and ducked back inside. The doors ploughed shut. Race went to the grey steel lockers across the lobby. There was a chair by the window with a plastic woven seat and narrow steel-tube legs. He put his satchel on the green and black plastic weave and caught sight of Panos through the window crossing the lawn below. All the other actors, some of them in costume, went straying over the lawn and into the hall. Race put his satchel in a locker and locked it and crossed the lobby where the descending lift was pinging again, but before the lift door opened he had gone down the stairs and he crossed the lawn where the actors had passed and went in the other direction into the ferny shadow of the admin block and down the spiral stair to the base-ment. The waiting area was empty. He was sent straight in. The old doctor listened and said nothing. He was huge, obese, old and mighty. The students laughed at him: Bormann, they called him, or even Goering, but they were a little scared of him. He never spoke to them or asked questions. He was huge but his suit was still bulky on him. When he leaned forward to write, his collar yawned. How had he managed that, how had he got there, to be so big and old and incurious in his huge old suit? The lining at the cuff had yellowed. It must be peaceful being an old German, Race thought, you could hardly worry about death having seen so much of it. Bormann – which was unfair, Race thought, he might have been a refugee from the Nazis – leaned forward to write on his pad. Student legs – bejeaned male, bare female calves – flicked past in the ferny oblong window above the doctor's head. You couldn't hear their steps. The doctor pushed the paper across the desk without a word. Race took it and went through the empty reception area and up the spiral marble stair. The treads were pink and grey and veined like brain tissue. Race stepped on each one, thinking. At the top of the stairs there was sunlight again and the halls went in four directions. Race stopped. Either way, there was no hurry now. He went through to the back lawn. It was always damp there, the tree-ferns were always in shadow. The grass looked like moss. The clock high above the lawn struck. Race crossed the lawn and looked in at the door of the hall. Panos was on stage with a tall woman. He was in ordinary clothes, she was in a black gown and white collar. Panos declaimed:

> *'How many cowards, whose hearts are as false*
> *As stairs of sand, wear yet upon their chins*
> *The beards of Hercules and frowning Mars?'*

In the absence of an audience, his voice went echoing round the hall. Two or three people were sitting in the front row with clipboards in their hands, staring up at the stage. One or two people were alone elsewhere in the body of the hall. Panos saw Race at the door and made a little gesture with his hand, a kind of down-patting movement that meant 'don't go away'.

> *'Ornament is but the guiled shore*
> *To a most dangerous sea, the beauteous scarf*
> *Veiling an Indian beauty—'*

'I still think it's racist,' said Panos.

'The play's about race, Panos,' said one of the people in the front row, a woman, or a man with a high-pitched voice. 'It's a play about racism. But thank you. For your comments.'

'If I was an Indian . . .' said Panos.

'You're not Indian,' said the woman in lawyer's robes.

'People,' said the person in the front row. 'Panos.'

Race withdrew from the doorway. He folded the doctor's prescription and put it in his shirt pocket. He touched the folded paper through his shirt, then went back and watched from the door.

'*What find I here?*' said Panos, his voice echoing around the hall. '*Fair Portia's counterfeit! What demi-god hath come so near creation? Move these eyes? Or whether riding on the balls of mine—*'

'Yes, yes, I know, it's all very hilarious,' said the man or woman in the front row. 'I hope you're over it by Wednesday, that's all. Less than one week, people. Then we'll be doing this – for – real. All right. Back here two o'clock sharp.'

The actors sort of stood at ease, changing into other selves. Panos jumped off the stage and came up the aisle to Race. He led the way into the vestibule.

' "*People*",' he said. 'I hate it when people say "People" like that. How was that?'

He looked closely into Race's eyes.

'Good, good,' said Race. 'You're what's his name?'

'Bassanio.'

'He's good. He's OK, Bassanio. Maybe he shouldn't sort of crouch over those things.'

'The caskets?'

'The caskets.'

'He's not crouching. He's thinking.'

'Good. That's – good.'

The tall woman in black robes approached them and swept past, talking to another woman in Renaissance costume.

'She has this phobia,' she was saying. 'Hot-water bottle covers. Tea-cosies. Anything like that. It's a phobic reaction.'

She did not look at Panos as she passed.

'You're in love with her, right?' said Race.

'Bassanio is.'

'What about you?'

'No,' said Panos. 'There's just no chemistry.'

He watched her go across the lawn.

'Where's the chemistry?' he said.

They stood in the vestibule while other cast and crew members went out.

'I'll cook tonight,' said Panos.

'Good idea,' said Race.

'It's not an idea,' said Panos. 'It's a dire necessity. None of you cook.'

'I cook.'

'Busoni doesn't cook.'

'He can't cook.'

'He doesn't try.'

'I try.'

'Can you grab something, I don't know, green on the way home?'

'Green?'

'Leeks, peas, beans. Leeks would do. Peas. Where're you going now?'

'Movies,' said Race.

'What movie?'

'I don't know yet,' he said.

'On your own?' said Panos.

'I like the movies on my own.'

Panos was looking at him with his big Greek gaze but he was thinking about Portia and the caskets.

'What was that about Morgan at school?' said Race.

'What at school?'

'Did you say he was expelled?'

'He was expelled,' said Panos.

'What for?'

'I don't know.'

'You don't know why he was expelled?'

'I don't. I didn't know him. I didn't even like him.'

'Oh,' said Race.

'Why?' said Panos.

'I don't know. I just thought of him just then, getting expelled.'

'So pick up something green,' said Panos.

'I'll try,' said Race. He felt bad then. He thought of the big dark dining room at King Street where at night the light bulb never seemed able to beam all the way into the corners. Busoni and his dog on the sofa. Race lifted his hand.

'I'm off,' he said.

'Where you going?' said Panos.

'Library, then movies,' said Race.

He lifted his hand again and went across the lawn into the library and up to the lockers. He took his satchel from the locker and looked down through the window at the lawn. There was no sign of Panos or any of the actors. Race went out the other entrance and through the park to the city. In Queen Street he went into a pharmacy. The girls in the cosmetic section were like beings from another sphere, their lustrous nails, lavender smocks, violet eyeliner, *we do not speak your language earthling* look. He went past them and handed in the prescription and waited.

After a while the pharmacist darted out from the dispensary and looked at Race over his glasses. '*One* only, at night, as needed, swallow with water,' he babbled, reading from the label, his brow furrowed as if he had never seen such a thing. Race took the bottle and put it in his satchel and went back through cosmetic space-time, the swivel mirrors, the girls not looking at him, and into the street. He crossed over Queen Street and walked up Victoria Street to the western ridge. It was a part of town he didn't really know. He went along Nelson Street and into a bar he had been to once before. This was where Race had last seen Bonnie. He had been in there with Busoni and Panos one night when she and her husband walked in. She looked excited, radiant. She was sailing to England that same night on her husband's ship. She was wearing yellow and had a corsage on her breast. In a way she was very old-fashioned, Race thought. She had seen him and come straight over.

'Race!' she said. 'I want you to meet my husband.'

Race shook the husband's hand. They had chatted for a while, and even had a drink together, and then the couple left. The ship was sailing at midnight. Race watched them go out the door and thought: 'I'll never see her again,' and then he thought: 'I don't even care.' Yet here he was, back again. What had he come for? The place was empty. There were some empty glasses on the tables. The barman was standing at the bar, his head hunched over the racing paper, fingers outspread on the pages. He did not look up when Race walked in. Race asked for a beer. The barman looked up, only swivelling his eyes. He sighed, then unhunched, went to the beer-tap, poured the beer, took the money and resumed his position over the pages. Race took the beer to a tall table with four tall stools and sat there. There was a sling-shot of rain against the windows, and it stopped, and blue sky went past again amid bruised clouds.

'Maybe something will happen,' he thought, 'and then I won't do it.'

A young woman came out through a little low door behind the bar.

'Pick up them glasses,' said the barman without lifting his head.

'Pick them up yourself,' she said. 'I'm a barmaid not a Mrs Mop.'

She went back through the little door, then she reappeared fast.

'I told Brian that,' she said. She was shaking her forefinger. 'I said, "I'm bar staff, Brian, and I'll go in the public bar, but I'm not collecting." '

She went away again. The barman then muttered the conversation again, wobbling his head as he spoke. 'I'm bar staff, Brian, but I won't collect,' he said.

Race thought of Bonnie. He remembered the day they broke up. She had called him on the phone and asked him to come over in the mid-afternoon. He was pleased and a little puzzled. It was the first time he had ever been there during the day. Bonnie said she wanted to go out for a walk. They went up the street to the park on Mount Victoria and sat on a rock in the grass.

'He's coming back,' she said.

'Who?' said Race.

'You know who,' she said. She touched his arm. 'So now we stop seeing each other.'

'*When?*'

'Now, Race.'

The park was just a patch of long grass, unkempt, below the black pines of the town belt. It was a still, dry, cloudy day. Away across the harbour a US carrier lay at anchor, greyer than the rock of ages. Bonnie began to unpeel an orange. She had brought it with her in her bag and took it out. Her fingers, nimble, clever, divided the segments neatly, never breaking the integument.

'*Now?*'

'His ship is back this week. Maybe tomorrow. The letter came today. So we won't see each other any more.'

She prised off a segment of orange, like a cradle, an eighth of the moon, fat as a baby.

'Oh, Race, look at you,' she said. 'You'll find someone. A nice-looking boy like you, a *student*.'

'She's lying,' Race thought. And it was true, he couldn't see her any more – he couldn't look at her, only at her fingers, nimble at their work. 'She's a liar,' he thought. 'I'll never find anyone else. I found her, and she's all I want, and she's said *no*.'

'I'm going now,' she said.

'No,' he said.

'Race.'

'Where are you going?'

'Home. I'm getting *married*, Race. He's my *husband to be*.'

He couldn't even remember her walking away. He was alone in the park. Even the peel had gone. She must have scooped it up, the bright curl, as neat and organised as ever. The US carrier had swung on its anchor and was pointing its bow straight at him. And so that was the end, he thought. And when he met her again a year later, by chance, he felt nothing. 'So it was all an illusion,' he thought, sitting in the bar on his own. Then he remembered the statue of the queen and the trolley wires curving up the hill in the dusk and something moved in his heart.

The double doors to the street opened. The rain slung at the windows again, and the girls who came through the door screamed, rain lashing their bare legs. They clattered in.

'Ladies,' said the barman, pushing himself back on his finger-tips to survey them. They ordered rums and coke and went away to the lounge area and sat at a low table. One of them crossed her legs then moved her head to one side to look at them.

'Tarts,' said the barman without looking up, hunched over the racing paper. Then he looked over at Race, his pupils hard black rings in a blue field. A clock struck somewhere down in town, but Race wasn't sure he had heard the first chime so he couldn't be sure of the total. But he knew nothing would happen now and that now he didn't want it to. He stood off his stool and picked up the satchel and went to the doors. The wood around the door-plates was darkened by touch and scarred densely as a palm-print. He pushed the brass plate and went out.

He walked back through town and up through the park and the campus again; the rain came down briefly, and Race went on further up the hill and arrived at the apartment building where he and Panos and Busoni had lived a few months earlier. He let himself in through the street door and stood there, listening. There was a radio on in one of the ground-floor flats.

He unlocked another door in the foyer and went up the stairs quietly to their old apartment. No one had been in there, as far as he could see, since they had left. The rooms were bare apart from a mattress left behind when they moved out.

He took the mattress into the sitting-room and put it on the floor in one corner, then stood there for a minute or so. Then he went back to his old bedroom and stood looking, listening to the radio downstairs. There was a marble on the floor by the wall. He picked it up and took it to the middle of the room and laid it down. It rolled away and touched the wall. *Click.* That was why the building had been vacated. The whole block, four storeys of apartments, was on a lean. It was slated for demolition and the site would be turned into a car-park. Race went back into the sitting-room. The leaves of the gum tree that grew right past the window ticked against the pane. Race stood there. He was thinking about the tenants of the ground-floor flat. Of course they hadn't moved out, he thought, Eloise and Ken. Eloise was a fighter. She would give battle to the evicting powers. Eloise was only twenty-five but she had the manner, and the clothes, and the weight, the solid round calves, of a matron. She was wealthy as well. She flew to Sydney to see Fonteyn and Nureyev – 'darling Rudi' she called him – and once a month a black car came to pick her up and off she went to court in a black suit and a wide-brimmed hat. It was some tremendous court-case about a family trust and raggedy cousins with their hands out. Of course Eloise was still downstairs, Race thought, she'd be giving the developers merry hell. As for Ken with his thick gleaming glasses that concealed his eyes, he did whatever Eloise said.

Race went quietly to the top of the stairs and looked down at the mottled-glass door at the bottom. Had he locked that or not? He didn't want Eloise or Ken coming up to see who was there. The late sun struck through the door and coloured the stair-carpet a rich ruby red. It was almost five o'clock. He went back and picked up his satchel and went into the kitchenette and opened the bottle. This was easy now, it was easier and easier. '*Finally*,' he thought. Finally meaning *at last* and finally meaning *finally*. He saw that the small window above the stove was broken. Did we do that, he thought, or the wind? He began to take the pills, one by one. There was no glass or cup in the kitchen. He drank the pills down with tapwater cupped in his hand. Then it was done. Jazz was playing on the downstairs radio. Ken with his black-rimmed glasses was a jazz buff.

So this is it, thought Race. Five in the afternoon. Jazz, and a red carpet . . . At five in the afternoon, his father said, on a signal, the whole city of Warsaw burst out in gunfire. From every house, every window, every door. The uprising had begun!

But then Race felt bad and he didn't want to think about his father. Or his mother. Or Panos and the greens. Leeks will do, said Panos, peas will do. He thought of the dark dining room where the light never made it into the corners and he felt bad about dinner. But it couldn't be helped, he thought, this had to be done, and he saw the darkness where the Chev broke down, the lovely, lightless, starless dark.

He went and lay on the mattress and thought '*the dark*, no, *the unlit*, no, *the profoundly unlit* coast,' and then Ruru 'It's not safe nowadays, son, not in lifts,' and he almost felt like laughing and then he felt the cold. An icy sunset wind was coming in from the broken window in the kitchen.

'That could be a problem,' he thought. Though not much of a problem. Or rather, not much of a problem for very long. But then for a long time it was, and he lay there and, apart from everything else, he was aware of the cold.

Then the darkness came, and for a long time he was aware of nothing.

* * *

When Race woke Panos was standing in the sitting-room doorway, staring down at him with his black Greek gaze. There was daylight in the room. There were other people behind Panos; Panos seemed angry.

'I've been all over the place looking for you,' he said.

The other two – Eloise and Ken – said nothing. They were looking down at Race on the mattress with puzzled expressions. Panos was still standing in the doorway in front of them. He gazed around the room but did not step in.

'What are you doing?' he said. 'You stay here the night?'

'Yes,' said Race.

'No bus money?'

'No,' said Race. He wondered where the pill bottle was.

'You could have walked,' said Panos.

He stepped into the room. He was looking puzzled too, but lofty and bitter at the same time, as if forced into an ignominious role.

'We tried to find you,' he said. 'Busoni and me. Last night we went everywhere, bars, pubs . . .'

'Why?' said Race.

'There was a phone call for you,' said Panos. 'We waited round for hours then we came out to look for you.'

'Why?' said Race.

Panos looked down at him, still angry.

'Morgan Tawhai's dead,' he said.

5

'May I? Excuse me. May I?'
            'Sure,' said Race.
'Sorry—'
'No, sure—'
Race half stood and leaned back, and tucked in his chin as well
as if that would further reduce his presence, while the man beside
him stood and leaned across in front of him and snapped a picture
through the window.

'Beautiful thing, that,' he said, sitting down again heavily. 'Pratt
and Whitney.'

'Oh, yeah,' said Race. He looked out at the aircraft engine. It
seemed fine to him. A fragment of blinding sunlight was dancing
on the casing. Beyond lay the high blue horizon of the Bay of
Plenty.

'Rex,' his neighbour said. He shook Race's hand. He had a
great freckled heavy hand. He lifted it and sent it diving into
Race's hand as if it were a plane.

'Nineteen thirty-five,' he said; '1935 this plane went into
production and she's still going strong! She was in the Berlin
airlift.'

'This plane?' said Race.

'This *model*.'

'Oh, this model.'

'Hundreds of tons of meat and butter they flew in every day, right over the heads of the Russians.'

'Oh, I've read about that,' said Race.

'The old DC3, eh!' said Rex, laughing and shaking his head as though it was his own doing. 'Coffee!' he said. 'Eleven tons of coffee a day. That's what Berlin drank every day.'

Race saw a giant named Berlin drinking eleven tons of coffee at a wooden table. Rex was the mayor of Whakatane, he said. He was flying back from a mayoral conference in Auckland.

'There are several mayors on this flight,' he said. 'And I'm taking 'em all fishing. That's the mayor of Rotorua over there, and that's the mayor of Palmerston, and that chump down there – he's the mayor of Whangarei.'

The mayor of Whangarei heard his name; he half-turned his head, then he realised who was speaking and turned back again. Directly below them, below the plane, miles and miles of mountainous forest were gently lit by the afternoon sun as if a great secret was being disclosed. This was early on a Monday afternoon, two days after Race had woken to see Panos standing in the doorway, staring down at him on the bare mattress.

'He's *dead*?' Race said.

'He's dead,' said Panos. 'He fell. He fell off a wall or something. They found him on the footpath but he died in hospital yesterday. FitzGerald rang last night to tell you.'

Panos's gaze was moving round the room, from the mattress to the satchel to the broken window in the little kitchen, trying to work something out.

'We waited for you and then we went out and looked all over the place,' he said. 'We went to the Kiwi, we went to the Albion, we went to the Shakespeare, we went to the Roma . . .'

Then Race cried, shed tears briefly under Panos's indignant eye, because of what Panos had said and because he himself had woken in the world again, and because he was glad he had. Eloise came into the room behind Panos.

'*You* are coming downstairs with *us* and *you* are going to have *breakfast*,' she said.

She was a big woman, stout-limbed, soft-palmed. She took Race's hand in her small soft palm. Race stood up. The others stood back a little, in doubtful respect for the bereaved. Out the window, the trees were still leafless as if the whole notion of spring arriving the day before was an error. The woods across the valley in the Domain were the colour of an old wood-stack; above them the pillared museum stood on the crest of the hill, massive, certain, memorious, with its gloomy inscription: *The Whole Earth Is a Sepulchre for Famous Men*. Race went downstairs with Panos and Eloise and Ken. Then Panos went away and Race slept on the sofa in the downstairs flat for a few hours. Then Eloise drove him home in Ken's car and he fell asleep again and he slept for the rest of the day and all night until the Sunday.

When he got up and went down to the kitchen on Sunday morning, Panos and Busoni said nothing about the matter. He felt their puzzlement. What had he been up to? Why had he stayed out all night that night, of all nights? He said nothing. He didn't know himself. That afternoon the house was very quiet. Everyone stayed in their rooms. Race went out for a walk alone in the grey afternoon. He walked to Dominion Road and then decided to walk the whole length of it, three or four miles out to suburbs he had not seen before. What *had* happened, he wondered. He couldn't even re-create the mood he had been in two days earlier. 'Only two days ago,' he thought. 'And now I'm alive and Morgan's dead, and here I am on Dominion Road.'

A few months before, there had been a proposal to use Dominion Road, the longest straight thoroughfare in the city, as a model of the solar system. The sun would be marked by a brass plaque at one end and all the planets set in brass in the pavement along the way. But the plan had been vetoed by the local shop-keepers – they could not see how it would increase turnover. As he walked along, Race kept thinking about it. What size, for instance, should the sun be, at one end of a street four miles long, in other words in a solar system eight miles in diameter? A dinner plate? A cartwheel? And what about the Earth, what size should that be – a saucer, or a thimble, or an apple pip? And where should the thimble or apple pip be placed? By the carpet warehouse at the second intersection – or much further out, by the shop selling papers on the corner of Valley Road? Race walked half a mile or so and suddenly thought of Morgan at the fancy-dress ball, dancing alone, right up by the stage under the guitar necks.

'Maybe he knew!' Race thought.

He stopped on the footpath. He saw Morgan in his old cord jacket and needle-cord jeans, dancing to 'All Along The Watchtower'. What were the words? He couldn't remember exactly. *Time was short? The hour was getting late? Time was running out?*

'He knew what was going to happen!' Race thought. 'Of course, he didn't know he knew but some part of him, that he didn't know, knew he was going to die.'

'Morgan Tawhai!' he said aloud.

No one heard him. He was on the corner of Valley Road by the shop selling Sunday papers and milk and flowers. There were stocks and chrysanthemums in plastic buckets on the rain-darkened asphalt outside.

'Maybe that's what I loved about him,' Race thought. 'He was always keeping his appointment.'

He kept walking until he reached the far end of Dominion Road and then went down a side street or two just to see what was out there, well past Neptune and Uranus, at the end of the solar system. Then the rain began to fall, he looked at the little pastel houses in the rain, and wished he had a girlfriend to go and visit out there, in the region of Pluto so to speak, and then he turned, walked back in light rain the whole way, and packed a bag to fly to Morgan's funeral in the morning.

'One plane every thirty seconds,' said Rex. 'Meat, butter, coffee. Fish! They had to build another airport to take the traffic. There was an old radio tower in the way and the Russians wouldn't take it down, so the French rolled up and blew it to bits. The Russians went crazy. "How could you have done this?" the Russian general yelled to the French general. "With dynamite, my dear colleague, with dynamite." '

Rex shook with laughter.

'With dynamite!' he said. 'My dear colleague.'

He pointed past Race to the window. They were now flying out over the sea.

'May I?' he said again.

'Oh, sure,' said Race, flattening himself against the seat. Rex rose to his feet with his camera in his hand but the air-hostess saw him and sprang down the aisle.

'Seat belts *on*,' she said. 'We're coming in to land.'

Rex shrank back looking shamed. To be reprimanded by this girl! The hostess sat down herself, young, stern, incorruptible. The plane wiggled in the air and shuddered. Race could see breakers below with a timber-coloured backwash, then a narrow grey beach and there was the grass runway rushing up. A rabbit or hare went dashing into the unmown grass beside the mown. Then they were all out of the plane and walking across to the terminal. It was just a small-town airport sleeping in the sunshine. And there were FitzGerald and Tolerton waiting for him behind a cyclone fence.

They greeted one another with solemn expressions. Was he all right? Were they all right? But, then, suddenly translated hundreds of miles into the sunshine, into the spring, high spirits broke out.

'We're staying by the beach,' said FitzGerald. 'We're in a "family hotel". You should see this joint.'

'There was an old woman who lived in a shoe, with so many children – that's us,' said Tolerton. 'And she doesn't have a clue, actually. Mrs Brisco is her name. No "e".'

'No smoking,' said FitzGerald.

'No smoking, no drinking, no gambling, no dancin',' said Tolerton. '*Dancin'* – *dancin'*.'

Tolerton did a soft-shoe shuffle outside the terminal.

'Where's Morgan?' said Race.

Morgan! They had momentarily forgotten Morgan, exactly as if he was still alive.

Morgan's body was in a little church across town; he would be there overnight before they took him home.

They caught a cab from the rank outside the terminal. In the taxi, Tolerton became serious.

'It's bad,' he said.

186

'What?' said Race.

'Things are bad,' said Tolerton. 'There's a fuss. They found drugs in a jacket pocket or something. Where he got drugs from, I do not know.'

'The cops are overjoyed,' said FitzGerald. 'They think they're in New York.'

'What happened?' said Race.

'Human Sanity left him asleep on a path,' said FitzGerald.

'Is he here?'

'God, no,' said FitzGerald.

'Well, it was hardly his fault,' said Tolerton. 'You know what Morgan was like when he was drunk. Falling over everywhere.'

'If he'd fallen asleep on the footpath – fine,' said FitzGerald. 'But this clown leads him up a forty-foot cliff, *then* leaves him to sleep it off.'

'Well, I just don't know,' said Tolerton uneasily.

'He might as well have left him unconscious in the middle of the road,' said FitzGerald.

'That's hardly fair,' said Tolerton.

'On the white line in the middle of the road,' said FitzGerald.

There was silence as the taxi drove through town.

'Here's the beach,' said Tolerton. 'There's our hotel. Oh – there's our landlady at the window!'

'Hello, Mrs Brisco,' said FitzGerald, looking up from the taxi. 'We love you, mad as a hatter though you are.'

They went into the hotel and met old Mrs Brisco with her apron and her dark-flecked chin in the gloom of the hall. Race dropped his bag upstairs and they went out again, across the road to the beach, FitzGerald talking all the time as they crossed the sand.

'There's about ten of us,' he said, 'someone called Lily, and Tubby Rawlinson who flatted with Morgan for a while, and his girlfriend. And Sandra Isbister, she's here – she got to know Morgan quite well in the last month or two, she was telling me she met him at a nightclub and looked at him and just *knew* something was going to happen but I don't know about that – and of course Candy and Adam – poor old Griffin, he hasn't uttered a word for two days I don't think – it was his birthday on Friday, you can imagine what sort of day that was: Morgan died at five and Adam had to identify the body and then Mrs Tawhai arrived – how she got there in that time, I don't know, she must have flown bodily through the ether – and she turned on him, on all of us really. It was all our fault. Drinking. Leading Morgan astray. But, you know, it was her son lying there dead, and so no one said a word, and then the paper got hold of the story about the drugs and then the police decided there had been foul play. Hey. Hey! *Hey.*'

He called out to a little group of people away down the beach and Candy and Adam turned and waited for them. Candy looked at Race with her great eyes and said nothing and Griffin looked at him and said nothing either, his eyes red-rimmed and aggrieved. Then in the distance Race saw the girl he had seen helping Candy make a dress one day. 'The famous Sandra Isbister,' he thought. 'She's not as pretty as I remember.'

They walked down the beach away from the town. Race kept an eye on Sandra Isbister. 'She's quite ordinary looking really,' he thought, 'even quite plain.' Her brown hair was in an urchin cut; she had no make-up. She was wearing a simple cotton green and white dress. She walked along looking rather solemn and unsure of herself as if she did not really think she belonged there. Far across the bay lay another country of folded hills and gullies, tiny roofs, patches of bush. Everything there looked infinitely peaceful and innocent there, as if nothing bad had ever happened, no law had ever been broken, no one had ever died. Then an onshore breeze sprang up and the waves came pouring into the bay, rushing forward like the winged sandals of the wind that was driving them on, and Race felt happiness sweep over him as if they had travelled hundreds of miles that day not because of Morgan and death but to meet by the shore – he noticed Sandra Isbister had a kind of gaiety to her walk, as if, although she felt the solemnity of the occasion, the way her foot fell, the way her calf turned, she could not help being light-hearted – as the waves came pouring landward, in the sun, in the spring.

They turned and walked back towards the town. At the town end of the beach was a long breakwater of black rocks. They climbed up and walked along beside a railway track that led out to sea. The rails were rusty but apparently still in use, for wagons stood along them. The deep green water was slapping at the rocks. FitzGerald stepped behind a wagon and took out some marijuana.

'No!' said Tolerton. 'Not here. Not now.'

He spoke so sternly that FitzGerald grinned and looked unsure of himself which was rare for him.

'Why not?' he said.

'Well, I can think of a dozen reasons,' said Tolerton. 'Not least there's this: here we are in this one-horse town, bringing back a body, and you think everyone's not watching us like hawks?'

'But they can't see through cast iron,' said FitzGerald, and he rapped the rust-coloured side of the wagon.

'Oh, you do whatever you like,' said Tolerton, and he marched away on his long thin legs in the direction of the town. There was no one else in sight. Candy and Adam had come onto the break-water and they sat on the rocks down by the slapping green sea. They were keeping to themselves. Candy put her arm over Adam's shoulder and looked fully into his face. FitzGerald and Race and Sandra Isbister walked on. There were some Maoris fishing at the end of the breakwater: you could see the glint of their rod-tips in the sun before you saw them. A man of thirty-five or forty with a long, sparse, red moustache was standing on a pointed rock; an older couple wearing woollen jerseys were sitting below him. The woman's feet were bare. Some newly caught fish were in a puddle of seawater. The older man, still sitting down, reeled his line in.

The hook was bare.

'Might as well pack up and go and buy *fish*'n'chips,' he said, stressing the word *fish* and looking shyly up at the visitors.

'But you've got a good haul there,' said FitzGerald, looking at the fish in the seawater puddle.

'Oh, them,' said the man disparagingly, as if it was only good form to say so. His wife smiled, but slowly one of her bare feet curled: she was embarrassed by the newcomers. The younger man did not once look at them. He baited his hooks with intense concentration and then climbed further up on the black honey-combed rock and, with a very grave expression, his mouth down-turned under his moustache of sparse red hairs, he cast out. The line went sailing out far over the water and the sinker fell into the green sea with an audible '*plop*'.

6

That night, old Mrs Brisco insisted on strict segregation of the sexes. The boys were on the upper floor, in an attic dormitory. She herself stood guard on the landing below. The girls shared twin rooms on the second floor. Mrs Brisco demonstrated that all the locks and keys to the rooms worked and made the girls promise to lock their doors, but finally she had had to go downstairs and get some sleep and her guests then came and went as they pleased. Adam departed to Candy's room for the night. And since Candy was sharing with Sandra, Sandra came up to sleep in Adam's bed in the men's attic dormitory where they talked and laughed until after midnight. FitzGerald gallantly attempted to join her but was refused permission. He pretended to be dismayed and complained a little, but it was a narrow bed in a dormitory, and he was not really sorry, and his honour was satisfied.

'Where's Rod Orr?' said Race in the dark. He had suddenly noticed his absence.

'Rod's not coming,' said FitzGerald.

'I guess he never liked Morgan much,' said Race.

'It's not that,' said FitzGerald. 'He probably feels guilty.'

'Why should he feel guilty?'

'Morgan wanted to stay the night – and he should have stayed the night – but Rod said no.'

'Why did he say no?' said Race.

'Who knows? God knows. Something about a curtain,' said FitzGerald. 'But if he'd stayed on the sofa he wouldn't have died, and I guess Rod feels guilty.'

'Rod doesn't feel guilty at all,' said Sandra Isbister, from the dark. 'He says Morgan committed suicide. He says he jumped.'

'Jumped!' said Race.

'Or he was pushed,' said Sandra. 'He says there was a lovers' quarrel and he jumped or he was pushed.'

'A lovers' quarrel?' said FitzGerald. 'With Human Sanity!'

'Rod Orr would say that,' said Race. 'Rod has sex on the brain.'

'Everyone has sex on the brain, to some degree,' said Tolerton.

'That's not where I have it,' said FitzGerald.

'You,' said Tolerton. 'You'd have sex anywhere. At bus stops. In shop windows. In the forks of trees.'

'Sex in the forks of trees!' said Sandra Isbister, but this time she spoke rather sleepily, which made the others laugh, as if she had sped away into the borderlands of sleep but then, hearing the phrase from afar, had to come all the way back. And even when they all began to drop off, there was a ripple of laughter still in the room, but they were really only happy at being there together in the Brisco Family Hotel, under the sloping attic roof, and there was an odd sense of safety and contentment, and sadness as well, as if the final night, the last hours, of childhood were just then coming to their end.

And in the morning the mood was quite different. Everything was hurried and urgent; no one spoke much and they did everything quietly as if not to disturb other guests, yet there was no one else in the place except for Mrs Brisco who was downstairs making breakfast. You could smell bacon and toast to the very top of the house. It was still dark outside. Then the sky began to colour, but the lights stayed on inside all the same. There was a sense of getting ready to go on parade. They had to be at the church by six-thirty. The boys, the young men, were to be pall-bearers, and as pall-bearers they would be the guests of honour. They were bringing Morgan home. But Morgan was *dead*. They were bringing back a dead body. And were they not the culprits? They felt important and guilty and yet innocent at the same time, and about to undergo rigorous inspection.

Apart from Lane Tolerton, who had just started working as a law-clerk, none of the males had worn a suit and tie or formal black shoes, it seemed, for ages.

'Fitzy, have you got any—?'

'What?'

'I can't think of its name,' said Race.

'Whisky?'

'No.'

'Personal magnetism?'

'No.'

'What then?'

'*Nugget*. Shoe polish.'

'I *thought* you were going to say Nugget.'

'Why didn't you say so?'

'I couldn't think of the name.'

'Have you got any?'

'No.'

'I have,' said Tolerton.

On the second floor, the girls were dressing soberly. There was only one mirror in the shared bathroom and they put on their lipstick together without smiling or even imagining a smile. When they went downstairs they ate hardly any of the scrambled eggs and burnt bacon and burnt toast Mrs Brisco had prepared. Outside, it was startlingly cold. Mrs Brisco put the hall light on and the veranda light as well as they went out in the half-light to the taxis. At the church a crowd was waiting even though there was to be no ceremony, merely lifting and carrying the coffin out to the hearse before departure. This was done. The pall-bearers were watched intently – Morgan's friends, all white, all six of them – as they came out of the little weatherboard church and carried the coffin down a concrete ramp and across to the verge. Then suddenly the sun was up and shot its beams on the frosty grass and on the puffing exhausts of the cars and the chrome door-handles of the hearse and on the flowers inside on the coffin-lid, and then off they went, the whole cortege, heading out of town. Candy and Griffin were in the first car behind the hearse. In the absence, as yet, of any family members, they had the role of chief mourners. In the car behind were Race, FitzGerald, Tolerton and Sandra Isbister. They were being driven by one of Morgan's cousins – a distant cousin, he admitted, even very distant – 'I wouldn't have known him if I saw him in the street.' His name was Gideon. He was wearing a rumpled grey suit, and a red sweater under his jacket because of the frost, but soon, when the sun was up, the car became too warm.

Gideon began to mop his brow. He wanted to take off his jacket but that, it turned out, was not possible.

'I can't stop the car,' said Gideon.

'Why not?' said FitzGerald.

'Those other buggers will pass me,' he said.

He hadn't meant it as a joke but everyone laughed and the mood, once again, became quite ordinary and cheerful. They had left the town behind and were on the coast, passing hoard-ings with pictures of beach property for sale, and then the real beaches themselves, cold breakers purling on the clean sand. Gideon was a wool-classer, he said. He was thirty-five, separated, father of two – he declared his whole station in life in a minute. He liked to go fishing, he said. He had been fishing everywhere along this coast – there off the rocks, and away out there, and just around that point – although whenever he could he went out by boat.

'My great-grandfather used to fish off this coast,' said Tolerton. 'One year he lost his signet ring overboard. It was a very valuable ring. But he came back the next summer and caught a big snapper at exactly the same spot and took it back to the hotel. Well – you can imagine everyone's amazement when the cook cut the fish open and the ring *wasn't* inside.'

Everyone laughed at this, except Gideon who shook his head and said: 'You students!' He had a plump, round face with numer-ous black dots like pebbles dashed over it. A few miles on he glanced out the corner of his eye at Sandra who was in the front seat beside him. He asked if she would mind if he smoked.

'Of course not,' said Sandra. 'I might have one too.'

'Oh, well!' said Gideon. 'You can light mine for me.'

She lit a cigarette using the lighter on the dashboard and passed it across, a little lipstick on the filter. She lit one for herself and then, on impulse, leaned forward again and pressed the knob of the dashboard radio.

When the train left the station
There was two lights on behind

'Oh, I *love* this,' said Sandra, and she began to sing:

'*The blue light was my*—'

Then Sandra was aghast. She clapped her hand to her mouth as if she had done something quite wrong. Music – in someone else's car – on the way to a funeral! She jabbed at the chrome knob, trying to turn the radio off again.

'No, leave it on,' said Gideon.

'Leave it on. Leave it on,' said Race and FitzGerald together.

'Oh!' said Sandra. Then she laughed at her foolishness, and took a puff on her cigarette and exhaled lightly to show she didn't care. Race saw that her hand was shaking very slightly. She was sitting half-curled on the front seat, in a fur coat. It was probably her mother's or from an op-shop, Race thought – in any case it was slightly too large for her. The coat completely hid her form and yet Race thought just then he could almost see her naked, or at least that it was easy to imagine her naked and that this was not even sought by him, or by her for that matter – it was the way she held herself, it was unconscious, it was in the micro-muscles, and then some classical phrase – 'nymph of the fountain always wet' – came into his mind – but from where? – and in that minute, cruising along the highway in Gideon's old Velox, the sidelong sun lighting the chrome dashboard and the blue cigarette smoke, Race thought: 'My God. I've fallen for Sandra Isbister!'

A little further on, the car in front of them stopped abruptly in the middle of the highway. Gideon slammed on the brakes. They all slewed forward in their seats.

'What is it? What's happening?' said FitzGerald, craning to see past Gideon's head.

Standing across the road were four or five men, silhouetted by the morning sun, idling there, barring the way.

The hearse began to move again, but instead of going on down the highway it turned off the road and in through a gate.

'What is it?' said FitzGerald again.

'Oh, they're just the boys,' said Gideon. He put the car into gear and moved forward. The young men who blocked the road looked at them impersonally, like car-park attendants with no interest in the people in the cars, just the vehicles themselves. Gideon drove through the gate after the hearse and they went slowly rocking across a grassy field.

'What's happening?' said FitzGerald. He seemed alarmed for some reason.

'It's just the people here,' said Gideon. 'They want to keep the body. They say: "We loved this boy and now look what's happened to him. So *we're* going to keep him safe with us." So we'll have a little *tangi* – a little cry – together, then we'll all drive on.'

In the corner of the field a woman came out from the porch of a house and began to call out in a long, high-pitched cry. The other cars were coming in through the gate. They parked in rows and everyone got out and stood on the grass.

The woman on the porch was calling out, crying out, and then, without any warning, everyone in the crowd of visitors, who had formed several ranks in front of the parked cars, began to weep. Tears were streaming on every face. It was so sudden and unexampled that Race, even through his own tears, felt amazement. 'How does *this* happen?' he thought. Yet his own grief – and presumably that of the others – was quite sincere. They were weeping for Morgan, there in the glassy hearse in front of them, and for themselves, standing in the cool sunlight that slanted across the grass, and also weeping, so it seemed to him, because in their thousand-year isolation the Maoris had discovered a certain pitch of the human voice, like that of the woman whose chant was still rising and rising in the air, which instantly and without exception made anyone who heard it cry.

Then the chanting stopped, and, abruptly, so did the tears. Race looked around him. Everything looked the same at first, but then he thought that things were subtly different. The shadows were sharper. Yet everywhere it seemed it was business as usual. Gideon was standing with his legs planted wide, jingling change in his trouser pocket as he chatted to a man in a black blazer with red piping on the collar. A few fields away a man was ploughing with a tractor, turning up sharp lines of wet black earth. A black dog squeezed through the lower bars of a gate and went racing after him, its body stretching and then closing like the symbol – Ω – of an ohm. And plump Rawlinson, who had shared a flat with Morgan the previous year, and who a minute before had been sobbing openly, was now looking down at his light-meter with a frown, and at the same time pulling with his thumb at the brown leather camera strap which was a little tight around his neck.

In the distance were the roofs of a town, and a tall green hill stood to the north. The wind was blowing and, as he watched, Race saw a white cloud was continually forming on the peak of the hill and streaming towards the sea. So this is the *world*, he thought. It was the first time he had seen or thought of the world as a single place. Yes, it was a great lit-up room which you come into and from which, in time, you leave. That was the proposition, and the effect, of the tears that had just been wept for Morgan: the world was one great room.

'Time to go now,' Gideon said to Race, and he and the others walked back over the grass to the cars, Rawlinson still pulling with his thumb at the dimpled brown strap which was just a bit too tight around his plump pink neck.

Part IV

2004

1

'My darling, I cannot live without you,' said a man's voice. 'I am in love – don't you see? Why can't we leave this awful place and go away together. Shall we go to the seaside? Do you not adore the sea?'

Toby turned around to locate the source of these endearments. Two seats behind him a man in his late thirties and wearing a panama hat with a pink band was addressing Candy. Candy, eyes lively, was drinking in every word. The man was one of the guests at the wedding. Gillian was getting married that day. The man in the panama had just flown in, he was telling Candy, from a film festival in Romania. Only the day before he had been watching a film in competition – he was on the jury – when a woman slipped into the seat beside him and began to whisper in his ear.

'I am mad about you. Why not leave this awful place and come down to the sea? Do you not adore oysters? Do you not adore the sea?'

'A few minutes of this,' the film man was saying, 'and I'd had enough. I got up and moved away to another seat. But she came after me: "Look into my eyes. Do you not see my love for you?".' That was it. I got up and walked out. But she followed me into the foyer. "Madam!" I said. "You have entirely ruined that film for me." "I am so sorry," she said. "You did not like my translation? I was sent to translate the film into English for you." '

Candy gave a little scream of laughter. At the same time she was looking through the windows into the courtyard, which was shaded by high pines of some Mediterranean species.

'Where's Race?' she said. 'Where's Chadwick? Holding everyone up, as per usual.'

The mini-bus was nearly full. The one which had been parked in front of them had already left: it shot off out of the courtyard and disappeared down the hill back into the city. Toby, meanwhile, had flushed a deep dark red. The man behind him talking to his mother must be Jojo's new lover. Toby had never met him but he knew he was in his thirties, and English, and in the film business. He could not imagine how he, Toby, had come to sit right in front of this fellow without realising it. *'Fool,'* he thought. Though of course it was just like Candy, as well, to tangle everything up, befriending Jojo's Englishman. As if it was not difficult enough that Jojo had even been invited to Gilly's wedding, much less to be there as a bridesmaid, at the centre of everything, and not only that but to bring along her new 'partner' as well. Toby had not seen Jojo for nearly two years but somehow, during that interval, she had become Gilly's closest friend. At times Toby suspected it was her way of taking revenge on him. At other times he wondered if it was not more than that. She did not want to leave, to lose, his family. Might that not be construed as a reflection on Toby himself?

'Oh, just go,' cried Candy to the driver. *'Go!'*

She waved her hands, with her fingers downward, as if saying *'Shoo.'*

'Ma!' said Toby.

'They can catch the next one. They can come by cab. We can't wait here all day.'

Candy couldn't bear to miss a moment of the wedding. The service had just been held in this little chapel amidst the mountainous suburbs and now they were heading for lunch in a sports club – which was not, apparently, a sports club at all – down on the Corniche. Off they went. Candy would like to have said she'd planned every minute of this day for the last year, but that would not be true. In fact she hardly knew what was going to happen from one moment to the next. She'd flown into Beirut only the day before, like most of the other guests. Everything had been decided and arranged by Maro's family, who were very well-off and well-connected and knew how things were done in this place. Gillian didn't mind. She was delighted with everything. She had, in Candy's view, suspended all critical faculties, but maybe that was just another definition of love. The mini-bus driver, obeying Candy, took off. Down the hills they shot, winding round smooth boulevards and through sharp gorges. The Beirut street tarmac made a smooth hissing sound which Candy liked. It was a strange place, she thought. The outward signs of years of civil war had largely vanished but the town itself, the atmosphere, seemed nervous, careful, absent-minded, like someone who has experienced a psychotic episode. It was staggering as well, Candy thought – these thousand-foot mountains covered in villas, right up to the sky.

At the base of the hills, though, in the very centre of the city, lay ruinous plains, and a gigantic mosque was taking form amid cranes like a great grey egg. And then they were down on the Corniche itself, beside the sea.

They pulled up at Le Sporting, which seemed to Candy an odd name, and an odd place for a wedding breakfast, but what did she know? The real wedding feast was not until the next day, fifty miles away, at Baalbek, near the Roman ruins. Or was it the day after that? She could hardly keep track of the revels. '*Baalbek*,' her future son-in-law had said to her, as if the word was rich with poetry and allusion, which it might have been to him but wasn't to her. He was a nice boy, though. He was in trade, like all the family. He traded in *parts*. 'Parts of what, darling?' she had said. 'Plant,' said Maro. '*Plant?*' It was a mystery to her, though not one she was deeply interested in. But she liked Maro and she noticed that, unlike any businessmen she'd met before, in the US for example, he was interested in history, art, architecture.

'Baalbek!' Maro said to her. His eyes were large, dark and round. 'The greatest ruins of the classical world.'

But now here they were at Le Sporting, on the Corniche. And there, across a little sandy piazza, were the bride and groom, standing in the doorway and greeting the guests. Jojo and two other bridesmaids and Maro's three brothers were just visible behind them.

'This is my son, Tobias,' said Candy to the English film-man when they climbed out of the mini-bus. She looked Toby up and down.

'As you see, his luggage has gone missing.'

Toby was wearing jeans and a slightly frayed cotton shirt. Several other wedding guests were also exiguously attired. They had all got off the plane at Beirut but their luggage had wafted on, to Riyadh, to the Gulf, to the shores of India . . .

Candy was angry with Toby. Instead of going to a men's outfitters that morning to buy a new suit as she commanded, he'd taken a cab out to the airport to see if his stuff had turned up. And of course nothing had.

'The logo of Middle East Airlines is a very old cedar,' said the film-man in his English voice. 'An excellent thing in its own way, but not exactly a symbol of celerity.'

Toby nodded his head up and down during this speech, as if to hurry it up and get it over with.

'You going in now?' he said, indicating the door of Le Sporting with a gesture of his head.

'Well, yes, of course,' said the film-man.

'Cool, I'll borrow your hat,' said Toby and he took the man's panama off his head and stuck it on his own.

'*Toby!*' said Candy.

'Just a quick walk,' he said, and went off fast along the pavement of the Corniche. At all costs he did not want to enter Le Sporting just then and be greeted by Jojo at the door. Jojo hugging Candy, Jojo hugging her fat film-man, and then, what – my turn? He walked on. He needed to think about something else for a moment. Anything else. This Corniche is something else, he told himself. It's really something, even after years of war. The big palms had survived, although they had a war-torn look – they reminded him of those tattered and smoke-singed banners you sometimes see in English churches. Toby had already got to know the Corniche. He had been in Beirut two full days and he now thought of the great sea-front boulevard as his own territory. The other wedding guests were staying in a hotel much further up the hill, a thirty-storey monster the colour of pink ham. Toby could have stayed there, but he'd wangled a deal with Race by which he went to a cheaper hotel and Race let him keep the difference. He was down by the sea in a hotel whose ambient decor was not pink ham. There was a little thin marble here and there, but the main visual effect was of raw concrete. The rooms even smelled of raw concrete. Toby didn't mind that. He liked the smell. The Raw Concrete Palace stood in the sea air and on the previous evening, and again that morning, Toby had borrowed some shoes and shorts from the desk guy and gone out for a run under the great tattered palms, their fronds hanging down like those banners dedicated to the English god of war, and he had gone two or three miles along the wide seaward pavement of the Corniche, the surface of which, while not of porphyry or bronze, somehow seemed, even after years of war, sumptuously darkened with wealth. There were plenty of poor people in view as well; hot-food vendors on bikes shot out in front of the Mercedes and Opels; anglers, poorly clad – not sportsmen, just skinny guys hoping to catch supper – stood on the sea-edge of the fissured rock-shelf. '*Slosh! Wap!*' went the green Med in the slotted rocks. Every fifty paces along the sidewalk's gleam a beggar had set up his station. Toby had befriended one of them already – a multiple amputee who sat on a little wheeled tray and who wore such an expression, of both knowledge and anxiety, that Toby thought that he himself might now begin to understand the declaration *The meek shall inherit the earth* if by 'inherit' was meant 'comprehend'. His name, this beggar had told him, when Toby first stopped to give him some coins, was Tawfik. And here was Tawfik again, just up ahead. This was the third time they had met. Tawfik had already been at his post when Toby went for a run early that morning. But this time, instead of the look of dignity and gratitude, Tawfik shot him a beam of something like hilarity. Here was this brown-haired stranger again, this foreigner, this probable infidel, now wearing a hat banded in pink, and now – they were roughly the same age – they knew each other. They were almost friends. What a place the world was!

'Where you goin', boy?' came a stentorian voice.

It was Chadwick, who sometimes liked to talk black. He was calling from a cab which had stopped on the other side of the road. Race and the third Mrs Chadwick were in the cab with him.

'See you later, Tawfik,' said Toby, handing him the coins in his pocket. Tawfik bowed his head over the transaction, as solemn as a banker.

Toby went over a crossing to the cab.

'Just some fresh air,' he said. He winced. The fresh air was a lie. For him there were great social difficulties involved in this wedding. Race and the Chadwicks were aware of that.

'You gave us the slip,' said Chadwick.

'Yep,' said Toby. 'We thought we'd got away.'

He stood there looking down at them. He put both hands in his jeans pockets.

'Get in,' said Race. Toby got in. They drove back along the Corniche and went into Le Sporting. Toby took the panama hat off and handed it to the cloakroom attendant.

'What name?' she said.

'Celerity,' he said.

They went into the great dining room which was dark and crowded. There were to be no ceremonies on this occasion, only eating. The spice of wealth was in the air. Many of the guests – Maro's friends – had flown in first-class, from Cape Town, Tokyo, São Paulo. Race, father of the bride, was seated with the wedding party. Chadwick and Mrs Chadwick and Toby found places at the remotest table. Some rich Spaniards were on one side of the table, on the other were the owners of a hunting park in the Limpopo. Many courses were then delivered, though in no clear order or sequence. Toby immediately drank off four or five glasses of wine. He kept his head down, and then suddenly sat bolt upright.

The Spanish millionaires and the South Africans had found a topic in common. They were talking about the cost of shooting different species on safari.

'Your leopard's pricey,' one of the South Africans was saying. 'The trouble with your leopard – he doesn't breed prolific.'

Everyone nodded. Toby nodded, too, and twirled the salt-shaker round on the table with his fingers.

'Plus – he has this vindictive streak,' said the South African. 'He'll attack the very person who's shooting at him.'

'Have you ever thought,' said Toby, 'has it ever occurred to you, just to leave the fucking leopards alone?'

'Now listen—' said the South African, half rising to his feet.

'Now,' said Chadwick. He put a hand on Toby's shoulder and glanced at the other wedding guest, who sat down.

'The people you have to meet,' said Toby.

'Now look—' said the South African.

'Sit down,' ordered Chadwick. The man sat down again.

'Come out here,' said Chadwick. He had his hand on Toby's shoulder. Toby stood up and went towards the terrace with him.

'I was rather hoping,' said the film-man who appeared at their side, 'to see my hat again.'

Toby went away through the club and came back with the hat and planted it on the film-man's head, pulling it down almost over his eyes.

'All right?' he said.

'Come on,' said Chadwick.

He led Toby away. The film-man stood there quietly for a second, then pushed his hat back up with two fingers, one on each side of his head.

'He's not a bad fella,' said Chadwick. 'I spoke to him before.'

'Everything OK?' said Race, who had seen Chadwick and Toby leaving and who came out after them.

'All is well,' said Chadwick.

They stood on the terrace facing the sea. It was much quieter that side, away from the traffic. There was a series of concrete steps and landings and banisters of stainless steel that led down to the rocks themselves, drenched and gleaming with the Mediterranean, a steep green sea going '*slosh!*' in the fissures.

'Byblos,' said Chadwick, looking along the coast, 'is somewhere along there.'

'Oh yes?' said Race.

'I've always meant to go to Byblos. It's where the Bible got its name, although I forget why.'

They walked down the steps. Further out on the rocks was a small wooden hut, neat as a sentry box, with its back to the land.

'The thing is,' said Toby, 'I didn't *lose* Jojo. I broke it off. I sent her away. I didn't want to be with her.'

'Well then,' said Chadwick.

Mrs Chadwick came down the steps.

'You boys all right?' she said. Laura Chadwick was slim and pretty and older than the forty on which she had settled as her definitive age.

'Sea air,' said Chadwick.

They walked out on the rocks towards the little hut. But when they reached it and went round the front and looked in, someone was inside. A youth, a soldier in uniform, with an old rifle, sat sprawled on a wooden stool.

He looked up at them with a helpless air.

'Oh, my goodness,' said Mrs Chadwick. 'How long has he been in there?'

'Don't talk to him,' said Chadwick. 'He's on duty.'

'What sort of duty?'

'Border patrol,' said Chadwick.

They looked at the sea. It was green and choppy, and, further out, a dark flecked blue. There were no ships in sight.

'What's he waiting for?' said Mrs Chadwick.

'The enemies of Lebanon, I take it,' said Chadwick.

He gazed into the sentry box at the youth. The soldier looked up at him with a furrowed brow. Chadwick pointed out to sea.

'Who?' said Chadwick. 'Who is coming?'

'*Quoi?*' said the soldier.

'*Qui est l'ennemi?*'

'*Ah. L'ennemi! Les Juifs.*'

'The Jews!' said Toby.

'Israeli navy,' said Chadwick.

'That's right,' said Toby. 'Watch out for the Jew-boys, son.'

'Oh,' said Mrs Chadwick.

'It's all right,' said Toby. He laughed a bit wildly. 'I'm the only Jew round here.'

'He's drunk,' said Chadwick.

'I have Jewish antecedents,' said Race. 'The Radzienwiczs were Jews.'

'You watch out for them Jews,' Toby said to the soldier.

'Steady,' said Race.

'Keep your eyes peeled,' said Toby.

'*Icepeeled?*' said the youth.

2

The next day in the middle of the afternoon all the wedding guests set out for the Bekaa valley and the ruins of Baalbek. They drove over a mountain, most of them in a fleet of mini-buses which had assembled at midday at the ham-pink hotel on the jacaranda-shaded slopes of moneyed Beirut. By chance rather than design, Candy, Race and Toby were the only ones in the last mini-bus that left the hotel forecourt. Toby had arrived late, on foot, from his hotel. Race had been out walking round the city and forgot the time; and Candy found at the last minute that she was not, as she had thought she would be and should be, included in the group – bride, groom, groom's parents – travelling by limousine. The three of them were in a subdued mood. The mountainous suburbs, the road-works, the rain falling at the top of the pass, the half-built concrete houses standing in the rain, the pylons on the lower plain . . .

'Thank God Chip didn't come, that's all I can say,' said Candy.

Chip had refused point-blank to attend his step-daughter's wedding in Lebanon.

'I like Maro,' he said. 'He's a good kid. I like the Lebanese. I'm pleased he'll be one of the family. But Beirut? The Bekaa valley? Kidnap Central? Are you kidding me?'

They looked out at Kidnap Central. Flat fields and glasshouses stretched away to a mountain's grey flank.

'This is the first time since I don't know when that we've travelled together as a family!' said Candy, turning up the brightness. 'How do you *feel*, Race? How did you feel, giving your daughter away? I was proud of you. You looked so handsome. You did it so well. Didn't he, Toby? Didn't he do it just beautifully?'

'You did it just beautifully, Dad,' said Toby.

Just then Toby looked very alone.

'He's stuck,' thought Race. 'He's afraid of something. What's he afraid of?'

'Hey, look at these guys!' said Toby.

A stern-faced cleric in a black turban came into view on a hoarding below the roadside power-lines. Then another, and another.

'The ayatollahs,' said Toby. 'The imams. They look like a fun-lovin' bunch. Just as well Uncle Chip's not here. He'd be calling in the air-strikes right now.'

'I was proud,' Race said to Candy. 'It's a cliché, but that's what I felt. My little girl, I used to carry her on one hand, and here she is a married woman, and she's *beautiful*. That's what I thought.'

'The fascinating thing,' said Candy, 'is this: Maro's parents knew each other at birth, but they only found out after they were married. He was an orphan and was taken in by this woman with a baby. She fed both of them together, one on each breast. Then he was taken off somewhere else and grew up and knew nothing about it, and one day he met Sonya and they got married. They only found out later: she was the baby on the other breast! Isn't that romantic?'

'It is,' said Race.

'It's more than that,' said Candy. 'It's like a myth.'

A jet went high overhead, making a hard solid sound in the sky like a marble rolling over slate.

'Israelis,' said Race, looking up at the clouds. 'They watch this place like hawks, according to Chadwick. They probably know exactly who's in this vehicle, right now.'

'Do you think he *remembered* her?' said Candy.

'Maybe,' said Race. 'Maybe she remembered him.'

'What do you think, Toby?' said Candy.

'I don't know, Ma,' said Toby.

'I think they *recognised* each other,' said Candy, 'in their hearts.'

The Palmyra hotel, half-hidden by vines and palms, was just across the road from the Roman ruins on the outskirts of Baalbek. 'The Palmyra,' Candy read aloud from a brochure she found in the mini-bus just as they were arriving, 'is famous for its air of faded grandeur and the ghosts of its illustrious guests, from Cocteau to the Kaiser, from Gertrude Bell to the Empress of Abyssinia, who still roam its lofty rooms.'

'Bullshit,' said Toby.

'*Don't*, Toby,' said Candy crossly.

'Well, anyway, you're there now,' said Toby. 'You don't read brochures when you're there. You read them when you're not there.'

'I read them just exactly where I please,' said Candy, but she put the brochure back in the seat-netting and climbed out of the bus and followed Race and Toby into the hotel. Toby carried Candy's luggage. After checking in, Candy hurried to the bar to see who was there. Race and Toby crossed the road to look at the ruins, but they found that they were fenced all round, and the entrance was locked.

'Five o'clock,' said Toby, reading a sign. 'They're closed. Three thousand years old and they close at five.'

He and his father walked along the highway into the town. It was only a little place but a maelstrom of traffic whirled through the central square – carts, motorbikes, motorised carts, scooters, sedans, jalopy trucks.

'It's drive-time, baby,' said Toby, gazing around.

'What do we want?' said Race.

'I should buy something,' said Toby. 'I haven't bought anything since I got to Lebanon. I've just been banqueting.'

'Buy something,' said Race. 'As your father I advise it.'

'I don't know what,' said Toby. 'Oranges? Light bulbs? Baby formula?'

He scanned the market's offerings.

'Shoelaces!' he said. 'I need some laces.'

He stepped into a little cavern and selected a pair of brown laces from a vertical tray on the counter.

The door darkened and Jojo and the English film director came in.

'Jojo,' said Race.

'Toby!' said Jojo. 'We've been here three days and I haven't even seen you. This is ridiculous.'

'Sorry, excuse me, I'm just buying laces,' said Toby.

'Have you met Joachim?' said Jojo.

Toby and Joachim shook hands wordlessly.

'I just, excuse me, have to buy these laces,' said Toby.

'Souvenir?' said Jojo.

'No. I need laces,' said Toby.

'These ones?' said Jojo, picking up a pair from the vertical tray.

'Yes,' said Toby.

'Don't buy these, Toby,' said Jojo. She ran the laces between her finger and thumb.

'Why?' said Toby.

'They won't work.'

'Jojo, they're shoelaces,' said Toby.

'They won't knot,' said Jojo.

'Not what?'

'Stop,' said Race to Toby.

'They're the wrong material,' said Jojo.

'Come on, darling,' said Joachim.

'One pair of shoelaces, please,' said Toby, handing them to the shop-keeper.

'They won't work, Toby,' said Jojo, laughing. 'They'll slide past each other.'

'Great. Sorry, I mean. See you again,' said Toby. 'Real soon.'

Jojo and Joachim went out the door. Jojo was still smiling, but Race saw a sadness slant on her like rain. Then she straightened and walked on.

3

So this was it, the high point of the wedding! After three days of nuptial celebrations, you couldn't say that there'd been a real climax. Neither Gilly nor Maro were believers, so the marriage service – a restrained transaction in the Protestant hill-top chapel – didn't really rate. And since they'd been living together for nearly a year, no one could pretend that the wedding-night itself was some big deal. But this was different. This was the moment, everyone felt it. The buses were outside the Palmyra hotel, the morning sun was shining, the guests came forth in their finery, they gazed in wonder at their transport and then climbed aboard. These were not the fussy little mini-buses of Beirut but local vehicles from the wild east, from Baalbek town and the gorges, much battered by calamity – here a bullet-hole in a window, there the upholstery stripped to bare metal. The door closed; the brigand at the wheel hit the sound system and accelerator; Arabian music – wild, aggrieved – filled the bus like the sunlight, and out they shot into the traffic and away across the floor of the valley. The wedding feast was not, in fact, to be held in the famous ruins of Baalbek. Even Maro's family, with all the strings they could pull, could not pull the one that might spread out a banquet on the porch of the temple of Bacchus or on the great platform of Baal-Jupiter. Earlier that morning, Race and Toby had gone for a jog through the ruins, but they were in a hurry and the precincts were too big to make much sense of in the time at their disposal. They themselves were busy, in any case, with other matters.

'You're going to have to make your mind up,' said Race. 'Do you want to end up alone?'

'*You* live alone.'

'Well, only after – I mean, I had you two first, didn't I?'

'I don't know what to do.'

'I think Jojo loves you.'

'Oh, yeah? What about Joachim?'

'Joachim! She just brought him along as someone to bring along. She doesn't care about Joachim. She loves you, Toby.'

'That's not the problem. I don't think I love her. I don't know if I can love anyone. Something stops me.'

'What stops you?'

'I don't know what it is. When I'm with her, the self I want to be – I can't find him. And then I feel afraid.'

'Everyone feels afraid sometimes.'

'Not when they're in love. Some Frenchman said people fall in love only because they've read about it in books. It's the opposite with me. I can't fall in love *because* I've read about it in books. I feel worried. It's like I'm sitting the exam.'

'Does that matter?'

'Of course it matters. You loved Ma.'

'Well . . .' said Race.

They stopped jogging and Race stood there, panting, but speaking carefully.

'In point of fact,' he said, 'I was in love with someone else.'

'Really?' said Toby. 'Who?'

'Just someone. And Candy was in love with someone else as well.'

'*Really?*' said Toby. 'Who?'

'Someone. Doesn't matter now. Anyway – both those arrangements fell apart, and then we sort of just ended up together instead.'

'*Instead,*' said Toby, trying to take this in. 'I don't think I want "instead".'

'But you aren't in love with someone else. I think Jojo's the one for you. And you're the one for her.'

Toby looked worried.

'We'd better get going,' he said. 'We better get changed.' He was now in his own running gear. His luggage had arrived in the course of the night by unseen agency. When he woke up, his old tartan suitcase, mute and much travelled, was in his room as if it had found its own way. He and Race ran on through the stony courts and the pillared wastes and back across the road and up to their rooms. Toby re-appeared outside the hotel in a dark suit of light-weight cotton. His English shoes, dark brown, were polished. He noticed, with an odd intensity of interest, as he stepped on the bus, that the laces had come undone. He stooped and did them up. He was thinking about what Race had told him. His father and mother had never been in love! Did that make a difference to him, his character, his nature?

He and Race were the last on board and went down the aisle of the bus. By now, on their fourth or fifth day together, the wedding guests were getting used to this – meeting in a different place every morning, feasting together, travelling on together, a pod of unrelated fish. Here now were the rich São Paulistas, dressed up as for an exclusive nightclub, and here were the English in crumpled linen, as for a picnic on a heath. Even Toby's South African foe stretched his lips and nodded his head as evidence of goodwill when Toby came past. Then the doors closed, the Arabian music wailed and out they shot into the local traffic and headed across the plain.

'*Wheeeee!*' cried Candy. They were leaving the borders at that moment, she felt, not only of what she knew but of what she had ever foreseen.

And there, right on cue, just out the window was a fleet of Syrian tanks parked in a field, muzzles pointing high to the east and to the south. Some soldiers, sallow kids in trousers and skimpy vests, were washing their clothes. Grey underwear was strung on lines between the gun barrels. For a moment they saw one another, the children of Adam, with fleeting recognition – the wedding guests in linen and silk, the skinny conscripts in their vests – and then parted for ever.

'Where *are* we off to?' cried Candy in a tone of joy.

'That's Mount Lebanon,' said Chadwick, pointing ahead. A grey and rumpled moor filled the windscreen, daubed here and there with streaks of snow.

'Mount Lebanon!' said Candy. 'Oh,' she said. '*Bernard!* He wanted to come so much. Poor darling! He said he'd always wanted to see the cedars on Mount Lebanon.'

Bernard had died three months before, at night, in his sleep.

'We thought of it. We thought of bringing him, although he could barely cross the room,' said Candy.

'He would never have managed the trip,' said Laura Chadwick.

'He never recovered from the fall he had,' said Candy.

'He would simply never have managed the trip,' said Laura Chadwick, as if she would brook no argument.

The bus slowed and turned and went down a pot-holed lane lined with poplars. Then they passed a wide pond in a bed of shingle and a grove of willows and came to an open meadow. The bus stopped. Everyone looked out the windows.

'My God,' said Joachim, his voice ringing out down the bus. 'The tents of the patriarchs.'

They climbed down and stood looking at the scene. A line of low Bedouin tents, open on three sides, richly carpeted and pillowed within, stood on the margins of the field. In the centre, under linen awnings, seven long tables were set with flowers, silver- and glass-ware.

'Too good for the working-classes, hey hey?' said Joachim.

A jet went whistling overhead, almost out of sight in the cirrus.

'Israeli,' said Chadwick.

'Lucky for us,' said Joachim. 'If it was the Americans up there now – well, no wedding party is safe!'

Chadwick set his jaw.

'Just kidding,' said Joachim.

'Unfortunately –' said Chadwick.

'Here comes champagne,' said Joachim. 'My God, is that *arak* they're making over there? And a sheep on a spit! It's Deuteronomy, baby.'

Candy had set off far away to the tables to read the place-cards. She made some brisk changes and then came back, wobbling as her heels sank a little in the turf. She took a glass of champagne. Far to the south stood Mount Hermon, gleaming with snow.

'I see it now!' said Race after a glass and a half of champagne. Mount Hermon shone in the south. Mount Lebanon rose only a mile or two to the west. Race thought of the hall of some old farmhouse, with a grandfather clock ticking. The Israeli jet, almost invisible, went back again in the cirrus.

'Arabs and Jews,' said Race. 'All this fuss. It's just an old family row over the will. Who gets the farm? Who gets the grandfather clock?'

'Not bad,' said Chadwick, nodding his head.

Everyone was circulating, walking around, looking into the tents. Some guests, the clubbers from São Paulo, the Madrilenas and Madrilenos, had already gone in and were lying back on the couches, as far, amid the pillows, from sunlight as was possible under the circumstances. Race went looking for Toby. He found him watching the patriarchs roasting sheep on spits. Some boys from the neighbourhood had climbed up the poplars along the lane and were watching the proceedings as well. There was a heady banter – the old men roasting the sheep and the boys in the trees were shouting harshly back and forth at one another, but whether in anger or play was hard to tell.

'I had the same problem as you once,' said Race. 'I thought I couldn't love anyone again. I was kind of worried about that at one time, but it turned out all right.'

'You fell in love.'

'I did fall in love.'

'But not with Candy?'

'This was before I married Candy,' said Race, speaking with care.

'The other woman,' said Toby.

'It was, in fact, yes, another woman,' said Race evenly.

'He's tougher than I thought,' thought Toby.

They turned away from the roasting spit and walked across the field.

'Who was she?' said Toby.

'Just someone. Well, she was someone called Sandra.'

'Sandra,' said Toby. 'Sandra who?'

'Isbister.'

'What happened to her?'

'I lost touch.'

'What was she like?'

'I was in love so I can't really describe her.'

'Is-bis-ter,' said Toby.

'Sandra Isbister,' said Race as if to himself.

'Silly sort of name,' said Toby carelessly.

'She's your mother,' said Race.

He stared at his son, amazed. He had spoken on an impulse so thoroughly controlled for twenty years that he never imagined it would defeat him.

'My – mother,' said Toby.

'She is your mother,' said Race.

Toby stared back at him.

'You never told me,' he said.

'I just told you then,' said Race.

He had that same tough look again, which Toby had very rarely seen in his life. Toby was not, in other words, at that moment, permitted to complain.

'My *mother*?' he said again. 'Where is she?'

'I told you. I lost touch.'

'You lost touch?' said Toby. 'With my mother?'

Race shook his head, not meaning that he hadn't but that there'd been no choice.

'Sandra was – wild,' he said. 'She ran away. She always ran away, from everyone.'

'Why?' said Toby.

'I don't know . . . She had this power over men that she didn't really want. She didn't even approve of it. But she enjoyed it too. And so she was confused, and off she went.'

Toby nodded. He felt that he somehow knew all that already. They had reached the edge of the field and they stopped at the gate and looked down the lane at the wide shingle pond.

'Who'd have thought it?' Toby said. 'Coming all the way here, to hear this. Does Candy know?'

'Does she know she's not your mother?' said Race.

'Dad,' said Toby.

'Sorry,' said Race.

'Does she know you were going to tell me?'

'I didn't know myself. We used to debate it once upon a time, but then there didn't seem to be any obvious point.'

'Why now?'

'I didn't plan it now.'

'But you did it.'

'Maybe you need something.'

'Like what?'

'A jolt,' said Race.

'How did I happen?' said Toby.

'Sandra and I were together a year or two. We had you. Then she took off. She ran. Sandra loved running off. And there I was, with a one-year-old. And Candy was free. She was on her own, I mean. So we just – tried it out.'

'Candy!' said Toby.

He gave a little laugh, perhaps comprised fractionally of a sob.

'She's been a very good mother to me,' he said.

'Don't say anything to her,' said Race. 'Not yet anyway.'

'I won't say anything,' said Toby.

'Do up your laces,' said Race.

Toby crouched. Then they went away to the feast in the middle of the field.

4

'The thing is,' said Joachim, squinting at the sun that was hanging in empty space above Mount Lebanon, and then holding up his thumb and forefinger to make a half-square and squinting again in a way that indicated he was now looking through an imaginary lens or viewfinder, managing further to irritate Toby who, nevertheless, was on his best behaviour considering the place and the occasion, and the state of his thoughts, but who still couldn't understand how Joachim and Jojo had happened to end up at this table, right on top of him so to speak – which was in fact Candy's doing – 'the thing is,' said Joachim, 'if you look at that mountain there and – now – you see those sort of odd streaks of snow–?'

'Yes,' said Candy, looking at the mountain.

'Well, don't you think – I mean don't you actually think – that they look like a script, a sort of proto-script, a kind of proto-Arabic you might say? Don't you think so?'

'They do!' said Candy. 'They look exactly like a script. How brilliant of you!'

'Then the question is, my darling,' said Joachim, holding out his wine-glass to be re-filled, 'what is the script saying?'

'"Fuck off, Joachim", probably,' said Toby in an undertone.

'Now,' said Chadwick.

'What was that?' said Joachim. 'What did he say?'

'Fuck off, Israel,' said Toby. 'Obviously. Fuck off, Israeli Air Force.'

'No, my dear chap,' said Joachim. 'What I think it's saying is this: "Fuck the Moderator of the Free Church of Scotland." '

And he then laughed so immoderately at his own remark that almost everyone up and down the table, without even hearing what it was, felt quite warmly disposed to him for his good humour. Joachim then began a long story about visiting Edinburgh – or was it Glasgow? – it was a long time ago – when he was a student at St Andrews and seeing the words 'Fuck The Pope' written on a brick wall under a railway bridge, but someone else had come along and struck a line through the word 'Pope' and carefully replaced it with:

Moderator of
the Free
Church of
Scotland

This recollection made Joachim roar with laughter again, and again some of the others around him felt themselves basking in the glow and the cheer. Candy had completely forgotten that she had moved Jojo and Joachim to this table only in order to bring Jojo and Toby closer together, at least for the duration of lunch, the final gathering of the wedding. Her plan was to show Toby to advantage: how could anyone prefer pink-faced Joachim, plump, scanty-haired Joachim who must be pushing forty, to her handsome son who was twenty-three and who, she firmly believed, was intended, desired, *required* by fate to marry Jojo? But now she was laughing along with everyone else, although she wasn't exactly sure what the joke was – a prim sectarian hand on a brick wall in Scotland – but she felt sure that it was funny. She trusted Joachim on that. Joachim, she thought, was charming, irresponsible, flippant, quite unlike the people she normally met in Washington. She felt flippant, irresponsible, herself. There was Chadwick for instance, going on about the Middle East crisis. She'd just about had the Middle East crisis, Candy thought, up to her ears.

'And if it *is* just an old family row over the will,' Chadwick was saying, 'then you should ask yourself: What are *we* doing involved in it? We might, perhaps, take the role of impartial judge, high above the fray. Instead we jump in and help one side beat up the other, and strip him naked. Did you know, for example, that every drop of kerosene used by the Israeli military is donated free of charge by the United States of America? Yep, those boys up there right now – all riding round on free JP-8 jet fuel, courtesy of Uncle Sam.'

'Oh, I wouldn't worry about that,' said Joachim. 'At least *they're* not going to bomb us to smithereens.'

Everyone round him laughed, which irritated Chadwick. For a moment he lost his courtly manner.

'Oh, wouldn't you?' he said. 'Well I do. And we may all have to worry about it. It's distorting and poisoning our relationships everywhere – even here, even now.'

'Not mine, dear boy,' said Joachim, 'not mine.'

Chadwick felt heat on his face. To be addressed as 'dear boy' by this scarlet-cheeked Englishman. Then he remembered himself and drew back. There was a phrase he'd once read about sixteenth-century Rome – 'Only in this city have men learned to differ in opinions without flying into a rage.' He smiled at Joachim, and nodded and then withdrew his attention. Joachim looked disappointed. He felt that he'd been on the verge of a great victory, on behalf of flippancy, but it had slipped away. In any case, the lunch was now reaching a fissiparous state. At all the tables people were beginning to leave their seats and go visiting. He heaved himself up and looked down at Candy.

'Must away,' he said. 'Splash the uh, the uh—'

'Now don't forget to come back!' cried Candy.

Jojo didn't look up. She leaned in towards Chadwick.

'What did you mean "even here, even now"?' she said.

'Nothing,' said Chadwick. He looked back at Jojo, golden-headed, sun-browned after only a day or two in the Levant. He was thinking about the war in Iraq. He felt weary for a moment even thinking about Iraq, much less talking about it to this young woman. That morning, at the hotel, he had had a call from a colleague in Washington, warning him that a scandal was about to break over prisoner abuse in Iraq.

'It's not pretty,' said his office colleague. 'You're in the Mid-East on vacation? That may not be the best place to be in the next few days.'

But here they were in a field in the Mid-East. It was warm. It was almost the beginning of May. The afternoon sun was still shining on the meadow. There were sounds of high hilarity rising here and there. A small dance-floor, of the best polished wood, had just been revealed near the tents, and the dancing was about to begin. The music had started already. The dance-floor was still empty but as soon as the first dancers arrived it would be instantly thronged. What was he doing talking about war to tall, pretty, Jojo, the tops of whose breasts, he couldn't help noticing, were sun-browned as well. Chadwick had no desire to alarm her. But Jojo was serious. She was from the film world where no one she knew – she was in wardrobe – talked about things like this. She looked at him seriously. And Toby was there too, listening. They were there sitting together side by side, at last, and after all. Chadwick relented.

'This foul mess we're in,' he said. 'This fiasco in Iraq. How did *this* happen, you have to ask. How in God's name did we get to here?'

'To where?' said Toby.

'US war crimes. Murder at checkpoints, mass arrests, thousands kept hooded all day in the sun, then vanishing into prisons. Rumours of torture . . . How on earth did they manage it?'

'Who manage it?' said Toby.

'Seven or eight people who took over US policy after the twin towers came down,' said Chadwick. 'But I have to say they did it brilliantly. They left the rest of us for dust.'

Toby had gone pale. He had just realised a fact which until then had somehow escaped his notice: he was not Jewish. He put it another way – he was no longer Jewish. He was no longer Candy's son. He felt strangely, unjustly, deprived. He was also annoyed with himself. His stupid remark – he could hear it now – laughing at a name . . . *Isbister*. 'If only I hadn't said that,' he thought, 'Race might never have let the secret slip.' And he, Toby, might have stayed as he was, perhaps for ever. But it was too late now. He was no longer Jewish. He was an Isbister instead. An Isbister! He wanted to steal a look at Jojo to see if she noticed the difference, or even if she seemed different now as well, but he didn't.

'After the towers fell,' said Chadwick, 'there was this incredible noise and confusion. Everyone had their opinion. I know what

I thought: this was the result of a terrible foreign policy. It was time to change. Americans are not fools. We don't want to see our cities under attack from maddened strangers. What should we do now? And that was more or less the first response. We had to change our Middle East policy. We had to settle Israel-Palestine. We had to be *fair*. But then, all of a sudden, that changed. Attack Iraq. Attack Syria. Attack Iran. Leave Israel alone! All the good ol' Uncle Chip stuff. And they won! They've got their way. It was brilliantly done.'

'How?' said Toby.

'It was all over in a couple of months,' said Chadwick. 'In fact, it was decided in a single week. I remember that week, although I didn't know exactly what was going on. I had an inkling but I just couldn't see it clearly. You were both there, I remember that.'

'We were there?' said Toby.

'You were there,' said Chadwick.

'How can he not love this girl?' he thought, looking at Jojo, tall and slim with her clear eyes fixed on him as if fixed on the facts.

'The week Bernard broke his leg,' said Chadwick.

'We were there,' said Toby. 'We saw the meteors!'

'*We*,' thought Jojo.

She remembered Caspar standing on the truck-bed. 'These here are *American* shootin' stars.'

'Thanksgiving,' said Toby.

'Thanksgiving,' said Chadwick. 'That was the day the President, President Bush – God help us all – said *Get me the war plans for Iraq. And – keep this a secret*. The only thing that had appeared in public that week was an article in the *New Yorker* by old Bernard Lewis. He was a friend of our Bernard. They grew up in London together. "That old fox", Bernard used to say. Lewis writes a piece in the *New Yorker* that week linking 9/11 and Iraq. Iraq was 'deeply involved' – almost everyone in the Middle East thought that! And that America was too frightened of Iraq's terrible weapons to do anything about it. Oh, it was a beautiful piece of incitement. And the very next day, on Thanksgiving eve, Bush says to Rumsfeld, "Get me the war plans for Iraq. Keep this secret." You might, in fact, make an argument that that week the *New Yorker* all on its own pushed the US into war.'

'Thanks, fellas,' said Toby.

'But the campaign didn't end there. It was rolling right along. There was Bletchley Two, for instance. Ever hear of Bletchley Two?'

'I never heard of Bletchley One,' said Toby.

'Bletchley Park,' said Chadwick, 'was where the British broke the Nazi codes in World War Two. And Bletchley Two was the name these people gave to a secret conference to analyse the meaning of 9/11. See how good they are? What happened on September 11 wasn't an act, it wasn't even an event – it was a code. It was a mysterious signal from outer darkness which needs decryption. And they are the fellas to decrypt it for us. And a real rogues' gallery they were too – old Bernard Lewis again, Wolfowitz, various hacks and think-tankers. And so they *de-code* 9/11. And guess what? It was nothing to do with American policy. It was evil attacking good, lightning out of clear blue sky. What to do? There's a swamp in the Middle East. A delta of terror. Drain the swamp! Smash up the Middle East. Burn it down! Start with Iraq! Impose the free market! It doesn't actually make any sense, it was a series of mad non-sequiturs, but the White House – that ship of fools – bought it.'

'Wolfowitz, Lewis,' said Toby. 'So that's your argument, Uncle Chaddy? *Blame the Jews.*'

'Oh, Toby,' said Chadwick. 'I'm not an anti-Semite. I'm not even anti-Zionist, if the project was carried out with decency.'

'You,' said a voice, 'are wanted.'

A hand fell on Jojo's shoulder. It was Maro's father, Anton.

'Young lady, you must come and dance,' he said. 'Look over there! Everyone is dancing.'

'Oh, Anton,' said Jojo.

'No "no"s,' said Anton. 'Gillian has even put her veil on again. How can the bridesmaids not dance if she wishes it? She has sent me to get you. This is an order from high command.'

They looked over the way. The little dance-floor was crowded. The beat was pumping. A white veil could be glimpsed among the moving heads. Jojo stood up and looked into Chadwick's eyes for release but he had no power to grant it. Away she went in her beautiful dress with Anton, wilting slightly, as one condemned.

5

By this time almost everyone was strolling around or on the dance-floor or installed inside the low-slung tents, and the few still at the tables drinking coffee or *arak* – there was no sign the waiters were ever coming to clear up – now felt like those lost souls who stay on in a ruined city; then Chadwick and Toby got up too and left, and went strolling around the field, and ended up at the gate to the lane where the buses were parked. They stopped and looked down at the shingle pond which was already in shadow.

Beside the pond was a man in a green corduroy suit, sitting on one of the carved dining chairs, his back to the festivities, a fishing rod in hand.

'Look at that,' said Chadwick. 'Only an Englishman would bring a trout-rod to a wedding breakfast.'

'I know him!' said Toby. 'He's one of Gilly's friends from Cambridge. He's a don. He's very clever. He's very clever, and very bad-tempered – that's what I hear.'

The thought of this combination for some reason made them both laugh. The Arab boys who earlier had been shouting from the tops of the poplars had come down to the ground and were now gathered round the fisherman in green corduroy, although keeping a respectful distance. Toby and Chadwick stood leaning on the gate watching him as well.

'He has these tremendous rows with his girlfriend,' said Toby, 'so I hear.'

'Does he now?' said Chadwick with the faintest hint of sarcasm.

'He knows!' thought Toby, who heard the hint, and realised how well Chadwick knew him. 'He knows I'm not Candy's son. He's probably known that my whole life. He probably knows my real mother!'

But he said nothing. They watched the fisherman in silence. Then there was a shout. The angler had hooked a little fish and up it came into the air, wriggling and dancing on the line. The boys were capering and shouting.

'Well, I'll be damned,' said Chadwick.

The angler stood up and unhooked the fish. He handed it to one of the boys. They crouched on the shingle bank. After a minute or so, a curl of smoke went up.

'They're going to cook it!' said Toby.

'Waste not,' said Chadwick.

They watched the boys.

'That was another thing,' said Chadwick. 'Remember that week in Washington? Remember the kids in Gaza, blown up on their way to school? And the Israelis saying: "Oh, yeah – we did that." I was puzzled by that. I couldn't understand it, but I had a feeling it was important. One day I decided to go and look at the place, to examine the scene, so to speak. The Israelis don't like it if you go poking round the territories but they can't really stop you – "US envoy inspects conditions in refugee camps" – that sort of thing – so off I went. I even made sure I was there at the same time of day the booby trap exploded. It was like the papers said . . .

tumbledown houses, sandy lanes, a few greenhouses, the sun coming up through the haze. I had an Arab driver and we found the place and I started to climb up the slope to the spot, but the slope was sandy and my soles wouldn't grip. I'd dressed the part, you see – US diplomat, dark suit, striped tie, new shoes I'd bought in Jerusalem, black Florsheim's, and I kept sliding down in my own footprints. My driver was cracking up. He wasn't a bad guy I guess. But I persisted. I could hardly take my shoes off, could I? American dignity was at stake. In the end I reached the top. I looked round. Now what exactly happened here, I thought. Five kids on their way to school. I could see the Israeli army post a few hundred yards away. The bomb was activated by remote control. Someone at that post had been watching those kids through high-power binoculars. The Israeli military have *very* good optics, don't worry about that. And when the kids reached the spot where I was standing – *bang*. Later on they held an inquiry and said, "Sorry! Big mistake. We did set off the bomb, but we thought they were terrorists threatening Jewish settlements." And I stood there, looking round, and wondering what happened, and then I remembered the blue shirt. Five boys from the same family, the eldest thirteen, the youngest six. The youngest, Akram al-Astal, was wearing blue jeans and a blue shirt. I knew that from the papers. It was a very big bomb, you see, and it blew those kids to bits. Akram's mother said: "We knew it was Akram only because we found scraps of his sky-blue shirt." And that was it. That was the detail I needed. Because, you know, a six-year-old in a sky-blue shirt cannot, half an hour after sunrise, be mistaken for a terrorist on his way to kill Jews, even in Gaza. In other words, it wasn't a tragic accident. It was deliberate. The Israelis killed the children *because* they were children.'

'No!' said Toby.

'Unfortunately, I believe it's true,' said Chadwick.

'But why?' said Toby.

'They wanted a reaction,' said Chadwick. 'They needed some terrorism against them. The Palestinians had been quiet for months. Everyone was talking about the peace-process and Palestinian rights and so on. Prime Minister Sharon had to re-write the script. He was on his way to the US in a few days. He wanted some violence against Israel, and fast. And so he arranged something so terrible there must be a revenge attack. And he got it, right on time. He was actually sitting in the White House when the news flash came. Fifteen Jews killed on a bus in Haifa! I remember thinking: That's incredible timing, Ariel, how did you pull that off? I was half-joking, but in fact it *was* incredible timing. The man's a master choreographer. And it worked. Bush fell for it hook, line and sinker: "Israel's war on terror is America's war on terror!" Now – five Palestinian children have been slaughtered, and fifteen Jews effectively murdered by Ariel Sharon but, you know – it was worth it. That's the thinking. Fifteen Jews die – it's terrible, it's awful, but it's a sacrifice we can bear. "In war, force and fraud are the two cardinal virtues," said Hobbes. Fifteen dead? But America's on our side again. Forget the peace-process. Forget the Palestinians. And that's just what happened. Make war on terror! Attack Iraq! And as for Akram al-Astal in his sky-blue shirt – well, everyone just forgot all about him.'

Toby was silent. He felt a wave of melancholy about everything just then. Murdered children. The dance music, Jojo, himself. He turned from the gate and looked back over the field, and the great valley beyond, and the sun which was about to sink behind Mount Lebanon but which still sent its beams down through the air and lit up the slopes and the gullies of the mountain, and the flights of birds crossing far away in different directions, and something like gossamer in the air which glinted here and there as if threads of silk a hundred feet long had been inserted into the wind to reveal its hidden currents.

'In war, force and fraud are the cardinal virtues . . .' said Chadwick. 'You know, if I blame anyone for this mess we're in, it's not Israel, or the Israel lobby, or the crazy people in the Pentagon, but a single, solitary Englishman.'

'Who?' said Toby.

'Thomas Hobbes,' said Chadwick. 'Ever read Hobbes?'

'No,' said Toby.

'You should,' said Chadwick. '*The basis of all morality is fear. Man is ruled by two passions – fear of violent death, and pride. The prince – Leviathan – exists to rule over the proud.*'

'Is that what you think?' said Toby.

'No, Toby,' said Chadwick patiently. 'It's the exact opposite of what I think. But it's now the philosophy of the United States government, with one modern amendment – America itself is to be Leviathan and rule the world. That's the theory of the Pentagon gang – Wolfowitz and Cheney and Rumsfeld and so on. "Nature renders man apt to invade and destroy one another . . . Man deceives himself as to the horror of his natural situation by weaving a cocoon of vain dreams about himself." There you are. Hobbes in a nutshell.'

'I doubt that Bush or Cheney ever heard of Hobbes,' said Toby.

'No, but Wolfowitz has,' said Chadwick. 'He was the brains behind this war. And he was a pupil of Leo Strauss, who idolised Hobbes. He must have been some guy, Strauss. In fact, he didn't have pupils: he had *disciples*. Everyone fell for him. There are novels written about him. He's in the latest Saul Bellow – '*That slight person, triply abstracted, mild goggles covering his fiery judgements*'. And now his disciples are in power, and those fiery judgements are burning up the Middle East. Tell lies. Make war on the least suspicion. Assassination. Bulldozing houses. Torture. I'm hearing bad, bad stories out of Iraq, Toby. Prisoners coming in for interrogation covered in third-degree burns. They've been arrested by our troops and they're brought in tied across the hoods of Humvees like deer. The engine-heat burns them and our boys don't care. That's the Leviathan for you. There is no providence, there is no mercy – no idle chatter about goodness as Strauss would put it – only fear, and power. Perhaps you can understand it in Israel's case. That country was built by people who'd been in Auschwitz. But what is terrible, what I can't stand, is that it should be the basis of our policy as well. Force and fraud. Lies and fear. The United States of America! No! It's not acceptable.'

'You mean it's all right for Israel?' said Toby.

'I mean it's understandable,' said Chadwick. 'Those people came out of Auschwitz. Buchenwald. Treblinka. No – not out of Treblinka. No one got out of Treblinka. Treblinka wasn't a camp. It wasn't even a place. It was a thing – a machine. If you got near it, it killed you within two hours. There was an alley lined with flowers and fir trees, and SS men. The Jews had to walk down the alley and in the sand they could see the footprints of the people who had just gone before and who had already ceased to exist. And there was a little man squatting and laughing and dancing in front of them. "Children, children! Hurry, hurry! The water's getting cold in the bath-house!" A million Jews died at the end of that alley. The children of Israel . . . And Israel can't forget that. It's not behind them – it's still in front of them. That's what the world looks like to them.'

'So it is all right for them,' said Toby.

'No, Toby, it's a disaster for them. They're in a Hobbesian world and they can't get out, but as for us . . .'

Chadwick went through the gate and Toby followed and they went down the lane a short way and watched the boys by the pond. The smoke came over to them. One of the boys ran up the slope with a piece of burnt fish in his hand. He was in a red jersey with tremendous holes at the elbows. He held out the fish. Chadwick put up his hand like a traffic cop.

'Not for me,' he said.

The boy had sooty black eyebrows and grimy hands. He proffered the fish to Toby, laughing.

'Oh God, OK,' said Toby.

He took the bit of fish and ate it. The boy then ran back down the shingle slope to the others. The fisherman had stood up and was packing up his rod. He left the dining chair where it was in the shingle and he came up to the lane. He was a handsome little man with a frown on a strongly formed brow. He nodded curtly to Chadwick and Toby and went past them through the gate. Toby and Chadwick turned back as well, and stopped again to look at the scene in front of them. The sun had just set and the valley had abruptly grown darker: far away across the plain little ruddy flames were glinting here and there, as if from the mouths of caves, and the indentations on the moors of Mount Lebanon now looked like great thumb-prints left by a potter. But the disco music was going as loudly and cheerfully as before.

'What people forget,' said Chadwick, 'is just how *weird* Hobbes was. He was the original crooked man. Both his slippers, someone noted, were worn down on the *same side*. And he was fantastically timid. He admitted that himself. It was the result, he said, of his premature birth. His mother thought the Spanish were about to invade – this was six months before the Armada – and she panicked and went into labour. Hobbes was *congenitally* fearful. Hence, I suppose, his whole philosophy of fear. Isn't that wonderful? Five hundred years ago a woman in a white ruff panics and goes into labour, and we're still dealing with the consequences.'

Chadwick did not see Toby fall. He was looking away out over the plain where little fires were glowing red in the distance and Toby buckled and slid silently to the ground just behind him. The long day, the surprises it had held, the *arak*, and the sudden depth of the past – a woman in a white ruff! – for the first time in his life he fainted away.

'Nor was Hobbes even a very good exegete,' said Chadwick, his back still turned. 'He thinks, for example, that the Leviathan in the Bible means the king *over* the proud, who will subdue the proud, but in fact it means the king *of* the proud; in other words, the *most* proud—'

He turned to Toby and then saw him on the ground. Chadwick gazed down at him. 'He's asleep,' Chadwick thought, 'how very odd,' and without realising it he put his hand out to expostulate, unintentionally like a figure in an old painting. Jojo was running towards them. Later she thought that she had known something was going to happen before Toby fell, but she was never sure. She had been on the dance-floor and from time to time had turned to glance at Toby and Chadwick talking by the gate, then going out of sight, then coming back. She wished she could be there, but she didn't like to go over uninvited. And then she saw Toby crumple, and she ran. Later she also said she had been frightened. In fact she was thinking: 'This *is* the Middle East!' She thought of the jets overhead and the boys in the trees and she had a moment of dread, absurd as it seemed, that Toby had been shot dead. And even so, at the same time, she was pleased she had an excuse to leave the prison of the dance-floor and go to Toby. She ran past Chadwick who was still standing looking down at his godson in surprise, and then Jojo was on her knees, in the grass.

'Toby,' she said.

Toby was quite white.

'Where's he gone?' she thought. 'Where *is* he?'

'Toby!' she said.

His eyes opened and then shut again. For a long moment he knew nothing – only that he had been down in the dark and that he had needed to go there for a long time, the illustrious dark. For he didn't know anything just then – where he was at that moment, for instance, or even exactly who he was—

Then he opened his eyes again and he did know something: he was looking into the eyes of someone he loved.

He wanted to say so, to tell her that, but no words came.

And he knew that was why he had fainted – in order to wake up and see the world with an ignorant eye. He was then aware of the sea. In his mind's eye he saw the sea – grey, flat, about thirty miles away, and also girdling the whole earth. And he saw Jojo's eyes looking at him and he was aware of her breasts and he wanted to laugh then and felt like crying as well and no words came but then out of the slowing babble he began to hear words form. 'So that's all words are,' he thought. 'Laughing and crying, slowed right down.'

'Toby!' said Jojo.

'It takes a lot,' Toby said.

'What?' said Jojo.

'It takes a lot to laugh and . . .'

'*What?*' said Jojo.

'It takes a train to cry,' said Toby.

'Toby!' said Jojo.

'That's Dylan, Jojo,' said Toby, slightly peevish. 'It's a song by Dylan.'

6

The next morning Jojo and Toby met on the terrace of the Palmyra hotel. They met early and by arrangement. None of the other wedding guests was up. They had croissants and coffee for breakfast, and ripe figs that had come from Egypt. It was a cool spring morning. The grape clusters in the vine above their heads were still tiny and green. They had made the arrangement to meet drily, formally, and as though there was nothing special to it. This was intended to put everyone off the scent – not only Joachim, for instance, but if necessary Jojo and Toby themselves. They both knew that something had happened, but neither knew whether the other thought the same.

'Do you want more coffee?' said Jojo.

'Thanks.'

'My shower was cold this morning.'

'You can have hot water in the morning at the Palmyra, or the evening, but not both.'

'Look, that woman's baking bread on the hearth.'

'They do that here, but they're aware of the rustic charm and charge even more.'

'It's expensive for a hotel with no hot water in the morning.'

'The Kaiser stayed here. And de Gaulle. You have to pay for that.'

'Oh, God,' said Jojo. 'I forgot to see the ruins.'

'We can go see them now,' said Toby.

'They'll be shut.'

'We can try.'

They finished their coffee and left the hotel and went across the road. Behind a long concrete wall, great pillars of marble, the smokeless stacks of Roman power, stood against a blue sky. Jojo and Toby walked the perimeter of the site through a wasteland of goat-nibbled furze and broken stones.

'How's Joachim?'

'Asleep.'

'Do you like him?'

'I like him. He's nice. He's good.'

'He's a whale.'

'He's a lovable whale.'

'You *love* him?'

'I don't love him, Toby,' said Jojo.

There was a silence.

'You know that,' she said.

'I do.'

There was another silence. They had nearly done the full perimeter of the site and were back on the smooth road again. They stopped at the entrance.

'What about you?' he said.

'What about me?'

'You know that I knew.'

'What?'

'That you didn't love him.'

'I did. I mean I do.'

'Have we . . . changed the subject?'

'I think so.'

'We both just said "I do." '

'I know.'

'Come in, come in,' said a man beaming by the gate to the ruins.

'You're not open,' said Toby.

'For you – it is now open,' he said.

He was a middle-aged Lebanese man in a brown and green knitted cardigan, smoking a cigarette. Without quite knowing it they recognised in his disguise the one who verifies the presence of love.

'We only have half an hour,' said Jojo, further on inside the enclosure. The mini-buses would soon be gathering at the hotel to take everyone away. Jojo and Toby were holding hands again for the first time for two years. Ahead of them, as a result of that touch, waited Beirut, London, the world together. They went around the stone platforms and megaliths. The place was, strangely enough, not deserted. They caught a glimpse of another couple ahead of them in the distance, and they saw a pretty Lebanese girl, on her own, looking down from a high stone balcony into a field of long grass where two youths seemed to be loitering. The wind was blowing mildly through the trees.

'Fifteen minutes,' said Jojo.

'This,' said Toby, 'is the temple of Bacchus. Possibly. I don't think they really know. And there's the soffit.'

'The soffit?' said Jojo. 'What on earth's a soffit?'

'That's a soffit,' said Toby, pointing high above them. 'It's a well-known architectural term. It's the underside of an arch, I think. Look! There's an eagle up there, and a palm. And a god. It's supposed to be Bacchus. But I think it might be Cupid. It looks like Cupid to me. Do you think it's Cupid?'

'Maybe it is Cupid,' said Jojo.

They stood under the soffit, gazing up at the winged god and the eagle and palm carved high above them. Then they remembered the time, and went back down the stairs, where they stopped in their tracks.

Just round the corner from the bottom of the stairs someone was sitting in the dirt, leaning against the temple wall. But who was it? The figure was hooded, and was covered from head to toe in a sort of striped robe. Only the hands of the person were bare; they were dirty, and half clasped, but were they the hands of a man, a woman, a youth? You couldn't tell. There were some roses, very dark red, growing nearby in the dry earth. The figure was silent and quite motionless. There were no eye-slits in the hood. All the same, Toby and Jojo felt they couldn't stand and stare. They moved away.

'How strange,' said Jojo. She felt a little frightened. It was so very odd, the motionless figure in the eyeless hood. Who was it? Why were they there? What were they *thinking*?

Back in Beirut by noon, the wedding party immediately began to disperse, swirl away to the ends of the earth never to form again. Some people went straight to the airport. Others took tours, to Byblos, or up into the wild gorges. Gilly disappeared into a grand Beirut world which was now hers, preparatory to flying to Brussels where she and Maro were to live. The rest of her own family and the Chadwicks went to their hotels, having arranged to meet for a late lunch at Le Sporting.

At one o'clock Jojo arrived at Toby's hotel with her luggage. She had left Joachim.

'Where's Joachim now?' said Toby.

'He's seeing the minister of culture,' Jojo said. 'Joachim adores ministers.'

Toby came out of the shower and dressed and they went out and walked along the Corniche. It was not even May yet, but the air was hot and dim and somewhat salty.

'Look, there's Tawfik,' said Toby. 'He's a friend of mine.'

'Where?' said Jojo.

'Just here,' said Toby.

Jojo could see no one immediately ahead, only a beggar without legs, on a little tray.

Toby bent down and said hello to Tawfik. If truth be told he was rather proud of his acquaintanceship with Tawfik. It seemed to him a mark of distinction – that he and this beggar, a man in another world, so to speak, should recognise their brotherhood. Jojo, he thought, would just have to be impressed.

But Tawfik looked Toby straight in the eye and did not return his greeting.

Toby fished some money from his pocket and proffered it.

'No,' said Tawfik. He looked away into the distance. Toby flushed, then he straightened up and walked on with Jojo.

'Search me,' he said, foreclosing any discussion. A little further on, he shook his head. They reached the entrance of Le Sporting and went in past black-suited security. The others were sitting at tables in the sandy plaza. The outdoor furniture, wooden and concrete, had been repainted in hornet hues of red and yellow. Toby had the impression there was some heavy weight hanging over the group.

Candy was the first to see Toby and Jojo. She had been watching out for them and she caught his eye and waved her hand.

'Toby!' she called.

'My mother,' he thought. 'Whether we like it or not.'

'Hi, Ma,' he said.

'Oh, Jojo, Toby,' said Candy. 'Sit down.'

She looked delighted, and yet she was distracted as well. They sat among the hornet furniture. Again Toby had the sense of something odd in the mood – something uneasy and burdened and slighted.

The waiter came with a tray of drinks and olives and put them down on the table expressionlessly and went away without a word. Everyone watched him go.

'It's not good,' said Candy to Toby.

'What isn't?'

Chadwick was sitting there like a sphinx.

'This,' said Candy. She held out a newspaper. At first Toby could make no sense of the story on the front page.

'A Few Bad Apples?' said one headline. There were pictures of naked people in a pile, with grinning white faces floating above them. 'Detainee Abuse Rocks US' said another headline above the fold. He looked more closely at the pictures: a naked man on a dog-lead; a weeping man with a dog's fangs at his face.

'Those *fools*,' said Chadwick.

'What fools?' Toby said.

'In the Pentagon,' said Chadwick.

'Oh, Toby,' said Jojo.

She was looking at one of the photographs which showed a man standing on a box. He was cloaked and wearing an eyeless hood. There were wires attached to his fingers. His hands were stretched out, as if to the whole world.

'Those *damnable* fools,' said Chadwick.

'But we saw him this morning!' said Jojo.

'Who?' said Candy.

'That man,' said Jojo.

Toby looked uneasy at this leap of the imagination.

'Where, darling?' said Candy, looking puzzled.

'At Baalbek,' said Jojo. 'In the ruins. By the roses.'

But she saw no one was listening.

'It will take us a hundred years to get over this,' said Chadwick. 'Maybe five hundred.'

'Under the soffit,' said Jojo.

7

Outside the supermarket in Camden Town the heat struck down. It was mid-July, the first hot day of the English summer. Instantly, the required temperature having been reached, bare London limbs – calves, thighs, arms, navels – navels especially that year – appeared in the streets. Far and wide into the gritty distance, up to Hampstead Heath, down to Euston Road, the semi-naked, navel-baring English flowed.

'Hello, darlin',' said a young black man to an old white woman coming out of the estate beside the supermarket. 'Everyone's tearing off half their clothes. Terrible innit? But what can you do?'

Toby raced into the supermarket. He had a lecture at two. It was now twelve-thirty. He had to pick up something in Sainsbury's then take the 91 down to Aldwych, and then he had to meet his father. Race was in town for the first time since Toby had come to live in London. He was coming to the flat at four that afternoon. Thinking through this schedule, Toby found he had forgotten what he had come to the supermarket for. What was it? Food, drink? Edible, vegetable, medical? There was enough food for them at home that night. Jojo was away on a film-set in Spain. When she came back tomorrow they would all go out for dinner. He roamed up one aisle and down the next, hoping for insight.

At Jams and Spreads two young women were clashing shopping trolleys.

'Cow!'

'Cow!'

'She hit me with her *thing*,' cried one. 'She is cow. Her mother is cow.'

Her little face in a brown veil looked like a flower in a pot.

'Get away from me,' said the other young woman. Her navel was bared and pierced. 'Go back to your own country.'

'Leave her, darlin',' said her boyfriend. 'Do yourself a favour.'

'You permit me in your country,' said the first. 'Now permit me to exist.'

'She hit me with her trolley. *Wiff* her kid in it! Shows how much she cares about her kid. She's a cow.'

'Cow!'

'Cow!'

'That's enough,' said Toby.

They stared at him.

'What's it got to do with you?' said the English girl.

'I can't get past,' said Toby.

There was a silence.

'Cunt,' said the boyfriend in a small voice.

'Optrex,' thought Toby.

'Optrex!' he said. 'That's what I came for.'

'Oh, yeah,' said the boyfriend. 'That's good stuff, that is.'

The woman in the brown veil went one way, the English pair another. Toby found the Optrex, paid at the self-service till. '*Thank you for using Sainsbury's self-service*,' all the machines were singing. '*Thank you. Thank you. Thank you.*'

He put the Optrex in his bag. Then he saw Jojo's books there.

'Damn,' he said aloud. He had meant to drop them at the library when he left home. Now he would have to go back up the hill. Outside the heat of the sun hit him. The sky had a bronze cast to it. The crowd at the bus stop was huge. The sun had not only brought English limbs out of hiding, it had brought forth the English themselves from a thousand rooms, basement squats in Camden Town, mansions on Primrose Hill. And the convertibles! Where had they been hiding? They came cruising down Parkway as elegant, as evolutionarily inevitable, as dragonflies above a pond. A flock of cyclists went scudding past. People were avoiding the Underground. There were rumours of more terrorist attacks. Jittery, bellicose, magpies clattered their beaks in the oaks above the traffic. A bus came up from the West End; the driver slowed, peered at the throngs on the pavement and drove on.

'*Fucker!*' sang voices in the crowd. Toby rapidly re-calculated. If he took a bus to King's Cross and dropped the books off there? Or went up to Chalk Farm and then took the tube south? The great shapeless city stretched out in his mind. Then three buses all came along together and he squeezed onto one with the crowd.

'Ow!' cried a girl with dark blue hair and pallid skin. 'Don't push me. If only you knew how much I don't like being pushed. OW!' Her voice rose to a scream.

'Shocking, that!' said a black schoolboy joyfully. 'Like she's havin' an orgasm!'

'Excuse *me*,' said the Goth girl. 'I hurt my *foot*.'

'Hurt your head more like,' said an old woman.

The bus braked sharply.

'Oh, God! Why did he stop like that?' said the Goth girl.

'Some of us have bad backs,' said the old woman.

'If there was a accident, we wouldn't have a chance,' said an old man. 'The Routemaster was better. Best bus they ever built.'

'They always brake like that, for fun,' said a Goth boy who was with the girl.

'Ooooh,' the Goth girl said. She reached up and tousled his hair. 'Shall we go to yours? I want to – you know – change your body.'

'You can change my body outside, but not inside,' said the boy.

The bus stopped by the pub on the corner of Brecknock Road. For some reason everyone peered out the window as if there was something important to see.

'I had a haircut up the Brecknock once,' said the black schoolboy.

'Watchoo ask for?' said another boy.

Toby got off at the next stop and walked towards the library. He stopped outside his flat and stared down the road. He was thinking of Romulus's homework: the sun rushing through the galaxy, the galaxy soaring on elsewhere.

'So we're never in the same place again,' he thought. 'Always somewhere completely new.'

Inside the library a woman in her sixties with a blonde perm was waiting at the desk. The librarian came out from a hiding place. Young, daffy, sweet, breathy, with thick glasses.

'Can I help you?' she said to Toby.

'This lady was here first,' he said.

'I've come for me book I ordered,' said the woman.

She handed a slip of paper to the librarian. The librarian took it and went away and came back with a book and handed it over.

' *'Ere!*' said the woman. 'That's not my book! That's the wrong book.'

'Oh dear,' said the librarian. 'Well – it's the, um, same title and the, um, same author—'

'Nah,' said the woman. 'It's not worth reading, that isn't. It's too fin. I wouldn't bother with a book like that.'

Librarian: 'Oh, well then, I'll just – um—'

She gave Toby a blind, helpless gaze.

'Cancel it!' said the woman.

'Well – *OK*,' said the librarian doubtfully.

'No wonder they don't advertise it,' said the woman. 'Book like that.'

'Still, it might be all right,' said Toby.

'You what?' the woman said. She stared at Toby. A fierce eye in a nest of dry wrinkles.

'It might still be worth reading,' said Toby. 'Even though it's so thin.'

'Blimey,' said the woman. 'You an American?'

'Yes,' said Toby.

'Oh, well,' she said. She turned to the librarian. 'I'll take it then. Just because of what the gentleman says.'

She took the book back and looked down at it in her hand, and laughed grimly at her folly.

'*Fin* book like this,' she said.

Toby handed in Jojo's books and paid the fine. Then he stepped outside the library and saw Race. Race was at the end of the ramp, staring up at him.

'Toby!' said Race.

'What are *you* doing here?' said Toby.

He saw his father just then as a stranger might see him, tall, sandy-haired, slightly lost in the London streets. His check shirt . . .

'I got in early,' said Race. 'My flight changed. So I just thought I'd – I'd – I'd just look around your neighbourhood.'

'That's fine, that's great,' said Toby. He felt like laughing for some reason. Then he saw the expression in Race's blue eyes. Race looked innocent, alarmed, uncertain – as if just then he had become the son and Toby the father, as if just for a moment they had changed places, as sons and fathers do.

Part V

2010

1

Jojo lay sprawled on the carpet. She was, in her own view, hard at work. Race, looking through the open double doors into the rumpus room, appreciated the sight. He loved his daughter-in-law and he was appreciative, as well, of her good looks. The long limbs, the shortish blonde hair which she flicked back with one hand as she studied the terrible puzzle. Her hair immediately, heavily, fell over her eyes again. The jigsaw she was doing was also rather beautiful – a long, narrow picture of the Empire State Building, rendered in a greenish hue as if seen under water; the colour was also reminiscent of dollar bills. Though how anyone, Race thought, had the patience to do a jigsaw of the Empire State Building, all those thousands of windows . . .

He himself was doing the dishes. It was his turn that night. FitzGerald had done them the night before, and Tolerton the night before that. The dishwasher had been stacked. Race was now dealing with the pots and pans, the roasting tray. The kitchen had an L-shaped bench from where, to the right, you could see into the rumpus room and, to the left, across the dining area and sitting-room, to an open deck beyond. Toby was in the far corner of the sitting-room watching a movie. Outside on the deck in the early evening were FitzGerald and his Danish wife, Inga, and

Lane Tolerton. Inga was drinking wine. FitzGerald and Tolerton were drinking single malt.

It was on this coast, along this road, perhaps near this very spot, that the old Chevrolet had broken down all those years before. No, they hadn't broken down, thought Race – FitzGerald had slammed it into a ditch. On their first night in this house, which they had rented for a month, Race went out on the deck after midnight and there, out to sea, was an ocean liner, a cruise-ship, passing silently, all lit up, far away. That sight had been unthinkable when they were last there, standing round the old Chevrolet trapped in the sand. The world had become much richer, and less dark at night. In a way he missed the darkness. So far on this holiday on the coast they had not gone out to the Tawhai farm. Who was out there now? What would they say to them? 'We've come to see Morgan's grave'? They kept putting the trip off.

They were also waiting for Candy and Chadwick to arrive. When Race announced he was going to take a trip to New Zealand, Toby and Jojo said they wanted to go as well. Toby hadn't been back since he was a child, Jojo had never been. Then Candy said that she had to come. Then Chadwick decided to fly in as well. But neither Chadwick nor Candy, arriving from different directions, one from the east and one from the west, had so far appeared. Chadwick was at a conference in New Delhi. India was essential, he said, the future counter-weight to a tyrannous China; the great fact of the next century might just be that India spoke English and was a democracy. Candy, meanwhile, had rolled over on her ankle and she couldn't travel until the bruising went down and the ligaments began to knit.

'I'm *amazed!*' said a voice. Without looking up, Race knew who it was.

'Inga,' he said. He was scrubbing the wire rack. They had had grilled lamb for dinner.

'I – am – astonished,' said Inga. She was standing on the other side of the bench, in the dining area, her hands on her hips. Race looked at her admiringly. He couldn't help admiring Inga – her appearance – the chic hair, the red lips, the amount of cleavage, richly tanned, on display, the good ankles – and her nerve. She has some nerve, he thought.

'You, doing the dishes,' she said. 'While he' – she pointed at Toby in the distance – 'and she' – she pointed into the rumpus room – 'are lying round doing nothing.'

'I don't mind doing the dishes,' said Race. 'Leave them. They're young.'

'Young!' she said. 'They're not young. They're twenty-eight.'

'Inga, this is not your business,' Race said. Though she's right in a way, he thought. 'That's my son,' he said. 'That's my daughter-in-law. Please don't interfere.'

'I'm going to say something.'

'I've asked you not to.'

Inga marched into the rumpus room.

'Inga,' said Race.

'You're lazy,' said Inga to Jojo, who was lying poised above the Empire State Building. 'You're lazy and you're spoiled. You haven't lifted a finger all day.'

Jojo said nothing for the moment. Carefully she inserted the topmost section of the mast on the Empire State Building in its place in the great puzzle.

'Gotcha!' she said.

Then she looked up past Inga, to Race.

'She's really quite grumpy, isn't she?' said Jojo.

Inga had found the house in the first place and arranged to rent it and agreed the terms and conditions and paid the deposit and collected the keys. That, Race thought, might have been a mistake, if it meant she was now going to throw her weight around. She stood looking down at Jojo, then turned and marched away. She came into the kitchen and poured herself another drink.

'*I* have no interest in being here,' she said to Race. She held her glass between her breasts. 'I only organised it for your sake. I wasn't on your trips here a hundred years ago. I never knew this Morgan person. But I kept hearing about him from FitzGerald, and then, with all the rest of you showing up . . . Frankly, I couldn't care less about him. Was he gay?'

'I don't think so,' said Race. 'The last time I ever saw him he was boasting about this girl he'd just slept with.'

'Oh, that,' said Inga. 'That was probably just a cover. Rod Orr says he was gay. He says he killed himself, jumping off a cliff. Or was pushed in a lovers' quarrel. He says—'

'You know Rod Orr!' said Race. 'I haven't seen Rod for years.'

'Of course I know him,' said Inga. 'He's a darling.'

'I suppose he never liked Morgan,' said Race.

'He was jealous,' said Inga.

'Jealous?' said Race.

'He wanted *you* as his friend.'

'Me!' said Race in amazement. He had never thought of this.

Toby burst out laughing in the far corner of the sitting-room.

'What's he doing?' said Inga.

'What are you watching?' said Race.

'*Ghostbusters*,' said Toby.

That afternoon he had found a trove of old video tapes in a cupboard.

'I was right,' he called out. 'It's pure prophecy. The Stay Puft Man in a rage looks just like Dick Cheney in a rage.'

'Let's see,' said Race.

'I'll wind it back,' said Toby.

'Don't worry,' said Race. 'I take your word for it.'

He stacked the wire racks and roasting trays on the bench to drain. 'Done,' he said, to the dishes. Inga watched the proceedings closely.

'Frankly, I'm not the slightest bit interested myself,' she said. 'I had my own friends, thank God. But since we're here, for God's sake go out and see the place. Just go. Stop this pussy-footing round.'

Race nodded. 'She's right,' he thought. He walked out through the sitting-room. Inga followed. Race bopped Toby on the head with one finger as he went past. Toby, intently watching the credits roll, took no notice. Race and Inga went out on the deck above the sea. The sun had just gone down but the night was already quite dark. The sea was calm – a rolling, soft-footed calm, breaking on the rocks as if reluctant to make any sound at all. You thought of a parent watching sleeping infants, or a burglar waiting on the sill.

'So here we are again,' said Tolerton.

'We should go out there tomorrow,' said Race.

'Not me,' said Tolerton. 'Not with this foot.'

He had been stung by a bee in the grass in the late afternoon and his foot had swelled up twice its size.

'My own fault,' he said. 'Going round barefoot.'

'You're sure you're all right?' said Inga. 'You're not going to go into anaphylactic shock on us, are you?'

'I'm slightly allergic, that's all. It will go down in exactly three days. This whisky is extremely good for it.'

The next day a violent wind was blowing in from the tropics. Each of the headlands, one after the other – Horoera, Wakatiri, Cape Runaway – stood out to sea under a bonnet of shining cloud. Everyone was going on the expedition with the exception of Tolerton who came to the carport at the back door to see them off. He was in a red dressing-gown and walking with the aid of a stick. He had one foot in a running shoe, the other was bare as no shoe would fit it.

'Are you sure you'll be all right?' said Inga. 'We might be away for hours.'

'Of course I'll be all right,' said Tolerton. 'I'll be glad to get some peace and quiet, you lot out of the way. I have some work to do.'

Tolerton was a High Court judge. He had been able to get away for only a few days and he had brought some judgments to write. Now he raised his walking stick like the starter at a race-track and the cars set off, FitzGerald and Inga in the lead in a smart new silver sedan, Race and Toby and Jojo in Tolerton's old Land Rover. Toby and Jojo were not in fact going out to the Tawhai farm. They had strapped their kite-surfing gear on the roof-rack and were planning to jump out at one of the beaches along the way.

'Here, Dad,' Toby kept saying. 'This looks great. Just stop here.'

'Wait,' said Race. 'It gets better.'

He had been along this road now, he calculated, four times in his life – twice in daylight – and he remembered great sweeps of empty sand, the surf breaking for miles. No, *six*, he thought. Three times in daylight.

Toby meanwhile was getting agitated. Race might have been here before, he thought, but what did he know about wind-surfing? Look at those waves, look at those caps.

But the further towards the cape they went the stronger the wind blew.

'Here we are,' said Race, thankful that his memory had served him: two, three, four miles of sand stretched before them, not a soul, not a footprint to be seen.

Toby and Jojo jumped out, took down their gear from the roof, waved and were gone, over the low dunes without looking back. Inga and FitzGerald's silver sedan was a speck in the distance. Race followed it and turned left at the crossroads and took the road to Cape Runaway. Everywhere he looked, the lie of the land had shifted, as if everything had swung slowly at anchor over the years. That roofline, that had not been there before, surely – yet the house was ancient, falling to bits in fact. This little creek he didn't remember, with its white concrete bridge. And the cliff road, when he came crawling around it, was not nearly as high as it used to be . . .

And then, round the corner of the coast, there was a church with a scanty wooden belfry which was simply not listed at all in his memory.

In the distance he saw the silver sedan parked in the driveway of a newish-looking house by the road. Race stopped at the gate and got out of the Land Rover.

The wind here was direct, tremendous. He went up the path: all the new plantings – the flax and the giant grasses – were bending and shaking as if speechless at the wind and then, coming round the corner of the house, there was Morgan. But of course it was not really Morgan. 'It's only his brother,' Race thought, but all the same he was startled, and impressed by the fidelity of the silent codes of inheritance. The man coming round the corner of the house looked just like Morgan might have, decades on. He had a startled expression on his face too, although he knew who Race was, he said, and he had come out to meet him.

'I'm Lucas,' he said. 'I'm the big brother. You better come in out of this.'

They went into the house. FitzGerald and Inga were already there, installed in armchairs in the sitting-room. They sent up a sort of high-chinned twinkle as if to say 'We're ahead of you here.' Lucas fussed around, bringing out tea in a teapot, cups and saucers and biscuits, all on a wooden tray with handles of chrome. He was a big, strongly-built, grizzled man. His eyes checked the tray, the biscuits; he was anxious everything should be done as well as if his wife was there. Lucas had just retired, he said. He had taught mathematics for thirty years at the University of New South Wales.

'Your mother was a mathematician,' said Race.

'You remember that?' said Lucas.

'I remember Morgan teasing her about it.'

'*Did* he?' said Lucas. 'I would never have dared. But Morgan could get away with murder. He was her favourite. He knew exactly how to get round her.'

'Morgan was – wild,' said Race suddenly, expansively. He thought of Morgan on the limo roof, Morgan in the fog looking for stolen jewels. He decided not to mention those. 'Didn't he get expelled from school?' he said.

There was a silence. Race had blundered.

'Something to do with tennis shoes?' he said. That was so trivial, he thought, who would mind?

Lucas looked unhappy, all the same. Family honour seemed to be at stake.

'Well, you know,' said FitzGerald, 'Morgan was brilliant. He just knew more than the rest of us. *What is the name of the liquor that flows in the veins of the immortal gods?*'

The house shook in the gale. You could hear the surf thunder and speak on the beach.

'Just *look* at your windows,' said Inga. 'They're all salt.'

'I was divorced last year,' said Lucas, rather humbly, as if that might explain things.

Inga left the room. After a minute or two she appeared on the veranda with a hose in her hand. She began to sluice down the big panes.

The men then laughed.

'My wife!' said FitzGerald, not without some pride.

Lucas beamed, in order to conceal what he was thinking: 'My precious tank water!'

'What a nerve,' thought Race, admiringly.

'There,' said Inga, coming back into the room. 'Now you can see yourself think.'

'Would you like to see the grave?' said Lucas.

They went out into the booming gale. The sun was hot through the rushing air as they set off across the paddock, FitzGerald and Inga going on ahead. Race noted Inga's air of elegance as she walked away over the rough turf. Then he smelled an ammoniacal tang and he saw the roots of the big tree, dark-ribbed and polished bare in places, wisps of sheep's wool caught in wood fissures. He liked exposed tree roots, Race thought, they were a natural form which appealed to him. Then suddenly he stopped. He was struck by a thought. It was odd, he thought, he had never seen the tree before, never noticed it, the 100-foot pine standing alone in the middle of the Tawhai front paddock. He must have looked straight through it on his previous visits, crossing the field first with Morgan on a summer morning long ago and then, within the year, coming back again with a coffin, he must have blotted it from view – a poor old Norfolk pine, the city councillors' favourite, which by some error of chance or judgement had been pitched there on the Tawhais' front doorstep. And yet now, walking out beyond the tree's shadow, he stopped to look back and saw how wrong he had been all those years ago: it was beautiful, this great tree, branches stirring tautly in the cloudless rush, the dark mast beaded with resin, and he thought, 'Of course, genus *Araucaria*! The monkey-puzzle, the hoop pine, the Norfolk . . . Straight from the Jurassic.'

Lucas had stopped and was looking up at the tree as well. He had forgiven Race his *faux-pas* about the tennis shoes. It was true, Lucas thought, Morgan *was* wild, in a way they had all run wild –

'We used to climb that when we were kids,' he said, stretching his head back to look at the very top of the tree. 'We'd climb right up there and then jump off.'

'Jesus, Lucas,' said Race.

'Yes, we'd just jump and drop down through the branches to the ground. Or we'd go out to the lighthouse and swing by our fingertips from the balcony. Twelve, fourteen, we were. Our parents? They never knew.'

At that moment Race felt a kind of cheerfulness, almost a wave of relief: all his life, he thought, he had never been sure what happened to Morgan on the night that he died, but now he thought that whatever had happened it was all right, at least it was all right now, and maybe it was even all right then, and then, still standing there with Lucas beside him, he saw a pair of magpies appear in the upper branches, one after the other, villainous, defiant – you thought of a pair of bouncers caught out in the daylight in their tuxedos – and then Race remembered the first time he had ever seen Morgan, walking round FitzGerald's room, slinging couplets back and forth with Griffin – *The moment when we choose to play/ The imagined pine, the imagined jay.*

'That was the start,' he thought, 'that was the beginning of the story, for me at any rate, the story of Morgan, and now it's coming to the end . . .'

But what was the end? Lucas had turned and walked on after the others. In the distance Race saw a red car come hurtling along the road, a cone of dust rising behind it. It seemed to speed up even more as it approached the gate, then it braked sharply and slewed in the gravel before coming to a stop.

'Candy!' Race thought at once. 'She should never be allowed to drive,' he added, automatically, in his thoughts. 'Never be permitted behind the wheel of a car.'

The red car had stopped behind Tolerton's old Land Rover. Out stepped Candy, and Chadwick, and Tolerton.

Race stood still in the paddock, then he began to walk back towards the newcomers. The others, FitzGerald and Inga and Lucas, also stopped and turned to watch, but they had gone too far to come all the way back.

'We made it,' cried Candy, coming through the five-barred gate. 'I simply couldn't bear it if you were here and we weren't.'

'We made it,' said Chadwick. He was in a lightweight suit, and striped tie. He looked extremely serious and important as if the fate of nations was in his hands.

'You're here too,' said Race to Tolerton.

'I had to come,' said Tolerton. His face was red. 'Chaddy's never been here before, and Candy couldn't remember the way. I was therefore required as navigator.'

He was still in his dressing-gown, with one bare foot.

'We're going to see the grave,' said Race, and they set off again, all of them, Inga, FitzGerald and Lucas some way ahead, and Candy, and Tolerton in his dressing-gown, and Chadwick and Race bringing up the rear. Candy had a walking stick. Tolerton was also on a walking stick. They marched across the grass, those at the rear going into the shadow of the Norfolk pine and out again, in procession, and then, no one knew why, they fell out of step with each other and ended up in single file crossing the big paddock, each with their own thoughts.

Inga was thinking: '*I* did this. I hope they're grateful, that's all. It means frankly nothing to me, but if I hadn't been here to organise them—'

FitzGerald was suddenly feeling guilty. 'Morgan knew I'd slept with Candy,' he thought. 'I wonder how. But that was why I gave him the pot that night. I gave it to him and maybe that's what killed him. Was *I* to blame for his death?'

He had never thought of this before and a strange quizzical expression – he could feel it – came to his face.

Lucas was wondering just what it was that had brought these people here, and what he thought about it. He wasn't sure that he liked it really, though he didn't know why. 'After all, they were his friends,' he thought. 'They came and buried him, and I didn't even know he was dead.' Lucas had been overseas at the time. 'And now I see them,' he thought, 'I know what *he* would have been like if he'd lived. My kid brother!' And it felt to him, meeting these strangers, that he had lost Morgan in another way, which he'd never thought of, long ago.

Candy was looking brave, but she suddenly felt afraid. She remembered a dream she'd had of Morgan after he'd died. He'd come to her angry, accusing, even dangerous. His hands stretched out to her neck. She'd woken in terror. 'What did *I* do?' she thought. 'Did he hate me for some reason? Or was it that he was in love with me!' After Morgan died she and Adam almost immediately had begun to fly apart. 'Was it Morgan who kept us together?' she now thought. 'Was it *him* that I really loved?' She didn't know the answer. 'Did I ruin my life?' she thought. She went on bravely.

Tolerton was hobbling along on a stick, in his gown. His foot was now rather painful. It didn't seem a good idea to be walking on a naked swollen foot over the rough paddock. 'I should have worn a flip-flop,' he was thinking. 'I shouldn't really be here at all. And not only did I have to come, I had to endure Candy's driving. She should never be allowed behind the wheel of a car, that woman. Never. Plus – I should have stood up to Rod Orr that night and let Morgan stay on the sofa. What was the problem? Something about a curtain. A *curtain*! But still – look at this place! It's completely unchanged!'

Chadwick wanted to swing round and talk to Race but something inhibited him. 'I've never been here before,' he was thinking. 'I wasn't even at the funeral. We weren't friends. I didn't want to be.'

A secret stirred in him then. He had not wanted to befriend Morgan out of snobbery, even racism. He, Chadwick, black, an outsider, though from exciting California, had felt his star might be dimmed by the other outsider, a Maori boy from the back of beyond. It then struck him that he had been sorry about that for the rest of his life. He had never rid himself of the memory of Morgan with his sign, an arch in red and blue, saying: ALL YOU NEEDIS—

'Hardly a coherent programme for a foreign policy,' he thought, 'and yet it mattered at the time. That was an important moment. The people who hated it' – he thought of the students of Strauss – *triply abstracted, mild goggles covering his fiery judgements* – 'got into power and have brought nothing but disaster. I set myself against them all my life. That's what made me who I am. But Morgan and I were never friends.'

Race was coming along last. He was thinking about the great tree behind him in the paddock which Lucas and Morgan used to climb as boys, and then he remembered climbing up around and around the trunk of a tree himself, with Morgan climbing above him, right to the top, which was as slender as a whip, the final handhold trembling—

'*That was the tree!*' he thought. 'It was here all along' – and he remembered waking from the dream in the airless cottage which Panos had never come to, and feeling the heat of the sun on his face at that perilous midnight hour, which had apparently known about the tree there in the paddock, and perhaps had even known about the heat of the sun beating down on them now decades later in the gale, and just then he felt the presence of that rarest form of authority: the authority of a dream.

The sunlight was magisterial.

They were now approaching the graveyard. Race couldn't remember the actual interment. He and the others were the pallbearers, they must have carried the coffin to this very spot, but of that he had no recollection. And then, at the end of that grey afternoon, they had all gone away, and none of them had ever been back. Race, surprisingly, had then almost immediately forgotten all about Morgan. It was early summer. He was in love. He was in love with Sandra Isbister! Sandra was still, admittedly, with FitzGerald, but when summer came she left him and took up briefly with Panos, then she left Panos and took up with Race. At last, Sandra was in his arms. She was in his bed. This was *his* summer of love. But it lasted only a few days, a few hours it now seemed, looking back, and then she was off again. It was the beginning of a ten-year pursuit, Race following Sandra around the world. She was in Melbourne, she was in Perth, she was on her way to India. At first, for a few months, Race had remained in Auckland. He was saving for a ticket to India. Everyone else was flying off in different directions. Candy and Adam were still officially planning marriage but they were fighting all the time. FitzGerald was in Benares. Rod Orr was in California. The Gudgeons were in London. It was 1970. The autumn came. It was cold and rainy in Auckland. Race walked the streets of Ponsonby between rain storms. He went to the park, making his plans – India, Sandra – and there, one day in the park, six or seven months after the funeral, he met Morgan Tawhai.

What are we to make of these illusions – as persistent across history as love or fear – of sightings of the dead? *The earth hath bubbles as the water has and these are of them.* It was not, in this case, love or fear. He had not thought of Morgan for months. Yet in some way he was not surprised. He sometimes had had a feeling that there was more to come, there was unfinished business between them. And now here was Morgan, in the park. There was a short preliminary, in fact, to his arrival. A flock of sparrows was on the grass – they suddenly all flew up together, on the slant: Race had the impression of a curtain being lifted. And there was Morgan, just visible against grey cloud. Of course, it was not Morgan in the flesh. It was a kind of picture of him, an image, although conscious, autonomous. And he was in trouble, Race could see that at once. He was in great trouble. He was drifting in the wind and Race saw that he was lost, he was moving this way and that, but his eyes were shut and he had no idea where he was, or where he was going, and then Race thought with a kind of dread that Morgan had been blowing this way and that in the dark without knowing where he was for weeks and months until he had come to this place where, so it seemed to Race, they were meant, for a moment, to cross paths. But why? This was the question. It struck him, again with a kind of dread, that there was something he had to do. There was some deed he could perform to save Morgan. But what was it? And then he knew that he wasn't allowed to know – he had to agree first, and not only that, but the cost would be high: if he did, if he agreed, if he said 'yes', the penalty would be very great, not of ardour or exertion, but of shame, ridicule (and that was reason, he thought, now, approaching the graveyard, for that stern, searching gaze that Morgan had directed at him – *are you up to the test?* – in the dream when they were climbing the tree (so the fearful vivid midnight in the airless cottage had known about that as well, he now thought, had foreseen that test, and had warned him, and then woken him to review the warning in the silence and solitude of the cottage which Panos never visited, had stayed away from, detained by the hairdresser and the beautician solely perhaps in order that Race should receive and review the warning in silence and solitude)) and then there was no more time left to consider. Race had to decide. He could agree or he could refuse. The choice was his. Only moments were left: Morgan, the image of Morgan, autonomous, sightless, was already drifting and fading away, and unless he, Race, accepted the conditions – shame, ridicule – then he would be gone and would wander on in the sightless wind, for ever.

One by one, everyone had now reached the graveyard and stood outside the picket fence. More introductions were made.

'Just look at that olive tree!' said Inga. '*Never* have I seen an olive that size in this country.'

They looked at the tree on the sheep-terraced slope just outside the graveyard.

'My great-uncle brought that back,' said Lucas. 'He went away in the First World War and he brought that olive home with him.'

'Shoot or stone?' said Inga.

'That,' said Lucas, 'I don't know.'

'Look at the fruit!' said Inga. 'Do you harvest them?'

'We don't,' said Lucas rather wearily. 'It's just not something we got the hang of.'

'What a waste!' said Inga, and she set her mouth.

'What a scold!' thought Race.

FitzGerald laughed at his scold of a bride. Lucas bent and turned on a tap by the fence and washed his hands, then unlatched the gate and the others followed him through.

The wind was immense, it poured down over the hill, pounced on them, there was an aureole around the sun in the spume-filled air, the leaves of the olive and the pines and pohutukawas on the hill were streaming.

'I could have agreed, or I could have refused,' thought Race. But there had been a third option as well. 'I could simply have declined to believe it at all.' That would have been the easiest, the most ordinary and straightforward – just reject the whole thing – the image of Morgan, the threat, the conditions – as an illusion. And yet suppose . . . suppose . . . it *was* true. There was Morgan fading now, and blowing away in the grey sky and then there was no more time to consider and so Race – because what else could he do? – accepted the terms, whatever they were, and said 'yes'.

At that instant, Morgan's eyes opened. He saw something – he looked straight across the sky – and Race saw that he saw and he turned to see what he was looking at, and by the time he turned back Morgan had gone: he had gone, fast as a hawk to its prey, as fast as sight, as fast as the lightning that says 'Here I am!' – and there above the rooftops outside the park Race imagined another figure, tremendous, triply abstract – he first thought of the judges of the three races of mankind, Rhadamanthus, Minos, Aeacus – but then he thought there was only one, and then this phrase reached him from some far nursery: '*into the bosom of Abraham*'.

It was there, he thought, Morgan had vanished.

That was his puzzle as he came last into the graveyard, and closed the gate with the latch. The latch was metal in the shape of a half-moon. He had said 'yes'. But what was the deed that he must do, and what was the punishment? Ever since, he had been expecting the bill to arrive. But perhaps, he thought now, for the first time, it had. He had said 'yes'. He had agreed, in other words, to believe. Perhaps that was the deed, and also the penalty: belief itself, poor, much mocked, richly ridiculed belief.

And there had in fact been a heavy cost, he thought. He once tried to tell Sandra the story, and later Candy, but he had lost them both in the telling. Sandra looked inscrutable. Candy had simply laughed at him. It was one of the reasons, he thought, they began to drift apart. In the end he kept it a secret, the story, his story of Morgan, camouflaged it, hid it away, almost from himself, in the absence of a single verifying detail. And then he had stopped just back there and looked at the top of the tree, as slender as a whip, and Lucas pointed: 'We used to jump off there, Morgan and I . . .'

ALSO AVAILABLE BY PETER WALKER

THE FOX BOY

'*The Fox Boy* is a triumph'
INDEPENDENT ON SUNDAY

In 1869, after an English defeat in New Zealand, a five-year-old Maori boy was captured. This little boy was to be adopted by the Prime Minister and educated to become a lawyer and an 'English gentleman'. This is the story of little 'William Fox' and his crucial role in New Zealand's history.

'Walker builds a strange, touching narrative about the collision between two cultures'
FINANCIAL TIMES

THE COURIER'S TALE

'A splendid debut'
FINANCIAL TIMES

As the King's young cousin, an aged scholar living in Italy, it falls to Reginald Pole to make the case for Henry's divorce from Katherine of Aragon. And it falls to the hapless Michael Throckmorton – the younger son of an impecunious titled family – to become Thomas Cromwell's messenger to Pole in Rome. This dubious privilege makes of Throckmorton's life a tragicomedy of endless journeys back and forth between England and Italy, but it also makes him a canny observer of the great figures of his time. And like his King he too [has] desire.

'Wild and desire.'
DAI

ORDER BY PHO[NE]

DELIVERY IS

Acknowledgements

With thanks to Randall Cottage Trust and Creative New Zealand.

The author and the publishers acknowledge the following permissions to reprint copyright material:

Extracts on pages vii and 12 taken from 'All Along The Watchtower'. Words and music by Bob Dylan © 1967. Reproduced by permission of B Feldman & Co Ltd/ Sony/ATV, London W1F 9LD

Extract on page 14–15 taken from 'The Man with the Blue Guitar' from *The Collected Poems of Wallace* Stevens by Wallace Stevens, Copyright © Wallace Stevens, 1954, copyright renewed 1982 by Holly Stevens. Used by permission of Alfred A. Knopf, an imprint of the Knopf Doubleday Publishing Group, a division of Random House LLC and by permission of Faber and Faber Ltd. All rights reserved

Extract on page 78 taken from 'Chantilly Lace'. Words and music by J.P. Richardson © 1958. Reproduced by permission of Glad Music, USA, Peermusic (UK) Limited

Extract on page 121 taken from 'Heartbreak Hotel'. Words and music by Mae Boren Axton, Tommy Durden and Elvis

The latch closed with a click. The others had gone in ahead of him. Suddenly, surprisingly, everyone was in a good mood. Here they were in the sun, far from their usual lives and about to visit Morgan who had never really left their thoughts. The wind was blowing through all the trees outside the graveyard, and all the bushes inside were bowing this way and that. In his mind's eye Race saw Toby and Jojo on the other side of the hill, wind-surfing on the swirl of the waves. The wilder the better – that was Toby's view. Race saw all the brushstrokes of the wild sea, and he thought of his son and daughter-in-law with a pang of dread.

'But what can you do?' he said aloud.

'What *can* you do?' said Tolerton, who was sympathetic, as a general principle, to all.

Then Race thought suddenly – 'Toby!'

Maybe, one day, he would tell Toby. And he saw Toby and Jojo, no longer children – Inga was right, after all – going out of sight among the brushstrokes of the future.

And he and Tolerton went on through the bowing shrubs.

But there was another surprise waiting there, something that none of them had ever really thought of. The gravestone, a hundred yards from the sea, was wind-worn and sun-whitened and starred here and there with patches of silvery lichen.

'Oh, God,' said Candy.

Morgan's grave was old.